# WHEN THE TIGERS ROAR

Adrian O'Donnell

Cover photo by: Chris Rodgers, wildlife photographer.
info@tigersafaris.co.uk

*For my wife Jo and for the real Melissa Jagger and Tom Cookson. Also a mention to my number one fan, Angie Haylor, and not forgetting all those loved ones missing across the world.*

# CONTENTS

# PROLOGUE

The saw sliced through the flesh and bone with that unique sound and smell and still, after months since beginning training to be a butcher at 1096 Madison Avenue, New York City, he was repulsed by the process.

Lifting a leg, he peeled back the skin before cutting off the foot just above the first joint. He wanted this meat to be the best quality and kept the skin folded back to avoid contamination - the first thing the master butcher in the store had taught him.

Proceeding to the gutting of an animal always made him feel nauseous as a seventeen year old boy and he'd had to train his own stomach to stop doing flips every time the blade slid into the gut cavity releasing that putrid smell.

He remembered vividly the first time he had to slice around a pig's anus before cutting it off to separate good meat from faecal matter before it was expelled during the gutting process. It was revolting but necessary and the more experienced butchers had cheered as he held the ass aloft after five minutes of struggle and gagging. This was a real New York initiation.

The only thing left to do was to hoist the carcass up with his chain and winch before separating the choice cuts. It was never going to be the career he longed for but as his father told him at the time, *'It's a skill for life, you never know when it will come in handy.'*

As a kid you doubt the words of a parent while they try to impose their own will upon you but this time the old guy had made a good point.

# CHAPTER ONE

Brandon pulled up the collar of his new five hundred dollar jacket, an early Christmas present from Mom - partly to celebrate his first job in the adult world, but mostly to keep out the ten below freezing temperatures covering the Chicago area. Rushing across the city to complete his debut assignment, and desperate to impress Mr Paul Grayson, the editor of the Chicago Press newspaper, Brandon practised his questions in the back seat of the warm cab. Until this point, the first month of his life as an eighteen year old journalist had mostly included filing old news stories in the haunted back office of the building and searching the internet for upcoming court cases in the area. Neither task ticked the boxes for his inquiring mind, but the flu bug sweeping through the office had at least presented him with an opportunity. Five reporters were at home recovering at the moment so grabbing that opportunity with both hands, he envisioned greatness as even at his young age he could tell that his fifteen minutes of fame had arrived early.

This task looked straight forward at first glance; the city was experiencing high numbers of veterans returning from Iraq and Afghanistan without support or housing, disappearing through the cracks in the well maintained, expensive pavements. As a result, the crime rate had soared and street violence was threatening to tarnish the name of the city even further. The mayor, Lori Lightfoot, was demanding action from Federal Government and the paper was all out to support her. She was a person the editor described as the best mayor he'd seen, high praise indeed from someone who verbally delighted in shooting politicians down.

The cab ride into the centre was its usual stop start due to the early evening rush hour causing heavy work traffic across the bridge, together with snow that had began to drift down and add to the problem. Tough weather for anyone let alone a rough sleeper. He checked through his hastily written notes again, butterflies appearing in his empty stomach. Mr Grayson had provided Brandon with a contact name and the agreed meeting area. The assignment was to interview a military veteran who ticked all the boxes to get the public behind the campaign. Tommy was a former sergeant in the Marines, decorated for bravery during a fire fight in Helmand Province, Afghanistan. For reasons that he wasn't prepared to explain on the phone, Tommy had bombarded the news desk with calls for the past few days. He demanded an interview and today was his day to tell his own story, whatever that might be.

The story of Tommy was not uncommon; Paul Grayson was a war historian and the picture for war heroes throughout time was similar. When the battle drum of the nation roused them from their homes, they stood bravely to face the machine gun or musket fire. But once the smell of gunpowder had drifted from the valley, the warrior was forgotten. And so the story continued; here was a decorated hero now faced with the humiliation of begging on the streets for food and maybe a warm bed in a shelter if he were lucky enough. He was once a person who you wanted to see in a fire fight, taking up the war on terror. Now, you held your head down and ignored his cardboard sign as you walked past.

For the past week Tommy had been forced to take up residence on North Michigan Avenue near the Cheesecake Factory, a popular chain of American restaurants which were growing throughout the country. It was the only place that he could find in the city which still had large numbers of people brave enough to face the cold weather. On a good day he could pick up a few bucks from visitors to the city and if he was lucky, sometimes even a decent amount from guilt ridden customers with full bellies - not that he could remember what one of those was. His cardboard sign was simple, it read - *'Hi I'm Tommy, Homeless Veteran, Hungry and Cold.'*

The cab pulled up in the brightly lit street, the Christmas cheer shared by those scurrying past but long forgotten by the cold figures trying to hustle a few bucks. Paying the fare, Brandon opened the rear door, a cold blast of wind cutting into his fresh, warm face. He shuddered before watching the taxi pull back into the traffic.

He scanned the street trying to orientate himself, seeing rough sleepers sitting in every warm place they could find before suddenly spotting a hunched figure sitting at the arranged meeting place. He was a big looking guy huddled in a filthy green jacket, the hood pulled tightly over his face to try and keep out the cold. He sat on a folded cardboard box with his back to an electronic board advertising Pandora jewellery. Wearing military boots that had seen too many miles and dirty blue jeans with holes which were not designer, his whole body seemed to shiver in the biting temperatures as he peered at Brandon from the shadows of his dark hood.

"Hi Tommy, I'm Brandon. You sent a message to the newspaper that you have a story that you would like to tell." As the words tumbled from his mouth, he realised that they seemed out of place and he sounded like a holiday rep on a sunny beach, encouraging guests to take up an overpriced tour. Kicking himself, he wished that he could start again but it was too late for a second take.

"You look about twelve years old man, have you got the food? That was the deal, a meal and a hundred bucks." His voice was deep and croaky.

"I can get you a meal Tommy, but I can't pay you the cash until we find out what you want to tell us. I'm guessing it's about your situation? I'm writing a story about vets so maybe you can help me?" Shit, he had done it again, this time coming over like a desperate kid....*calm down.*

"Veterans?" The man sniffed before giving out a chesty cough. "No one gives a shit about us, that's not the story. If that's what you've come to talk to me about, sorry, can't help you, but have a great Christmas, Junior." He pulled his hood more tightly around his face as though to shut himself off from the keen young reporter. Brandon felt briefly humiliated but composed himself again; he wasn't going to screw up for a third time.

"What's your story, Tommy? Can you share it with a twelve year old? I guess that you're hungry...."

"Always hungry, Brandon." He gave a rattling cough again. "My story? I have seen things happening but the police didn't want to hear me out. You see Junior, I'm a bum - look at me - people don't give a bum the time of day."

"What sort of things have you seen Tommy?" A sigh came from inside the darkness of the hood.

"People are going missing, Brandon, lots of young people. No one is looking for them, no one gives a shit. But I know what's happening, I've seen what's going on. I have watched him doing it and he's still doing it and no one can stop him."

"What is he doing?"

"Not so fast. I asked for food, what can you do for me?"

"How about a McDonald's? I can go buy one now." He bent closer, trying to catch Tommy's eye in the deep hood of the jacket, but the smell of stale breath and tobacco forced his face back. Tommy caught sight of his reaction - he never missed a thing - his fresh, clean pink face screwed up by the smell of the streets and he realised Brandon was disgusted by his appearance. He was a kid, what did he know about life? He would be sleeping in a warm bed tonight tucked up by Mommy, lucky bastard.

"Whatever man, go large on everything, it may be a while till I eat again," he replied, his sunken eyes now scanning the pavements for unseen dangers.

"Sure thing, can you tell me anything else before I go get the food?"

"I could tell you everything I know," he coughed and spat onto the sidewalk, "but not until I've eaten. And one more thing, I saw the look on your face when you spoke to me. When I was your age I was kicking doors down and shooting the bad guys out in places you have only seen in your fucking nightmares so don't you dare judge me by how I look today. You were thankful for the likes of me, you remember, in the good old glory days, when we were kicking ass and flying the flag over Baghdad. I was there, same age as you are now. Just don't judge me or the rest of the guys. We have nothing, but we gave everything."

Brandon kicked himself again, his first assignment and he was potentially uncovering a headline story. He repeated mentally to himself - *'Don't blow it man.'*

"Sorry Tommy, my ignorance, I didn't mean to offend you."

Brandon's pulse raced as he headed away, this had started as a simple chat but had taken a twist into something much larger. He ordered from the terminal before grabbing the paper bag from the counter and racing back to the street. The cardboard sign was still propped against the glowing advertising board but Tommy had vanished into the winter gloom. Brandon looked around hoping to catch a glimpse of him but he was long gone. One of the dozens of other homeless people in the area sat watching what was going on, a look of amusement on his face. Brandon approached him.

"Hey, did you see where Tommy went? I have food for him."

"He's gone man, give me the bag and I will tell you what he said to me."

"Tell me first; if you don't tell me I will give it to that guy over there," he said, pointing out another cold body across the road.

"Ok, Ok, some guys who are after him just appeared, he owes some young skateboarding punk money for drugs. He thought you were going to give him $100, that's what he owes. You won't see him again now, he'll be gone out of town. You die in this place for a hundred bucks, even if you are a hero."

"So what did he say?" Brandon waved the bag in exchange for the conversation.

"He told me to tell you to find Melissa Jagger near Austin, Texas as she knows the story. I don't know anything else." Brandon handed over the bag knowing he wasn't going to get anything else out of the man.

"Enjoy the food - if he comes back, ask him to contact the

paper again."

*Two weeks later.*

Melissa's home phone rang, she cursed and pushed a pile of paperwork out of the way almost spilling her cup of cold coffee.

"Hi, how can I help you?"

"Hey, my name is Brandon. I'm a journalist for a Chicago paper. I know that this is a long shot and this sounds a strange story, but hear me out for a second. I had an interview planned with a homeless guy in Chicago but he disappeared before I could ask him any questions. He left a message with another rough sleeper. He told me to phone Melissa Jagger from around the Austin area – you're the fourth I've tried so sorry to bother you if you don't know what I'm talking about."

She sat in silence for a couple of seconds before replying.

"Homeless guy? His name wasn't Tommy by any chance?"

"That's the man, what's the story? I'm confused…"

"He found me down here a few months ago, he told me that he had information about missing people but he vanished as fast as he came and I never heard from him again. Do you have a spare hour to chat Brandon? Maybe we can help each other out."

"Sure, tell me what you know." He heard her take a deep breath before speaking.

"Ok, my daughter Mia disappeared nearly a year ago, ten months, three weeks and two days ago to be precise. No one saw or heard anything and the police have dropped the hunt. Apparently they have concluded that she left after an argument, and she's eighteen years old so can make up her own mind. They don't give a shit."

"That's a disgrace, is there anything that you can do about that?"

"Hold on, let me explain. I started an online group for people in a similar situation and within a week I was flooded with desperate parents looking for their missing kids. But get this, during the past two years there have been at least two thousand people aged eighteen or over who have vanished into thin air in America. One day happily living at home with the family, next minute they have disappeared off the face of the earth. The police log them as missing people, but do nothing else." Melissa was in full flow. "Ok so back to our man Tommy – well, here's the big story. When I started the hunt to find Mia, it received some local media attention, partly because I had decided to set up home in a tent outside the police captain's house as a protest against no damn action or interest taken from their office. I had a five-foot wide billboard made free of charge from a local company. My daughter's face stared at him every time he left for work and he had me arrested twice - that is until the regional TV stations took an interest. After that he left me alone following local pressure from the town people.

One evening a homeless guy came calling to my tent, told me his name was Tommy Cookson and that he was a military veteran. He also said that he knew what was happening to the missing people. He said that he had seen it with his own eyes, just like that, completely out of the blue. Trouble was when I looked into those eyes all I could see was a cocktail of drugs whizzing around his brain. He said that if I gave him a thousand dollars he would tell me the story.

At that time, to me it seemed obvious that the guy was trying to get drug money, you know, shake me down. I told him to take a hike, thought he was full of bullshit, trying to hustle a desperate mom out of her last few bucks. As he was walking away he shouted across the road. *"She was wearing a black t-shirt with the word 'Scorpio' across the front. She was taken from the shopping mall car park - like I said, I saw it with my own eyes."*

And then he was gone, hitched a lift in a truck before I could shout for him to come back."

"Would anyone else have known that detail?"

"I did tell the police about her clothing, the fact is I thought Mia had gone to see friends in town, you know coffee and stuff. I didn't know that she had visited the mall so I asked the police to check CCTV and sure enough she was there, in the t-shirt this

Tommy guy had described, but she was alone. So strange - how would he know all of these details if he didn't see it?"

"So he could be the....," he stopped and stumbled over his words, "...the kidnapper."

"You nearly said killer Brandon, don't worry, you're not the first."

"It's not what I meant to say. He must have been the last guy to see her though?"

"He wouldn't have contacted me, or told you to contact me if he had taken her, that doesn't make sense. No, I just think he saw what he said. Trouble is, until today I didn't know where he had travelled to and now he has gone missing again. Back to square one I guess."

Brandon thought for a second, spinning his pen on his desk while he focused on the problem.

"Can I fly down to meet up with you Mrs Jagger? Maybe we can help with some publicity from up here?" Melissa replied immediately, she had developed the habit of snapping up all the help she could get.

"Sure, what do we have to lose? Give me a call when you come into town, I'm always around, and you can call me Melissa, I've never been a '*Mrs*', never much cared for marriage."

"Ok Melissa, I'll see what I can do and will hopefully be there in a few days." Brandon ended the call and knocked on his editor's door.

"Mr Grayson, can we talk?"

His editor was considered to be a good guy. Bald and just past his seventieth birthday, a slight well-earned paunch had developed over the past few years and was now showing under his neatly pressed white shirt. A former Air Force pilot during the Vietnam war, and now a solid go-to sort of man, he had married his childhood sweetheart when he returned home in the '70s and raised a strong family of five girls. Brandon had taken to him straight away, the type of grandfather figure he would loved to have had.

"Sure Brandon, how did the interview go with the veteran?"

"Not good, he didn't want to talk."

"Really? That's crazy. The guy phoned me like twenty times - did he ask you for a hundred bucks?"

"Yeah he did but I didn't pay, I didn't even have it. He ran away, apparently owed the money to some drug dealers from the city centre."

"Good, I'm glad you didn't pay. I told him that if he came up with a story that sold me three million copies, I would give him a hundred bucks."

Brandon laughed, "If I come up with a story selling you three million, I want more than a hundred." Paul smiled, he was growing to like this new kid.

"So what are we discussing?"

"It's a long shot, but I think we may have a big-time serial killer on the loose." Paul raised his eye brows; he was used to big claims made by hungry reporters.

"We haven't had one of those for a while; jeez Brandon, how can you be so sure?" Paul's tone of gentle cynicism was lost on the enthusiastic reporter.

"I just had a conversation with a lady from near Austin, Texas, a town named Fredericksburg. She's investigating the disappearance of thousands of kids across the country and this guy Tommy is a key eye witness to one of them. He seems to think that we have a serial killer with a long list of victims."

"Is this lady a cop?"

"No, the mom of a missing girl. I'm flying down to speak with her next week, so can I run a story?"

Paul put down his pen, his interest building.

"I'm not paying for your flight."

Brandon was unmoved, Paul was well known for counting every cent of the paper's budget and he shrugged as he replied. "Relax, I'll do it at the weekend and with my own cash."

"Ok, but be careful Brandon, these vigilantes can get a bit obsessed, I don't want you going missing." He laughed and continued, "Or she might be a cougar and eat you up for dinner."

At last seeing his editor's joke, Brandon smiled. "Very funny,

I'll let you know after the weekend Mr Grayson, that is if I'm still in one piece."

Sitting back behind his small desk in the large newsroom office, he checked the internet for missing people across the country. She was right, thousands of missing young people every year and the figure was rising. His mind went back to Tommy and his comment, *'He is still doing it and no one can stop him.'* He had obviously been following this guy, had he seen him kill more than once? And for a former war hero marine to say, *'No one can stop him'*, what on earth did that mean? He needed to find Tommy again and quickly, but he could be anywhere in the USA – the proverbial needle in a haystack.

Then it came to him; war pension, the guy must be getting some money still from the Government so he tapped - *Tommy Cookson, Marine* - into Google. A full story appeared alongside a bright eyed Marine Sergeant receiving a medal from the President of the USA. He looked the same height as Donald Trump, just a stomach that was a quarter of his, and a torso that looked ripped. A far cry from the guy he had spoken to two weeks ago.

He had a citation which would have made John Wayne proud, halting an advancing group of Taliban fighters while saving the lives of countless American servicemen and women caught in the ambush. Shot through the thigh, he continued to carry soldiers to safety while returning suppressing fire and calling in artillery bombardments; a true hero amongst today's snowflake celebrity generation.

After an hour of further research, he had his answer. Tommy was entitled to a full pension after the Marine Corps medically discharged him from service. However he vanished the same day without leaving any forwarding details. The discharging officer said that Sergeant Cookson seemed to have given up hope for any future and the money owed to him was still sitting in a military bank account awaiting his instructions. A phone number that he had given on the war pension data base system was never answered.

In answer to Brandon's query, the woman on the help desk tried to sound upbeat.

"He will resurface, these people sometimes just need some space to decompress. He knows that he has money waiting for him so he will make contact, they always do." This wasn't helping Brandon so he fired back another question.

"Next of kin? All soldiers leave a will and a letter before battle."

"Yeah, we have checked through all of that but unfortunately it doesn't help us. He only gave his mother's name and she passed away while he was serving overseas. We don't have any further details."

Brandon puffed out his cheeks in exasperation before letting out a sigh.

"Ok, thanks for your assistance, I guess we shall all just have to wait for Tommy to come through."

# CHAPTER TWO

The life of a dedicated, calculated serial killer was not as exciting as the TV Netflix series portrayed. Weeks of painful planning, hours of observing and hunting the target, the meticulous detail needed to avoid forensic detection; it was tiring, sometimes boring but then the satisfaction of the job came with a few minutes of calculated violence needed to take down the prey. The feeling of relief, the power surging through the body like a drug before every frustration flowed through the hilt of the hunting knife, along the glistening blade and into the dying girl.

He liked killing girls, the hunt was fun, their behaviour more stimulating than that of the only boy he had stalked. That had been almost predictable and he had taken him down in less than a week - it had been rather uninspiring how quickly it had happened. Girls, on the other hand, gave him a much greater sense of fulfilment. He had a plan, a promise that he would reach twenty kills and stop but he didn't; he just carried on regardless. It was evident that there was no one who could stop him - not even close. No body, no clue, therefore no murder; that was just the way it was.

Standing on the upper floor of the shopping mall in the town of La Mesa, he watched the pretty, blonde girl walking arm in arm with her friend. She looked in the right age range, eighteen or nineteen – he never took anyone younger, the police made more of an effort if a missing person was under age - probably in her final year at high school and it had taken a week of watching the girls going home at the end of the school day before selecting his target. This one always went home alone, always walking and always, always listening to music, oblivious to his presence. He had walked right behind her once, smelling her perfume, and looking at her glorious white flesh while she remained totally unaware of his presence. Following her to her front door had been a breeze but today he would take her down.

Sara took a seat in the mall coffee shop, running her fingers through her blonde hair. She and her friend Mel had filled a Saturday morning window shopping whilst trying on a few ridiculously expensive outfits they were never going to buy.

"I think that I'll have one of those new peanut butter hot chocolates, they look fabulous," she decided. Mel checked through her purse. "Yep, I can just stretch to one of those. I need to get the bus in thirty minutes though, Dad is taking me out to meet some of his buddies at a soccer match. Sounds fun, but cold fun."

"Rather you than me today," Sara answered as the waitress came over to take their order.

A few minutes later they sipped on the hot drinks. "Are you catching the bus with me?" Mel asked.

"No, I think that I'll walk home, my parents are away for the weekend so I'm in no rush."

"Come to the game with us, it'll be fun. One of Dad's buddies is super hot as well."

"No way, football is not my thing. Anyway, I have school work to finish - I'll see you on Monday." Sara stood up, pulling on her coat, scarf and gloves, ready to brave the elements on her walk home. Mel drained the remainder of her drink and they hugged before going their separate ways, unaware that they were being observed from above.

He was like a hawk stalking its prey - watching, waiting, swooping and eating. Timing was everything; attack too soon and the mouse runs and hides, too slow and it makes it safely home.

Anticipation surged through his body as he waited for the elevator to take him down to the parking lot. Reaching his van he stood for a moment, composing himself and controlling his breathing. This one felt special; some girls meant nothing, he killed them and discarded them without blinking. This one, however, looked like someone he once knew, a girl who had cheated on him and humiliated him. This one would suffer the consequences of a slut's actions from eighteen years ago. A girl he hadn't forgotten or forgiven, someone that still crept into his dreams on bad nights, someone he was about to perform an exorcism on.

The cold December air blew down from the mountains onto Sara's face as she walked towards home. It was a three mile hike and she had walked it numerous times, glad of the fresh air and exercise after a day in college or, as in this instance, a morning at the mall. As she walked the final stretch along a single track, her hands plunged deep in her jacket pockets and music playing loudly in her ears, she didn't hear the van stop behind her, but the unexpected scent of exhaust fumes in the clear winter air made her turn around. She froze for a second, not understanding what she was seeing before the hammer crashed into her forehead dropping her to her knees before she collapsed face first onto the frozen ground.

Casually he took her legs and dragged her to the back of the transit van before throwing her in, the rest a well practised routine with plastic ties applied around her hands and feet and a tight gag placed over her mouth. All in all, a well rehearsed drill.

Moving quickly and taking a shovel from the passenger side of the van, he removed the blood soaked frosted earth and tossed it into a ditch before checking the scene. He needed to be sure that all traces of evidence were removed; the difference between him and a lazy killer were the small details like this.

The hard ground had left no footprints, the tyre marks were practically invisible and would completely disappear in a few hours, plus he knew he had a day before her parents would return. His homework, as always, was impeccable, every tiny detail and conversation overheard had been stored for future use.

Reversing out of the single track road and hitting the tarmac, he gave himself a pat on the back for this one. Number twenty-five could be crossed off the list and now the fun part would happen. A small railway yard sat twenty minutes up the road, concealed at the end of a deserted lane and unoccupied throughout the weekend. As he had observed on previous weekends, the padlock was broken and therefore the gate was always unlocked. An ideal place for what he had in mind today.

Slowly Sara regained her senses in the back of the foul-smelling van; she couldn't see where she was but the pain shooting through her brain quickly made her remember her position. Struggling to undo the ties holding her legs and hands together only resulted in the plastic cutting in deeper so she stopped and looked for any tools to help. There were none, the entire insides of the van were lined with a thick plastic sheeting stuck onto the walls, the floor and the van roof. She knew why instantly - to hide any evidence and she started to freeze through fear of the situation. This wasn't just a random attack, he seemed too prepared for that. As blood oozed down her face and stung her eyes, the fog from the head blow was slowly clearing resulting in panic kicking in as her predicament became clearer.

The van stopped briefly and she could hear the sound of a gate creaking open before the vehicle moved a few feet, stopping again as the gate was closed by the driver. Sara sobbed as she tried to think of where he might have taken her; if this guy was going to rape her she still wanted to live so she needed to calm down and gain as much evidence as she could glean. He may win this fight but she would sure as hell put him in jail. The van stopped again; it seemed darker through the small gap in the door frame, as though they had pulled into a barn or other building and shuffling her back towards the far end of the van, she braced herself for the attack. She would submit and comply with every demand - she needed to survive. She just didn't realise that she was wasting her time.

The terrifying sound of a chainsaw starting outside shattered all hopes as the van doors were torn open revealing the true horror of her position. A bulky figure dressed in white police forensic clothing climbed purposefully into the back. She could see his eyes glaring from inside the visor on a yellow safety helmet as he revved the machine again, causing it to emit a high pitched roar before settling into a steady menacing hum, ready for work. He spoke then, the final voice she would hear.

"This will certainly hurt but I make no excuses, you sluts ask for all you get. But your death will keep others alive."

# CHAPTER THREE

Patrick Hunter, or Paddy as his fans called him, looked down the lens of the camera as he introduced the latest YouTube clip. He had a winning format whereby three times a week he discussed a different concept within tiger conservation. At thirty-six years old he had taken on the role from his father who had started the project of saving the Indian tiger back in the sixties. Pat had followed him around as a child in the early nineties and had become as fascinated and committed as anyone else on the team.

Today's show was a simple one. The Siberian Tiger - all six hundred and sixty pounds of it - sat ten feet behind him, Paddy protected by a solid glass, bullet-proof barrier as he gave a commentary to camera.

"Behind me sits the third largest carnivore on the planet; the only things bigger are the Polar Bear and the Brown Bear." He stopped speaking as the tiger moved to within a foot of the glass as a hunk of meat was thrown between the two of them sparking a close up view of the massive cutting teeth ripping the meat open before snatching it away and hiding in the undergrowth.

"Wooooooow, did you see what my baby just did to his breakfast? Glad this glass is tough. Let's hear some comments from our friends following online."

A list of messages trickled down the screen. Real fans were called *Paddy's Cubs* and they signed up for VIP offers and regular on-air mentions at a cost of thirty dollars a month. Others were encouraged to buy the tiger t-shirts or the Christmas line of goods on offer.

Filming finished for the day, he looked at the faces of the children and adults watching from outside the enclosure. He loved this part of the day.

"Let's go make those people happy, let's turn them all into Paddy's Cubs," he said to his camera man and off he ran, into the crowds of onlookers, talking to as many as he could and making hundreds of new friends and on-line followers. This was the area which he excelled in, his dad had felt awkward dealing with humans, his entire life was acted out in a tiger habitat, sometimes only a few feet from danger, but not many con men and hangers on were found out there, only honest, straightforward animals. Dad always used to say. *'Tiger's don't need much, just food, water, shelter and protection from bloody poachers.'* That's why he liked them, they both had the same needs and both liked the solitude of the wilderness. But then Dad had Pat and the more time father and son could spend together the better. Mum always stayed at home but put up with it and listened to the stories, always with a sparkle in her eye.

Mum had been gone for twenty-two years, but Dad had passed away only three years ago after a short battle with lung cancer. The world fell apart for the whole team until Pat stood tall and took over the charity.

Introducing social media was inspirational to the success of the work they undertook, helping the tiger population thrive throughout India, China, Russia and bordering countries. His infectious personality attracted over a million followers and the number was continually growing, plus his regular shows around the world were *'must see'* events.

He also hired himself out as a consultant to zoos around the world as between working for the charity and being a stay away husband and a father, he had to keep his own family clothed and fed. A non profit making charity was not the place to earn a good wage but selling his knowledge to others, however, kept them all comfortable. It also soothed his guilty conscience for not being at home where all the other dads seemed to be. His wife Jenny had long since given up on the thought of a normal relationship and she was tired of living as a single parent. Pat made constant pointless promises to cut back on the work but it never happened. There was no point in asking him to slow down as it wasn't just a job, it was a calling, his life's ambition and work. In the last of many heated discussions on the phone she shouted at him when he mentioned their son Danny.

"He will not become what you and your father are. He will make up his own mind in life. Your bloody tiger empire is not the be all and end all of bloody everything," before slamming the phone down on him.

The past three years had been especially stressful for everyone as his media persona had taken off. His views and opinions were broadcast worldwide and the TV companies loved him. It seemed that since the death of Steve Irwin no one else had stepped into the shoes of a celebrity conservationist. Pat was like a tornado on the screen and, loved by the public, politicians and fellow professionals. He was the real deal.

Only this time, the charity committee wanted to expand the brand further and the plan was simple - to make a documentary following a year in his life. Before this though, they would need to find the only professional thing Pat lacked, a media assistant, someone who could share a year of their lives free of charge. A big ask, but he put it out on the podcast anyway and, as always, he had a plan.

He pitched the idea live on TV one sunny Saturday morning in Dallas, Texas; an *Apprentice* style game show where a group of people would compete against each other to prove that they could cope with anything thrown at them. They would need to show good animal skills along with organisational and commercial prowess. The winner of the six week show would work with him as a close assistant for the documentary, with the once in a lifetime chance of helping Pat with a worldwide project afterwards. It took off like a rocket with twenty thousand applicants within the first twenty four hours – a totally unexpected response. The site had crashed twice so they reckoned the true figure of applicants could have been double that.

With this success came big time media attention with rival stations bidding to run the show. This resulted in great publicity for both sides and Pat got the best of the best tied up in a contract for twelve months. With the support of American TV stations, the idea could not fail to be a success, and the forthcoming film and book deal would make millions for the charity.

At the moment, the celebrity status did not come at too high a cost for him as without his trademark large brown bush hat and tiger-print shirt the general public didn't often recognise him in public. He and the family were able to live a hassle free life while still retaining the media fame he had started to crave. He even purchased his own book from a bookstore in the mall with Jenny during one of his rare trips back home. Not a single person recognised him from the front cover photograph and although he was pissed at the time, Jenny and Danny's constant laughing all the way home brought his ego back into check. He was just a guy who worked with tigers after all.

"Ok we have an hour before we go live, let's get to the enclosure and make ourselves ready, they are going to love the new addition to the place."

At a cost of one hundred thousand dollars he had installed a tiger proof glass observation booth in the middle of the enclosure, accessible only by a tunnel dug out underneath. With glass three inches thick and bolted securely to a concrete bed, it was a brilliant idea for bringing the public into the thick of the action. It was large enough to take five people and included interactive games and information. With the price for admission to Tiger Central being just five dollars per person, pre-booking had gone through the roof, the entire year was already taken and Pat believed it would pay for itself in no time at all. It was another imaginative idea, this time sent in from a viewer after seeing some GoPro footage that Paddy had taken for a bit of fun the previous summer from the same area.

Its positioning near the tiger's drinking and eating area was perfect, and being around fifty yards from the fence, the viewer felt a sense of danger and privilege, spending fifteen minutes in the bubble while surrounded by snarling, bone-crunching beautiful tigers - or in reality tigers sleeping which is what they did most of the day. But hey, nature was wonderful anyway.

# CHAPTER FOUR

The plane touched down at Austin-Bergstrom international airport and Brandon dialled Melissa to tell her he would be through shortly.

"Ok, I'll see you at arrivals, I'm wearing a red ski jacket, brown hair. See you in a minute."

Walking through the sliding doors he saw her immediately; he hadn't been sure what to expect, her voice sounded sad and he visualised an older looking woman, maybe with greying hair. He was surprised as a much younger woman was standing waiting for him in a thick red jacket and tight fitting jeans, maybe only mid-thirties - it was difficult to guess really. She looked pleased to see him and a large smile made him feel at ease as he walked towards her and shook hands.

"Hi Melissa, I'm Brandon."

"Pleased to meet you and thanks for coming over. I've a lot to show you which I think you'll find interesting. How long are you here for?

"I fly back tomorrow morning so I'll need to find a cheap motel for the night if you know of anywhere?"

"I do know somewhere, I have a spare room and you can have that for tonight. It's not much to look at but it's free."

His mind flashed back to the cougar comment made by Paul Grayson and he smiled at her as they made their way out to her car.

"Thanks Melissa, if it won't put you out, that will be great. Do we have a long drive?"

"No, it's ok, only around an hour twenty. You'll have to get the train back in the morning though as I have tennis. Is that OK?"

"Of course."

They reached the car park where the orange lights on a smart

4x4 flashed as they approached, and opening the back door, he was about to throw his bag onto the back seat when she stopped him.

"Watch the racquet Brandon, break that and you'll be walking."

He laughed, "I recognise the make, they are expensive. You must be a good player?"

"I was ok, but I just play for fun now," she said as she concentrated on finding her way to the barrier to get out of the typical maze of an airport parking lot. Brandon stayed silent until they reached the freeway.

"I play a bit - I was the high school champion which is my claim to fame," he laughed a little nervously. She glanced over at him,

"I played a lot when I was younger but it just became too much and meant I wasn't able to do anything else"

"Did your parents push you?"

"You really are a reporter aren't you? In the car for two minutes and you want to dig deep into my childhood." He realised that his eagerness had led to a brash introduction again so apologised. "Sorry, it's just becoming a habit. I was told by an older reporter that when I meet people I will have about five minutes to get their story and then I'm out." He laughed again. "I'll mind my own business."

"No, I need your help Brandon so you keep asking questions. You're here to find out about people going missing so let's chat about that." Brandon took the hint and focused on his potential story.

"Sure, I've been giving it a lot of thought. We need Tommy Cookson, he's a key witness to this stuff so I've spoken to the military pension's office. They have told me what we already know that Tommy has gone off grid. They think that he will turn up and is maybe just decompressing apparently." Melissa shook her head.

"I'm not sure, I think he's gone past decompressing, I think more like decomposing with the amount of drugs he has in his system."

"Yeah, but have you read about the guy online? It's an awesome story."

"Of course I've read about him, but that was then and this is now. The man is off the rails; if he were the runaway train he would have smashed through the station already, and that would be without blowing a warning."

Brandon persevered. "He told me that he has seen things happening."

"Undoubtedly; what did he say to you?" Brandon shifted uncomfortably in his seat as Melissa pressed him for an answer.

"He's told you that he has seen people killed, hasn't he?"

"I'm only repeating what he told me. He thinks that a lot of people may have died."

"Do you think Mia is dead Brandon, because if you do you can get out of my goddamn car and walk home. She is alive, I can feel it." Grabbing the wheel tightly with her knuckles turning white, she stared straight into the distance. The warm side slid away as quickly as it had arrived and a frosty draught hit him squarely in the face as a grinding jaw replaced her smile. Brandon struggled to think of what to say in response.

"I do think that she is alive Melissa and we need to find these girls - they need our help."

"Fucking right they do Brandon so let's get that message out there." She spat these words out as though he should never doubt her again and they drove the rest of the way in silence.

Entering a residential area just off the freeway, Melissa pulled into the driveway of a smart looking detached home with a white board exterior and a red tiled roof. A ten yard wide grass strip of lawn lay to the front where there were another fifty identical homes forming the neat street.

"Grab your stuff Brandon, this is my place," she instructed as she led the way through the black wooden front door and into a large open-plan ground floor. An oak wooden staircase on the left hand side of the room led upstairs while a modern kitchen with a huge marble island sat to the right. Between the two was a comfortable lounge area with double French windows leading out in to the backyard. Melissa walked over to the island, dropping her bag and keys on the surface.

"Drop your bag off in your room, it's the first door on the landing, it's not a large room but it will do for one night."

"I'm sorry for upsetting you Melissa, it wasn't meant like that," Brandon said, feeling awkward that he was now staying with someone he'd just annoyed. She looked at him.

"Forget it, it happens all the time. Go and get your bags sorted out."

He pushed the door open to where a single bed almost filled the room with a small, white built-in cupboard on the left hand side. Brandon looked through the window down onto the street in front of the house. There was nothing going on, no sound except for the distant buzz of the freeway. He pictured Mia standing here, seeing the same view.

A larger bedroom sat next to his, the door slightly open and glancing in, he saw that it still looked in use, as though someone was still living there. He assumed that it was Mia's room and he shuddered at the thought of what might have happened to her on that day.

Walking back down the stairs, he heard Melissa talking to herself as she sat in a cluttered office off the far end of the kitchen. He knocked and pushed the door open, noticing the mass of information scattered across her desk.

"So this is mission control?" he exclaimed, taking in the walls, every inch covered with charts of information, maps with lines drawn upon them along with photos of the missing girls. She looked up. "I guess so, the answers are somewhere on these walls Brandon, we just need to work out the clues. But the bastard who is taking our girls covers his tracks well; he never seems to leave any clues as to who he is."

The office was twice the size of his bedroom and he guessed that at one point this would have been a dining room for the family home, somewhere that maybe Melissa and Mia would have eaten with friends during better times. A shelf full of tennis trophies and photographs sat in amongst the paraphernalia of Melissa's search for her daughter.

"Hey that's Venus Williams with you, she's a tennis Goddess!"

She looked up again and nodded.

"Yes she is, a real legend." She then looked back down to her laptop on the desk. "I just need to answer a couple of messages and then we can get right on with the plan." Taking a seat, he wondered about the pictures and what the plan was but he didn't have long to wait as Melissa pressed send and closed the lid, giving him her undivided attention.

"Right Brandon, let me explain where we are and what I have planned for today.

The girls on the walls have all been missing for around eleven months or less, I have only been following these cases from the date Mia was taken. We have fifteen girls who have vanished from the planet during the past eleven months, can you believe that?" She looked up at the faces. "There are no clues and no present police operations to try and find them. It's an outrage so we're visiting the police chief today to find out what he intends to do about it. Fifteen young women and not a single question asked beyond the initial enquiries."

"Is he expecting us?"

"Not at the moment," she laughed, "but in twenty minutes he will. Are you ready?" Brandon was staring intently at the wall of information, his eyes moving from one part of the map to another.

"Sure, just one thing before we leave, is there a pattern behind any of the disappearances? From your diagram it looks like you feel that there is a similarity in all of these cases. It would help me to have some background information."

"I think that there is some kind of link emerging and this is what I need to discuss with him. Look at the map of where the girls have been taken from." She pointed out the line of pins placed across a map of the States. "It looks like the person is moving through specific areas. Look again, the path heads north, then a cluster of two or three cases, moves again, see

27

another small cluster, then nothing for two months before another larger cluster right here in Texas. What happened in those two months? Why is it that no one was taken then? We need to look at this time line and I have asked the police to interview all known sex offenders who were in jail for these two months. Something stopped this motherfucker taking girls in July and August and it has to be a clue."

Brandon nodded. "I agree; are the police aware of all this evidence you've put together?"

"They have stopped listening to me. I'm a drain on resources apparently. Let's go pay Eric Bent, our brave Captain of Fredericksburg, a visit - we could walk but the weather looks a little fierce out there so we'd better take the car."

They drove in silence through the residential streets until they arrived in the town centre. Pulling up in the parking area of the station house, Melissa looked at Brandon.

"You're about to see firsthand what I'm facing. Please feel free to jump in at any time once they get verbally heavy handed with me."

The American flags fluttered over a small two-floor brick building, two unoccupied police cars sitting outside. It was a typical small town police station, possibly home to at most, twenty police officers.

Melissa entered through the main white wooden door and totally ignored the woman sitting behind the reception desk. She had played this game a dozen times and knew where she was heading. The woman looked up and half stood up out of her chair.

"Miss, you know that you can't go in there." She was sick of repeating these words to Melissa, it happened every month, and every month she was ignored. She moved quickly around the desk and followed them both into the main office.

"Sorry Eric, I couldn't stop them." The chief looked up at the disturbance to his otherwise quiet day.

"Lora, you never stop them, it's ok, give us two minutes and then I think that we will be finished in here." It was the same story on every visit; Melissa made her point and was led out by uniformed police officers. They were kind enough to her but never listened to what she was trying to explain to them. He focussed his attention on the now very familiar woman standing in front of him.

"Look Miss Jagger, I am truly sorry that Mia hasn't turned up yet but nothing has changed and you can be assured that we will contact you if we hear anything."

She slapped her hand onto his desk.

"But you are doing nothing so what is going to change?" Eric looked at Brandon. "Is he a family member?"

"No Mr Bent, he is out of state press, I'm going public. I'm sick to death of you and your boys hiding the fact that we have a big problem." He bent down to open the bottom drawer of his desk. "Look at this Miss Jagger." He dropped a pile of thirty files on his desk top.

"What the hell are they?"

"These are people who were reported missing and who turned up safe and well within twelve months." Looking at Brandon he continued.

"Your daughter's file is a missing person's report. We have investigated and we can find no crime, not one shred of evidence to say anything bad has happened to her. Oh, that's except for the word of a drug-addicted petty thief who tried to extort money from you. There is nothing else we can look at. What more can we do?"

Brandon spoke up, "How about asking for extra help - have you spoken to the FBI for example? Do you know how many young people are missing within five hundred miles of this town?" Eric Bent shook his head.

"No but I guess that you're going to tell me?" Brandon felt a rush of power - he had completed his research before leaving Chicago.

"You have seven girls missing in this small area, and you think that they have all just run away after an argument? That's bullshit, something very wrong is happening under your nose and on your watch, Mr Bent. The American public should be made aware that a serial abductor is on the loose and you are ignoring it. How many more have to be taken until you see what's going on?" Bent jumped to his feet, almost knocking the pile of files to the floor.

"I'm not going to sit here listening to a kid lecturing me about how I run my police department. Get your ass out of my building, come back again and you'll find yourself sitting in one of my jail cells." Once again he had lost control of his temper.

Melissa stood. "Same answer every month Mr Bent, nothing changes and still young people are going missing. You have a daughter - I think her name is Jazz - she's in Mia's class in school. How would you feel if she didn't come home this evening? Would you sit back and wait for her to turn up? You know, sit on your flabby ass for ten or eleven months doing nothing, just waiting for her to jog back into your kitchen as though she has just visited the shopping mall. Or would you expect the local law enforcement departments to get out and find her? Mia and I didn't argue, I have told you that. Mia was happy, her friends have told you that. She was taken from the mall parking lot, a fucking witness has told us all that. Get out and find her, and if you can't, get help."

Eric Bent threw his hands in the air.

"Miss Jagger, I have tried and I will keep trying. I promise we will look at the evidence again and I will put out a notice to all areas to find this guy, Tommy Cookson. Without him we have nothing, and remember what he is at the moment, a desperate drug addict who will do anything for money. Apart from anything else, we need to speak to him about a number of drug offences in town. He may have been a war hero at one point, but today he is a wanted man."

They left the office and stepped back out into the freezing December morning. Melissa turned to Brandon in frustration.

"See? We are nowhere near finding out what's going on. It's the same every month, a heap of excuses and no action. Then he blows his top and throws me out." After seeing Melissa's imploring go unheeded, Brandon knew that this was a fight he was determined to get behind.

"We need to get this story out for people to read, raise awareness to the threat. Washington will hate it but hopefully it will stir up something, especially with a new administration in office. They will do what they always do, blame the last guy, while not fixing the problem. Let's get back home and go through the facts; I need to get an article together to give to my editor on Monday morning." Brandon felt her arm hook onto his as she led him out of the parking lot.

"Let's get a coffee from across the street first, I need to calm down a little before I drive. That bastard stonewalls me every time I see him." Entering the café, the smell of fresh coffee beans clung in the air and the sound of gentle country music weaved itself through the thick, warm atmosphere. It had a calming effect, something that Melissa desperately needed at that moment as she sat down and picked up a menu.

"This place serves the best freshly ground coffee, do you want a slice of apple pie to go with it? That's pretty good too."

"Sure Melissa, let's go the full American dream." His eyes wandered around the room, checking out the sepia photographs from yesteryear until they stopped on a pretty blonde girl sitting in one of the cubicles staring at her phone. He whispered, "Is she a similar age to Mia?" nodding towards her. Melissa turned around to have a look.

"Hell, I was just talking about her, that's Jazz, the Captain's daughter." She smiled, "She's a nice person, do you want to say hi to her? I know her pretty well." Brandon shook his head.

"No, I don't think so, we have things to talk about. Maybe next time."

She smiled again, sensing his attraction towards Jazz.

"Ok, whatever, just don't leave it too late. The pretty girls in this small town don't stay sitting alone for too long."

The girl stood and put her phone away before walking towards the door. She stopped and gave Brandon a quick glance before turning to Melissa. "Oh hi Melissa, sorry I didn't notice you sitting in here with your friend."

"Hi Jazz, this is Brandon, he's helping me with looking for Mia." Jazz looked back at the cute looking guy who didn't seem much older than her.

"Hi Brandon," she gave a small wave before turning back to Melissa. "Is my dad still being a jerk?"

"You know how he is Jazz, I just wish that he could help a little more instead of throwing my ass out of his office every month."

Jazz rolled her eyes and sighed.

"He tells me all the time that it's his boss's fault, they have taken away half of his guys and he can't even set up a road block without bringing in reinforcements from across the city."

Melissa shrugged her shoulders. "Well, that's not really our problem is it? My girl is still out there somewhere and so are a couple of dozen more. I have to keep pushing because if I don't, no one else will." Jazz put her hand on Melissa's and gave it a squeeze.

"I'm sure that it will turn out alright and she'll come home." She smiled at Brandon. "See you again sometime."

The café door closed, Brandon not taking his eyes from the girl as she left. He suddenly came back to reality, noticing that Melissa was looking at him and smiling. He continued with the conversation.

"Tell me about yourself Melissa, you didn't share too much information back in the car."

"What do you want to know? Oh I get it, the tennis stuff. Ok, well, I was a good player when I was fourteen, making it through to the junior national finals a couple of times but just falling short on each occasion - the story of my life! I turned professional at sixteen and went on the tour - not the sort you see on the TV with cameras and big audiences - I was playing in places that you have never heard of, mostly in front of a dozen or so people. The prize money barely paid for the expenses and my parents had no real money so I had to do it by myself. And then every now and then a new girl would appear, dripping with sponsorship and winning everything, and before you knew it she would be big league, mixing it with the top players and earning millions." She stopped for a second, sipping from the cup her thoughts a thousand miles away.

"That's when I realised that I wasn't going to get the big break. But......one year later I won a tournament in Germany - it gave me enough ranking points to play in a big tournament in the UK at a place called Eastbourne. All the top players used it as a warm up for Wimbledon. Somehow I made the quarters, beat a couple of good players and received a wild card into the main Wimbledon competition." Brandon was mesmerised.

She took another sip from the cup, her eye's lighting up in the memory of the moment. "I won the first two games easily before I was drawn against the world's number five player. I knew that if I could beat her I would be into the second week and earn good prize money" she stopped and laughed.

"She was such a good player - streets ahead of me. I was losing 6.1 4.0 and on my way out when I hit a little drop shot over the net. She raced in and tore her hamstring, she couldn't even walk. She carried on but I beat her 6.1 4.6 0.6. She just wouldn't give up and it was only afterwards that I realised her sponsorship would have been cancelled if she had. Their logo was *'Never Give Up,'* and her contract stated that if she ever quit in a game she was gone. Friggin' crazy - she was still trying to play the game with one good leg. Professional tennis is brutal, miss a few games and you are history - look at Andy Murray, he played until his body fell to pieces and was never the same afterwards." Brandon was still hanging on her every word.

"Then what happened?"

"I drew Miss Williams in the next round, she kicked my ass 6.2 6.2 and I was out."

"That's awesome Melissa, you actually took four games from her."

"Yep, I made some decent money that year and was invited to play in the Australian open and the French. A big company sponsored me for twelve months and it was fun, my tennis certainly improved when I hired a coach."

"So why did you stop?"

"The coach got me pregnant and when I tried to get back on the circuit after the birth it was impossible. I was back to playing in crappy venues, but I'd had a taste of the good stuff. The sponsorship went, so did the coach unfortunately when the cash stopped coming in and I was on my own. Mum and Dad had split and both died a few years later. It was tough but I had Mia. That was all that mattered."Her eyes darkened.

Brandon noticed the sadness which crept across her face and pushed the story on.

"And you never married?"

"Never found anyone who interested me enough, and the job with the sports agency was full on. I never had any time for anyone else apart from my baby girl."

"So who helps fund the campaign for finding Mia? That stuff adds up."

"It's just not Mia, there are a lot of parents with missing children so we get contributions on line but we also have a celebrity supporter, Pat Hunter, the tiger guy on TV. He has contacted us a few times. His niece disappeared a few months back so he has started giving us some publicity during his live streams. He has also donated some time and cash. He's a really good, kind man." She stopped for a minute as a thought came into her head. "Hey, do you want to meet him? He's filming in Dallas next month, running a game show where the winner will become his assistant for a year. The show will make him a household name, a real star. He has promised to drop by the house so maybe you would like to write something about it?"

"Sure," he took a drink hardly believing where this was heading. "That would be unreal, of course I would love to do that. I've seen the publicity for the show, it looks crazy - will he agree?"

Melissa nodded and smiled. "I think he has a soft spot for me, he will agree to most things I ask."

# CHAPTER FIVE

The man finally awoke at 06.30 in a nondescript motel somewhere off an equally nondescript freeway after a night of little sleep. He yawned stretching his arms and legs before scratching the stubble on his chin. He'd had a strange feeling all night in that stifling hot room, the weather outside was dropping below freezing but some smart spark had ramped the heating up to boiling point. It was a feeling that he hadn't expected to creep up on him so fast, he needed to find another victim. The need was pressing and the anxiety inside was growing.

Normally he could plan, prowl the streets and pick a perfect target, spend days on choosing a kill site and of course getting the perfect vehicle before burning it out somewhere else to avoid leaving evidence. All this before employing his own unique body disposal system, one which kept him from detection - a fail-safe mechanism to date. This time he could hardly catch his breath as an aching spread through every joint, like a drug addict craving a hit. He had to have it and it had to be now.

Checking out of his room and throwing his small bag into the back of his battered car, he headed for the nearest small town knowing this time it would be quick and ruthless. He checked the large sign on the side of the road, twelve miles until he could exit the freeway. It felt like forever, his body desperate for the release a killing would bring but suddenly, in the greyness of a winter morning, there it was, the road to his paradise. Flicking the indicator, he slipped out of the traffic onto the small road heading to town before pulling over in a lay-by and throwing the trunk open. The constant hum of traffic racing to unseen destinations continued, the occupants of the vehicles passing on the straight freeway oblivious to what lay a couple of hundred metres away from them…just a killer preparing to take another life. Nobody would give him a second look if they accidently came across him, a tall guy in casual clothes driving a battered car towards a farming town in the middle of nowhere - an everyday scene. The contents of the trunk said differently, white forensic clothing, plastic ties, and a large serrated butcher's knife, razor sharp and ready for cutting. He had added petrol and oil for the two stroke engine to his collection of equipment after the chainsaw murder when he had almost run out before he could remove her head. How embarrassing it would have been to fill up a fuel can dressed like a character from the Texas Chainsaw Massacre. Ironic really that it had actually been in Texas, but luckily the engine only died as her severed head fell onto the van floor.

Getting back into the driving seat, he slowly cruised past the fields watching the farmers ploughing up the rich brown soil before replanting for the coming year. And there she was, looking perfect, pushing an old bike with a broken chain. Checking in the rear view mirror he could see the road behind him was clear and he hadn't seen any passing traffic for over five minutes. He pushed the button and the window slid silently down as he pulled up next to her.

"Hi, do you need a hand?"

She looked at the smiling man a little suspiciously. She didn't know him, and this part of the country didn't have many strangers passing through.

"Nope, just bust a chain over at Friend's farm, I live just over the back." She pointed towards a building in the distance.

"That's still a couple of miles, we can throw the bike in the back and you'll be home in two minutes. Besides that, it looks like a storm is coming."

She looked skywards before returning her glance to the man. "Sure is, blowing over this way, it's going to rain heavy in about five minutes. Thanks all the same but I'm fine, my folks would get angry if I took a ride from a stranger." She set off again down the road as he crawled along next to her.

"Good advice. I have some tools in the trunk though and I reckon I could fix it good enough to get you home, if that's ok?" He laughed as he said it. "I have a daughter your age, couldn't forgive myself if I just drove through and left you to drown in this rain."

She stopped again, her mind racing, wondering what harm could come from taking a little assistance. Just then, the first drops of rain fell, pinging off the metal on her handlebar making up her mind for her.

"Sure, thanks for the help." He jumped out and opened the passenger door for her.

"Jump in, I'll be fine. I'll have it done in a minute, I'm always having to fix my kid's bikes so I'm a bit of an expert. Turn the radio on if you like, it's nice and warm in there."

Closing the door behind her, he walked round to the rear of the car and she twisted her head to see what he was doing. The raised trunk lid obscured her view so she just guessed he was doing as he said and she sang along quietly to a song until the words died in her throat as she realised instantly that she had made a terrible mistake.

A figure dressed in white pulled her door open and crashed a hammer into her head knocking her unconscious instantly. She lay slumped across the passenger and driver's seats, a terrified look frozen on her features as she bled onto the upholstery.

Tying her hands and gagging her, he threw her limp body into the trunk, muttering to the unresponsive girl as he did so. *"Ok little lady, let's go find somewhere to park up, we have a lot of work to get through now."* The rattle of an old exhaust pipe and the smell of the fuel fumes drifting across the muddy road signalled the last time she would be seen in this small town.

The tired police officer sat in his car five hundred miles south. He had twenty minutes until his shift ended at six thirty in the morning and he was counting every second as his radio cracked into life and his sergeant back at the station spoke.

"Hey Jake, we have a report of a car fire over in Cobb's Wood, looks like kids messing around again but a strange time for this to happen though. Can you take a drive over and check it out?" Jake started his engine and prepared to move out as he answered.

"Sure, I'll go and have a look, don't believe that it's kids though, probably a stolen car that has just been dumped. What kids are going to be messing around at this time in the morning?"

It was only a two mile drive along the roads which were normally surrounded by wheat fields in the summer time, but now in December, everything was ploughed back into the ground. He ruminated on what he might find when he got there - *Cobb's Wood, that's a strange place for anyone to be taking a car, the area is pretty boggy at the moment. I wouldn't even drive through there in a 4 x 4 at this time of year.*

Unusually, the gate leading to the single track was open, a broken padlock lying on the ground. Deep tyre tracks led down through the trees and out of sight, but the smell of burning rubber was thick in the air.

He got back on the radio. "Something is burning alright but I think that it's probably going to burn itself out before the fire guys arrive. Save them a trip, it's not worth calling in."

Opening the trunk, he took out his old hiking shoes and pulled them onto his feet before setting off down the track grumbling away to himself.

*"Fucking idiots, they'll be the death of me, nicking cars just for the fun of it, driving through the bloody woods at this time of year."* Every footstep met with a squelch as the glutinous mud sucked at his boots, doing nothing to improve his mood.

He soon saw the smouldering wreck which had obviously been burning for some time, a plume of dirty black smoke still spilling out from the blackened hulk. Occasionally a small pop from under the engine hood announced the demise of another component part.

"Jesus Christ!" He looked down to see a set of footprints in the mud disappearing into the distance as he pulled out his radio.

"Hi, it's Jake, doesn't look like kids, looks like one guy and he has hotfooted it past Johnson's farm. He looks long gone, probably a stolen car as we thought." Moving closer to the smouldering wreckage and taking a stick from the ground, he pushed the button to open the trunk before kicking it up with a muddy shoe. Something fell onto his right foot and he pushed it away quickly, gagging as he did so.

"Holy shit!" He staggered backwards almost stumbling onto the track as he scrambled for the buttons on his radio again.

"Guys, I need some support down here." He paused and vomited onto the muddy ground. "There's a butchered body in the car." He drew his gun, glancing around before continuing.

"Looks like a young girl," he made himself look closer at the horrific sight. "Oh Jesus Christ! What a fucking animal." The trunk lid fell shut again, hiding the grim sight. "And that mother fucker must still be around here, the car is still smoking." He scanned the area, a shiver running through him as he imagined the death of the young girl and he spoke urgently again into the radio.

"Get here now, we need to stop this sick fuck - he's on foot so can't have gone far."

A faint wail of sirens sounded along the road and a forensic officer ran a taped cordon across the gate before walking down to join Jake. "What have we got Officer?" Jake pointed to the car. "In the trunk, looks like the body of a young girl."

"How can you be sure that it's a young girl?" Jake stared at the man, his face a sickly green. "Because her head fell out onto my foot. It's in the bush over there.

The hotel light flicked on as he entered the cosy room, his need to kill partially satisfied. He had made a mistake this time, the old car he had used had broken down before he could dispose of the girl in his normal manner. She had been prepared so carefully, given the conditions and driven so far, but now the body would be found. What a waste. It had been a pointless exercise and her death without the end pleasure he sought from her mutilated body served no real purpose. Everything else had been destroyed so there would be no evidence but this must never happen again. He looked at himself in the mirror and carefully shaved his stubble and put his muddy work boots in the shower.

"*Never act on that impulse again,*" he muttered to himself, "*get caught and the fun stops, let's never stop.*

# CHAPTER SIX

Three weeks had passed in a blur and Brandon was again heading down to Fredericksburg but this time with an official assignment - a full on interview with Pat Hunter. Known all over the world for the Tiger Conservation projects, the latest YouTube sensation and breaking into main stream channels, this was a big deal and the editor had even paid for his expenses this time around. Melissa was standing in her normal position on the other side of the arrivals gate but this time the smile was missing.

"Hey, you look sad Melissa, everything OK?" he asked as he gave her a quick hug. She returned the hug before looking up at him, tears glistening in her eyes.

"No, it's been a tough couple of weeks, they found a body in the trunk of a burnt out car, she was badly burnt and cut up.... they thought that it could have been Mia." Her face crumpled. "But it wasn't her, it was another young girl who was taken outside a little town near Dallas and the bastard had driven her halfway across the country to dump her body. But it has to be the same guy, she was cut into pieces Brandon, like a butchered animal. I can't get it out of my mind - is that what has happened to my girl?"

Brandon pulled her into another hug before replying.

"We don't know that it was the same guy. Look, Mia is not dead, we just need to find her. You know that every time a girl is found they will contact you, and some other poor family will be going through hell when the police knock on the door."

They walked in silence back to the parking lot. As they fastened their seatbelts Brandon spoke again.

"Melissa, we need to get through this. If the other families see that you are giving up hope, they will give up hope too, then where will we be? No one will be doing anything. Stay strong, this is a massive weekend for us. We are marching on the Police Headquarters, families are coming from across the state to support you, and Pat bloody Hunter himself is coming to add his own support."

Melissa nodded and gave a small smile as she pulled herself together and started the engine.

As Melissa swung the car into her street, it looked like a carnival had hit town with hundreds of people gathering in the road and local TV station broadcast trucks running a live stream. Standing on the back of a pickup truck talking to the national press was the man himself, tiger-striped jacket and brown leather hat - a whole lot of media muscle. Black hair and clean shaven, with an impressively toned body, mid thirties and standing well over six feet tall, he was still tanned from an Indian adventure and was a handsome man. His familiar voice boomed around for all to hear.

"Hey everyone, here she is."

Heads turned as they got out of the car almost abandoned in the middle of the road. It was pointless trying to get into the packed driveway. Stunned, she tried to speak but the words were lost in the confusion and buzz of the chattering crowd.

"Melissa, get on up here with me," Pat shouted, holding out a hand to her.

She was shocked by his size, not just his imposing physique but the aura that glowed from him as she climbed up and hugged him before turning and facing the crowd.

"Hi everyone!" she yelled. "Are you all ready to go pay a visit to Captain Bent?"

They cheered their approval and raised their placards before taking the short march into town, chanting as they moved forwards towards the police house.

Brandon walked at the front between Pat and Melissa, a wall of noise spanning them on either side. Suddenly feeling a tap on his shoulder, he turned quickly and was shocked to see Jazz Bent beaming at him. Brandon smiled back, a flush spreading across his cheeks.

"Hey, won't your dad be a bit pissed that you are going to be protesting outside his station?" Jazz squeezed in to walk beside him.

"I don't care, I'm friends with Mia and I'm doing it for her, not him. Anyway, I wanted to catch up with you. What are you doing later?" Melissa overhearing the conversation shot Brandon a glance before answering for him.

"He's free tonight Jazz, what do you have in mind?"

Brandon looked back at her, raising his voice above the crowd noise. "Yeah, what do you have in mind for me?"

"Just a drink in the café, and maybe a film, that's if you would like to?"

"Is this how it works here, you are asking me on a date?"

She blushed a little. "I guess, you know as friends."

"Sure, sounds great." Melissa butted back into the conversation. "I'll make sure he's there Jazz. Seven o'clock on the dot."

The crowd moved forwards, gaining numbers and volume as they approached the Headquarters. The police had been taken by surprise yet again and some of the officers peered through the windows into the town square as the chanting intensified under Pat's urging. Eric Bent came through the door and stood at the top of the steps to a chorus of booing.

"Melissa, would you like to come inside so I can hear myself think?"

"Sure Eric, can I bring Pat and Brandon along with me?"

"Holy Shit, can things get any worse for me? The tiger guy, jeez why not?"

Sitting back inside his office Eric had lost the bullishness he'd had during his last meeting with her and offered his guests a seat before explaining how things had changed.

"So this is how it is Melissa. After the young girl's body was discovered the other week I have made some enquiries for further resources. The FBI are moving into my station on Monday morning." He looked at all three of them.

"They want to come over to the house and see all of your evidence, to try piece something together in the hope of tracking this guy down." Melissa stared at him.

"The evidence has been sitting there for a while Eric, as I kept telling you, someone just needs to join the dots up."

"Yeah, well I just hope that we can move forwards together. One day I will tell you my story, but if I told you now, I would lose my job." Melissa wasn't prepared to listen to his sob story and was quick to answer.

"Just like we have lost our children. Difference is, we're not scared to make a big noise to help find them." The captain seemed a beaten man as he now asked her to help him.

"Can you call off the folks outside, you know, tell them that we are getting help?"

"I can Eric, but we're going to stay outside for another twenty or so minutes, just to make sure Washington and the rest of our country hear our words."

They walked back outside where Melissa now stood at the top of the steps and gave the speech of her life. The crowd was silent as the words tumbled effortlessly from her lips. Eric Bent listened from the safety of his office, every word stabbing into his flesh like thorns. A knock on the door took his attention away briefly from her speech, but she had more than words, she had the power that only comes from someone who knows that they are in the right. She owned the crowd with the passion of that display, and they were in total admiration of her. He looked up and saw Jazz standing in the doorway.

"One day Dad you will be able to tell Melissa how hard you tried to get help, and how the bosses threatened to fire you if you continued."

"One day honey, just not today. Today is Melissa's day. She has deserved this moment."

A tidal wave of love flowed up the steps along with applause as the speech ended and Pat walked up to her before shaking her hand as camera lights flashed.

"Awesome delivery, all these people hanging onto your every word, believing and praying that their daughters will be found. I didn't realise that your place was a control room for gathering evidence. Can I come back and look, maybe use some stuff on my live streams to jog people's memories?"

"Sure, I think the plan is to head back to my yard and talk to other families, share experiences and hopefully share some more clues. Are you going to stick around for a while?"

"As long as you need me."

The crowd was now into the hundreds as they walked back towards the house. Some folk who were there just to support Melissa on the march climbed back into their cars and headed home but a hardcore of around fifty gathered in the yard, all discussing personal heartbreaking stories. Melissa again stood and addressed them all.

"Listen all, please help yourself to the few snacks we have laid on, feel free to chat and share experiences. Brandon here is a reporter; he will be coming around to hear your experiences before writing a story for a Chicago paper. Please tell him all you can, every bit of information can be vital, and as I said earlier, the FBI will be here on Monday. Eric Bent and his phoney police department have been exposed as incapable in this investigation so fingers crossed the FBI come up with something."

Walking inside to get a glass of water, she noticed her office door was ajar and pushing it fully open, Melissa saw Pat staring at the map where every flag sticking from the various states represented a missing girl. Sensing her behind him, he spoke without turning around.

"Jesus Christ, Melissa, every person taken is a young girl, between eighteen and nineteen years old. And the locations are crazy, this guy is not random, there's a friggin' pattern to it all. Why weren't the police interested in this chart?" Melissa came in and stood beside him staring at the map.

"They didn't even look, only you and Brandon have seen it. The guy is working the country in a logical manner, each disappearance leading to another state. He is organised, calculated and professional. He never leaves the police a clue."

"Maybe a delivery guy of some sort?"

"No, I don't think so, he stays around for a little while, takes girls in a cluster and moves on so once the pattern is solved we will have him. The FBI will make sense of this - they have profile experts who will virtually have a map of this man's life. If the man works for a company someone will know where he is operating from. If they go national with the story, someone will put two and two together."

"Do you have this all saved somewhere, on a disc or something?"

"No, everything I have is on the wall. I should, I know and I will ask their guys to do it for me on Monday. I.T. and me are not the best of friends."

Pat gave a sigh of agreement. "Amen to that, that's why I'm running this TV show next week, I need organising and the winner doesn't know what's going to hit them. What's the plan for this evening? I thought that we could go out for a meal, me, you and Brandon and maybe that Jazz girl who caught Brandon's eye."

"That's a good plan but we'll need to eat early, I think that they're planning a cinema trip tonight."

"No worries, I'll book a table for seven at the steak and rib place but right now, I need to go back to my hotel, Melissa. I have some TV work to finish before Monday morning, so see you later for steak?"

"Sure, and Pat, thanks for everything." She pulled him close and hugged him. "Whatever has happened to our girls, we need to find them."

"We will, if we stick together everything will work out. I have promised my sister that I will never stop looking – I'm no different to anyone else in the yard. We all need hope." And then he was gone, a lingering smell of his appealing aftershave clinging to Melissa's clothing.

Brandon checked his watch, it was a little after seven and the waitress was asking for their orders.

"Hope Pat makes it Melissa, he's paying." They laughed as the door opened and he walked in wearing a fresh pair of well pressed dark blue trousers and a white shirt which showed off his physique.

"Sorry everyone, I got held up at the TV studio. Has anyone ordered yet?"

Another waitress arrived looking upbeat and eager to please. She spotted Jazz and smiled.

"Hey Jazz, you didn't tell me at school that you were coming in tonight. I saw you guys on the march, it was so cool, and your dad's face...." She stopped when she realised that she had overstepped the line and continued to take their order. "We have a special tonight on beautiful rump steak and ribs - can I interest you in a drink while you decide?" She caught Pat's eye and gave him a smile as he answered.

"I think we have all decided, I will let the ladies go first."

A blur of blue flashing lights flew past the window as the waitress wrote the list down and she glanced up at the sound of the accompanying sirens.

"Wow, busiest day for a long time, you guys sure have kicked this place into life today."

Pushing through the swing doors the waitress disappeared into the kitchen as Jazz laughed. "She is such a jerk at school, she's only talking to me so that she gets a good tip."

Minutes later two more waitresses arrived, arms busting with plates and side orders and tucking into the feast the table chatted away for the next hour and a half. Just when they thought that they could eat no more, the dessert menu appeared and Melissa laughed as Brandon and Jazz ordered enormous ice creams with flaming sparklers stuck in the top. Brandon finished the last spoonful and flopped back in his chair. "I couldn't eat another mouthful. Thank you so much Pat, it was a fantastic meal. We're going to catch a movie if you two want to tag along?"

Melissa shook her head. "No, you two go ahead, I need to get back and sort things out for Monday morning, and I am sure Pat needs his beauty sleep before the cameras roll."

"I sure need it," he laughed paying the bill.

"Thank you for involving me in the group Melissa, keep in touch, I will do whatever it takes. And Brandon, give me a look at the article before your editor changes everything - I think that you are going to be a great asset to the paper. How about spending some time with me and the conservation project at some point? We always need a little publicity."

"Sounds great Pat, I would enjoy that." Brandon handed his newly printed card over to him. "Give me a call with what you have in mind."

"Sure, I was thinking about you working with me in the year after the TV show, covering everything. At the end maybe we can write a book together, make some good money. Have a think about it."

Brandon could hardly contain himself, "Sure, sounds like a great project." He was shaking with excitement at the ideas thrown in his direction. Melissa stood and took her coat. "I've had a wonderful meal with fantastic company, you two have fun tonight and be careful. See you back at the house Brandon, I'll wait up. Pat, it has been a pleasure, good luck with the TV show."

Melissa left and pulled her collar up against the cold as she walked the hundred feet to her car as more fire trucks rushed past. She saw why two minutes later as she drove into her road, where the family home was an inferno. The roof had collapsed in and all four sides of the building were alight. Silhouetted against the cracking bursting flames, the fire fighters worked frantically as a burly man in a white helmet approached her.

"Is this your home Ma'am?"

"Yes, what the hell happened?" she asked, the desperation in her voice interspersed with a sob.

"Are there any other people inside?" he barked out, taking Melissa by surprise.

"No, I'm living by myself."

"Ok, that's good. Just remain in your car for a moment please." He spoke on the radio and reported that the place was empty before lowering his head back down to the window.

"We're not sure how this started, a neighbour of yours phoned it in. They said that you had a party in the yard with a few dozen people?"

"It wasn't a party, it was a march for all the young people missing across the country."

"Yep, saw that on the news channel, sorry that it has ended like this. You don't deserve any more bad news."

Her thoughts ran wild about what would have been destroyed and suddenly she remembered her office. She jumped out of the car and started heading towards the house as the fire fighter grabbed her arm, halting her in her tracks.

"The map, and the evidence, it's all in my house. Is anything left inside? I need to get some things from my office, everything I have done over the past eleven months is inside." Shaking his head, the look on his face said it all.

"I'm sorry, it looks as though everything is gone, and what's not destroyed by the fire has been got at by the smoke and water. It's one of the fiercest fires I have seen - did you have gas tanks in the house? Something has really taken a hold."

"No, nothing, I don't understand this. I turned everything off myself, I know that I did."

"We will have a look once we put the fire out, we always find the cause, normally something simple, or an electrical problem. At least you're safe, Insurance companies will deal with the rest."

Melissa sat transfixed by the chaos outside the car in the flickering orange lights. Watching the mayhem as the walls collapsed into the building, it seemed like seconds before Brandon was banging on the window as two of the fire trucks drove past her car, heading back towards the station. The fire fighters looked filthy and exhausted as they glanced over at her through the soot stained windows, sorrow showing in their eyes. At last the flames disappeared, smoke and steam rising into the night sky, as the remainder of the emergency vehicles drove slowly past, leaving just a few fire fighters to stop any chance of it reigniting. She looked at the smouldering remains of her house where there didn't seem to be anything left that could burn. Melissa looked down at her watch. "Jesus, I've been sitting here for three hours while my life goes up in smoke." She broke down in tears again. Brandon put his hand on her shoulder; he wasn't sure what else to do.

"Brandon, I have lost everything, what am I going to do? Where will Mia go when she comes back? She won't know where I am."

Brandon stared ahead, hardly daring to look at Melissa, her pure raw grief too much for him to process.

"It will be ok, they can clean up the site and rebuild, that's what insurance is for. Mia will always have a home here."

"But we have lost all the evidence I had on the walls, everything is gone and it was our only hope. All the clues were there and now they are all destroyed - I have messed up because I didn't backup any of the information."

"We just need to put our heads together to see what we can remember. How many other people have seen it?" he asked.

"Just the people I trust, you and Pat. But the police knew that it was there and it makes sense that if the FBI saw what I had they would be asking Eric Bent some difficult questions. It all seems a bit too convenient, you know, if there is nothing to see, he has no questions to answer. My word against his, the whole thing stinks like a set up."

Brandon tried to offer some comfort. "But I've seen it and I remember some of the details .... we can start to patch things back together."

"Some things can be replaced but the clues to finding Mia are gone though. I can't show the FBI anything, it's all lost. What are they going to look at on Monday? All they will have is what Captain Bent gives them and we know he has nothing."

Black ash blew across the hood of the car, the soot staining the windscreen and the movement spurred Brandon into taking control.

"Sitting here isn't going to do us any good Melissa, let's book into a hotel and think about what we need to do." He checked through a list on his phone before booking a place online. "We're staying at the Sunset Plaza tonight, two single rooms next to each other. It's just out of town so we can get round to the house first thing tomorrow."

Sitting nursing a coffee while Brandon tucked into a buffet breakfast at the Star Line hotel the next morning, Melissa looked up as Eric Bent walked in and took a seat.

"Sorry for your loss Melissa, if there is anything I can do to help personally?"

"Thanks Mr Bent, that is very kind of you. Any news of what started it?"

"Yes, fire investigators found your electric heater had been left on in the bathroom, a towel had fallen onto it and ignited. That was the cause, someone had forgotten to turn it off after having a shower." Melissa stared at him.

"That's impossible, that heater was in the garage, I never use it." She looked at Brandon; "You were the last person in the bathroom, did you see that heater?" Brandon shook his head.

"I was freezing getting myself dry, there was no heater there, I swear."

"They have made a mistake Mr Bent, someone has moved the heater from the garage, it wasn't me and it wasn't Brandon." The police officer held his hands up as if to ward off her anger.

"Don't shoot the messenger, I'm just telling you what the guys found this morning. The heater was most definitely in the bathroom, I saw it myself and it was the cause of the fire. You need to speak to the insurance company about it although I'm not sure that they will cover the costs if it's thought that you caused it."

Melissa banged the table with her hand in frustration. "I didn't cause the fucking fire, a dozen people used my bathroom yesterday afternoon, it is not a big room and they would have fallen over the fucking fire. It was in the garage, I couldn't afford to use it. It didn't even have a plug on it!"

He looked at her quizzically.

"There is one thing that I can't understand though Melissa, the window on your back door, was that broken yesterday?"

"No, of course it wasn't."

"That's the thing, normally triple glazed windows like you have fitted do not shatter in a normal house fire, they just go a funny colour. They only break if there is a back draft and one of your windows, just above the door latch was broken inwards. The rest of the glass was black with soot but still in one piece so it looked to me that someone had smashed it before the fire. Is that possible?"

"No, I locked it before I left at around six fifty last night, it was all still secure."

"I thought that you would say that so I think that you've had a break in. Why would anyone want to burn your house down and make it look like an accident?" Melissa stared him down.

"Like I have been saying all along Mr Bent, nothing in your so called investigation makes any sense, and now you are asking me for answers when you have ignored me for ten months. Go out and do your job, find my daughter."

# CHAPTER SEVEN

The green room in Dallas TV studio four was buzzing, the applicants for the show had been whittled down to twenty although only twelve would be used with four on standby in case anything happened to the other contestants. The runner stood with her clipboard addressing those waiting.

"Ok, five minutes until the screen test, we will go in the order discussed this morning so keep cool everyone and do your best." She looked down at her board.

"Jane Palmer, please make your way into the studio."

The young blonde college dropout walked into the audition room where a number of lights and cameras faced her. She felt awkward and a little disorientated, partly from the studio set and partly due to the quantity of heroin she had shot into her arm the night before. Sitting on the floor stroking a large stuffed tiger was the man himself, Pat Hunter. It was the first time any of the contestants had set eyes on him and slightly taken aback, she hesitated before a voice barked at her from a chair behind a camera. "Act naturally, go over to the tiger and interact."

Walking forwards she knelt on the other side of the toy looking at Pat almost in wonder as he spoke effortlessly towards the watching camera.

"Tell me what you know about this beautiful tiger, Jane. Why should we protect it?"

Confused, she clammed up, hardly getting a word of sense out before collapsing in laughter. She was the only one laughing as Pat stood up looking angry.

"You're wasting my time and you have taken the place of someone who might have wanted to be on the show. Get out."

"I'm sorry Mr Hunter, can I try again?"

"Nope, no second takes. In my conservation work we need

to get things right the first time round, tigers don't wait for a second take, they either run away or eat you. You have just been eaten young lady. Please leave." She looked up towards the lighting rig before yelling at Pat. "Asshole!" He ignored her insults and shouted over to the floor manager.

"Next contestant please."

Jane left by the side door to the studio where the long alley outside led back to the main shopping street, and pulling on her hat, she strode towards the crowds before a hand clasped her shoulder.

"What did you just call me back there Jane? I gave you the chance to make some money and you messed it up, then you have the nerve to call me an asshole."

"Get your hands off me you fucking creep, touch me again and I swear I will sue you for sexual assault. It's my word against yours."

"Ok, I'm gone, just learn some manners, you are not a nice person Jane Palmer."

"Whatever tiger man, I have a life to get on with, you keep playing with stuffed toys. And by the way, I couldn't give a fuck about tigers, I just wanted a chance to be spotted on TV by a bigger company. It will happen, mark my words."

"Not with those marks on your arm it won't," he said, pointing towards a fresh injection site just visible on her arm.

"My life Grandad, everyone's shooting dope in this city, it's the only way to get through the day." She turned laughing and joined the crowds of shoppers.

"Pat, we need you back in here, we're ready to go again." The runner stood at the fire door, clipboard still in hand. He turned towards her, still shaking his head over the words of the girl who'd just left.

"Ok let's go again, Is Lilly-Anne the next one?"

It was a hard day for everyone, the crew had seen every type of person kneel by that moth-eaten tiger, thirteen candidates shone out, four more were put on standby and the rest sent home with a t-shirt and signed photograph. The producer faced the thirteen successful applicants.

"Ok, the last place is a straight fight between Suzanne Ryder and Beth Turner, the rest of you are all through. Report back to the studio for filming on Wednesday morning and thank you all."

Suzanne and Beth sat on blue plastic chairs outside a production office before a young man with a name badge telling them his name was Sam, came out and spoke to both of them.

"Ok, this is where we are, there is nothing to separate you on the scorecards. Pat is going to interview you individually; he and only he will then make a decision. Once he has done this the one not chosen will be on the standby list. Do you both understand?" Nervously they nodded.

"Who wants to go in first?" Suzanne raised her hand and entered the room, returning confidently five minutes later. "Good luck Beth, he just chats about the work, nothing to worry about."

Beth walked in to the bright office where Pat smiled at her before offering her a seat and beginning.

"Hi Beth, you did really well today. Why should I pick you as the final contestant?"

"Because I will suck your cock if you pick me." Pat stared at her for a few seconds before answering.

"I'm a family man Beth and this is a family show so I will pretend that I didn't hear your answer. However, this interview is finished so please wait outside."

"How did it go Beth?" Suzanne asked, looking concerned that she had only been in there for a minute or so. Sam passed the girls on his way back into the office, closing the door behind him.

"I think I messed up a bit," she smiled awkwardly. "I think I misread what he really wants." Almost straight away Sam came out again.

"Pat was impressed with both of you, however he is offering the final place to….." five seconds of silence, then - "Beth, well done Beth, see you back here on Wednesday. Suzanne, we will be in touch, you are the first reserve."

Pat sat alone in his car outside the studio, it had been a long day and the prospect of another night alone sitting in a hotel room felt depressing. The light from his phone illuminated his face in a yellow glow as it buzzed in the holder.

"Hey, how are you doing?" he asked his wife as her name appeared on the caller identification.

"We're doing ok, you haven't phoned us for a while."

"I'm sorry Jenny, work is full on. How is my boy? I'm missing you both, the TV work is not as exciting as I thought it would be." Jenny sighed before replying.

"You know, I think that you're right Pat, I have been thinking things over. This TV commitment has become a really big deal, but it isn't a big deal at all for me and Danny. We hardly saw you before, and now this is a whole year away from us. Can't you cut it down a bit, spend some time with us for a change?"

"I'm in a contract with a TV company Jenny, you know that. Just one more year and I will back off, we can then spend a lifetime together."

"Just like your mum and dad, I can read the story Pat and it has already started. Pat travelling the world, poor old me left at home to hear the stories, does that sound familiar?"

"You and I are different Jenny, it's not like that with us."

"Certainly feels like it. The only time we see you is on the TV. Danny had to paint a picture of his family at school yesterday. There were only two people in it, me and him. What's that telling you?" Pat sat silent for a minute, these types of conversations were becoming more frequent and more spiteful.

"What do you want me to do?"

"Come home and save what we have, a stay away husband and dad isn't a good base for a strong relationship. Come home and we can make a success of the other conservation work. One month away a year is better than what you're doing at the moment. I can live with one or even two, just not a year."

"I can't come home now, everything we have worked towards is starting to come true."

"And at what cost Pat?"

"What exactly are you saying Jenny? I am busting my ass off out here to make us money." His voice was now raised and more aggressive in tone.

"And I am busting mine off to try keep us together! Don't you get it? I'm tired of living alone Pat. I need my husband, not a TV celebrity." There was no way Pat was going to give up his chance of fame and this year of almost unlimited sponsorship towards his beloved tigers.

"Just one year Jenny, that's all, twelve months on the contract and you can have me back."

"You know what Pat, keep your contract, keep your work. We're through. You and your father are the same person, always will be. If you don't come home after filming, don't come back at all." He stared at the phone considering his options before coming to his decision.

"I can't come home, this is my job and if you can't accept this life then maybe it's for the better that we move on. I'm sorry for hurting you and Danny, I didn't mean to be a bad father and husband but if you are asking me to choose, I choose this. A life without completing my father's work is not what I want." There was a moment's silence before her voice portrayed her sorrow in what their marriage had become.

"And there we have the truth, your father's work. I don't know what our future looks like Pat, I need some time to think."

"Jenny, come on, that's not what I mean," he tried, but the line had gone dead.

# CHAPTER EIGHT

Alan Basher checked through his social media from his desk in the small New York investigation agency. It had being a tough start for him since his discharge from the Marines and a board full of photographs from distant places made up his *'war wall'* in his tiny office. Rows of smiling faces sporting heavy calibre weaponry stared down at him. In many ways, life had seemed simple, executing the will of the government while trying to sweep away whatever threats stood in the way of democracy. It was just that Alan had noticed that each time they marched in and saved the day it was only a matter of time before they marched back out and the terrorists returned it to square one.

A lot of American blood had been spilt in Afghanistan during his many tours and looking back today, he saw the areas which they fought so hard over back in Taliban hands. It now all seemed so pointless.

Today's life was a different proposition, the new investigation business had been slow to get off the ground with mundane tasks following cheating partners occasionally interspersed with a missing person or even a bit of commercial theft. This had not exhilarated him - the hours were long and he was certainly short of money and help. His proposed partner in the business had disappeared before they had even started. Months of planning and investing the Marine Corps salary had blown up in his face when Tommy was discharged from the military and went off grid. Everyone knew his story, but what the public didn't realise was the price he paid for wearing those medals.

Months earlier Alan had waited at the gates of Camp Pendleton, San Diego, to pick Tommy up and help him decompress from the horrors of his injury before flying up to

NYC to begin their second career. The only problem was that Tommy hadn't appeared.

Landing at the military airbase, Miramar, on a specially chartered flight, Tommy only needed to climb onto a military coach and head for Camp Pendleton, return his equipment and walk away a free man. The demons, however, were screaming at him to sabotage everything he had worked for. Why should he enjoy life while his friends had died for a handful of sand and an empty promise of a world free from terror? It was down to a guard on the gate to inform Alan that he had wasted his time after a three hour wait.

"I'm sorry buddy, your friend Tommy Cookson has left via a back gate, the staff couldn't talk him into meeting you. A passing truck stopped and gave him a ride almost straight away....it looks like he just lost all self control and ran." And that was the last time he had set eyes upon his former best friend.

A personal message from a mutual friend pinged on his ipad, bringing him out of his reverie.

*Have you heard about your old pal Tommy Cookson? Just been seen in Pensacola selling dope to kids. WTF??*

"How the hell has he come to this?" he mumbled to himself as he typed back.

*How can you be sure it was him?* A devastating reply came back a few seconds later.

*One of the guys saw him, Tommy ran away when he was spotted. He looked bad.....*

Alan checked his work planner but as normal there were no immediate jobs waiting for him to take on. The next investigation would start in six days time for a guy who wanted his son watched. He thought that he was involved in drugs and wanted him scared....was this the limits to his skills? More importantly, whatever Tommy was doing, they were blood brothers and he had a duty.

The gentle Florida weather was a blessing after the chill of Chicago, but the ambient temperature was the last thing on his mind. Tommy had gravitated down towards the Aragon Court area within the city, a low income housing project built in the 1940s. Originally an all white area as opposed to the Attucks Court area which was all black, he didn't care about social barriers so long as they bought his drugs. Business was tough, it always was working on the streets, but the few bucks he was able to make paid for the roof over his head, a single room in a tumbling down block. The rats and roaches ensured that he was never alone.

Rolling off the putrid mattress and sitting on the floor strewn with rat droppings and other general filth, he took a small bag of powder and mixed some in with a little water over a candle. It made life a little more bearable, numbing the pain in his damaged thigh and helping him forget the shit storm he lived in. Sliding the needle into a vein in his foot, he winced before flopping backwards onto the bed.

He had a more pressing concern to worry about than the rats however, as if he was to continue in this world, he needed some hard cash for this evening. The last of his supply had nearly gone and without more, two things would undoubtedly happen. Firstly the rent would not be paid and secondly he would start to withdraw - neither was a good prospect.

Taking out a battered phone from his pocket and cursing himself for losing the charging lead, he estimated that he had possibly one call left before the battery would die for good. He made the call.

"Hi, it's Sergeant Tommy Cookson again. I phoned yesterday, I need my money." He listened while the call centre operative lectured him again before replying.

"No, I've told you before, I do not have a bank account. What do you mean you can't let me have any money? It's mine!" The phone cut out leaving him frustrated.

"Shit!" He needed five hundred by tonight for rent and a drug debt or there would be a problem. The heroin was already melting away from his senses as he pulled on the only half clean t-shirt he owned and tried to look decent.

Heading off out into the sunshine he would have to take a risk; the large gymnasium that had recently opened on 9th Avenue had given him an idea and waiting for a client to push in their card, he followed them through the door before quickly hitting the changing rooms. Forcing a number of lockers open, he grabbed whatever items he could pocket before spotting two sports bags sitting on a bench and swinging these over his shoulder, he quickly walked back through reception and out onto the street and away.

Arriving back home, he opened the first bag hitting the jackpot as he discovered a wallet full of money - six hundred bucks and a number of credit cards. Flicking through the pockets and finding nothing more of interest, he threw it into the corner of the room while he checked the second bag. *"Jesus Christ!"* he muttered as he pulled out a bag full of powder the size of a pool ball tucked in a side pocket. The guy was obviously in the same business as Tommy, just a few leagues above him. *This bastard is going to be so pissed when he finds the bag missing, what an idiot, leaving it on a bench ready to be stolen. His bad luck.*

Knocking on the door of the room next door, Tommy stood with a smile on his face. He and his neighbour led their own lives but helped each other out when they could, each understanding the desperate need for the next fix.

"You want to get high, free? I'm giving you a dope challenge."

"I get free drugs, are you shitting me?" The young lad gawped as Tommy entered the room which was in as bad a state as his own. He sat down on another stinking mattress and pulled up the drug paraphernalia to cook up the powder and load the syringe.

"See what you think of it," he said as the teenager applied his tourniquet to raise a vein. The needle had barely left the kid's arm when he began to vomit and froth at the mouth before falling dead at Tommy's feet.

"Oh Jesus, wake up man, don't do this," Tommy implored him, pumping on the still chest until it was evident that he could do no more.

"I'm sorry man," he muttered as he left the room and went down into the street to find a phone box, anonymously calling the paramedics. He watched from a distance as the body bag was loaded onto the ambulance, his heart thumping from what had just happened. *Fuck, that could have been me, what the hell is in that shit?*

However he wasn't the first person Tommy had seen die by a needle, and sympathy didn't get the bills paid. This stuff might be lethal but it could still have a price. Once he was sure all signs of the emergency services had left his building he headed off to meet up with his guy, a man who would buy anything at the right price. He took out the plastic bag, explaining what had just happened. "Test this man, whatever it is, it's strong."

The small piece of paper turned a strange colour while they both waited for a result. His dealer was pretty impressed.

"Tommy, this stuff is pure, over eighty percent brown. No wonder the kid died....what you would normally shoot would drop an elephant." This was good news to Tommy who saw another of his problems being dealt with.

"What can you give me for the bag?"

"Bearing in mind your position, I'll give you five hundred bucks, two hundred in cash and the rest I'll use to write your debt to me off."

"Done," Tommy agreed, his immediate problems being solved.

Alan arrived in the city and it didn't take him long to find Tommy's regular haunts. For fifty dollars he was even given his address. He had patrolled better maintained areas in bombed out Baghdad years before and checking the door numbers, he soon found the place he was looking for. The block was exactly where the guy had described it, sitting beside a pile of overflowing bins in a rat infested corner of Shitsville.

Tommy's door was already half open as he tapped on the peeling paint. There was no answer so he pushed it open a little more and found just a single room with hardly any furniture and drug equipment sitting on open display on the top of a rusting heater that was clearly broken. It was a filthy hole, bereft of any human warmth.

"Hey, what are you doing?" a shout sounded out behind him as Alan spun round and saw Tommy coming out of a filthy rest room.

"Tommy, what the hell is going on brother?"

"Go back to wherever you came from Alan, I don't need you guys," Tommy told him before turning and slipping out of the building and into the warren of side roads surrounding the area. Alan followed him out and shouted after him.

"Come back Tommy, I'm just here to talk." The words bounced back at him from the graffiti covered walls as Tommy didn't turn back but instead headed straight out of the city and into hiding again.

Tommy sat begging outside McDonalds in New Orleans. The drugs were wearing off and the six hundred bucks he had stolen had long gone. The low was crushing him, the same as it did every time he took them, and every time he vowed to stop doing it ever again. He thought through his predicament. Somehow Alan had caught up with him but he wasn't ready to face up to friends just yet, he didn't need anyone looking down at him, criticising the way he chose to live, but he would need help at some point.

*"I need to sort myself out for God's sake,"* he muttered as he plunged his hand into a torn pocket and pulled out a few bucks, not enough for a hit, but enough to get him something to eat and a phone call. Walking inside the fast food chain, six chicken nuggets with BBQ sauce went down without his stomach even recognising that he had eaten and at this point, he knew this was it. The decision was made in the early hours of a freezing morning; he was not a bum, he was a decorated member of the Marine Corps who had risked his life to save fellow Americans. He couldn't even remember why he had started with drugs, it was lost in the blur of a foggy brain and far too many pills and powders. But one thing was sure, at some point he would be on

the other end of the dope challenge and when that happened, the next body bag better be an extra large one.

A folded piece of paper which he kept in his tired wallet held a phone number for salvation, a help line for Veterans suffering substance abuse issues and he certainly ticked that box. Although he still had a battered phone in his grubby back pack it had long since given up any hope of life - the battery hadn't been charged up since Florida - but he couldn't get rid of it, he had filmed a kidnapping, the taking of Mia Jagger nearly a year ago. He had tried to report it to the Captain in a small town near Austin shortly after it had happened, but the guy had thrown him straight out, not wanting the stench of his unwashed body polluting his office. He had then tried to chat with the girl's mother in her tent outside the police HQ. He had been shunned again so he did what he always did of late - vanished into thin air.

"Fuck it," he mumbled as he stole a padded envelope from a store while buying a can of beer, "that little mother fucker can pay the postage and sort this shit out." Scribbling on the envelope and pushing it into the post box, his phone was on its way to the Chicago Press, c/o Bradley, Reporter. Inside was a hastily written note,

*This is what you need from me, have it free of charge, God's speed. Tommy.*

Finding a phone booth on the street near a small jazz bar in the French Quarter, he dialled the number on the well thumbed, soiled piece of paper that he had once placed in his wallet while sitting on a plane, flying back into the country from another war zone. He remembered the day well, a captain had passed it to him during a conversation, he had taken it through good manners and stuck it into one of the pockets of his wallet. After a couple of rings the call was answered and Tommy started his road to recovery.

"Hi, my name is Thomas Cookson, former Sergeant in the Marine Corps. I need help, my life has fallen to bits and I think that I might die without you."

"Where are you Thomas?"

"I prefer Tommy, I'm homeless down in New Orleans. I'm cold, hungry and addicted to as many drugs as you can name - do I fit the criteria?"

"You do Tommy, can you get up to see us for an assessment?"

"Where do I need to come to?"

"New York, it's a long way but it will be worth the trip."

"It's going to take me a while to get up to you - I have an address on a piece of paper for a place in Queens, is that still you?"

"Sure is. Get up here friend, let's see what we can do together." The calm voice offered Tommy the sort of hope he hadn't felt in a while as he hung up and contemplated his future for the first time in a long while.

Sitting on the curb outside a truck stop in the back of nowhere wasn't the ideal preparation for recovery. He had watched the sun float across the sky while drivers ignored his pleas for a ride. The temperature was beginning to plunge and his old demons were telling him how to shut out the cold with a last shot when an old bearded driver pushed him in the back with his boot.

"Where you heading son?"

"New York, or anywhere close."

"I can take you half way, better than freezing your ass off out here, not many drivers are left in there to pick you up."

"Half way is better than no way mister, thanks for the ride." He got up and followed the guy to his rig where he climbed up into the cab. Before he turned on the engine, the old guy turned towards him, wrinkling his nose.

"Hell, you don't smell too good boy, maybe you should get in the back, that stink will make me throw up before we cross the state lines."

He got back out and climbed into the back of the truck which was filled with boxes for an engineering company. The driver followed him round.

"No offence boy, here's a blanket. Try get some rest, it's going to be a few hours."

It was cold in the back, but still warmer than life on the

streets. The truck ploughed on for hours until he heard the hiss of the brakes before the doors opened and a torch shone into his face.

"We need to stop for a while, I'm going to get a few hours rest in the cab. Just one thing first boy, even though you stink like a skunk I need you to do something for me, it gets lonely out here at night and a man needs a little comfort. You take care of me and I will let you sit up front with me in the morning."

"What do you mean take care of you?"

"I've given you a lift out of the kindness of my heart, it would be nice if you repaid me with a bit of man love. You know what I am talking about boy?"

"Yeah, I know - what do you want from me?"

"Suck on my lollipop and I'll give you the money to ride a bus from our drop off, all the way to New York. No one will ever know." Jumping up into the back he pulled the doors shut and flicked on an internal light.

"We got a deal boy?"

Tommy broke the man's neck before he could undo his belt, his body flopping lifeless onto the floor. Making a space behind a wall of boxes, he dragged the body in and hid it after first removing the guy's shirt, boots and trousers.

"Yeah, guess I just broke the deal," he said as he hopped out, closing the doors behind him.

The engine fired up and Tommy headed north towards the Big Apple. A fat wallet sat beside him on the passenger seat, probably a thousand bucks, maybe the old guy's wages for the trip, or just pocket money for drink, food and whores. Either way, it belonged to Tommy now. He typed in the new destination and SatNav spoke to him. He had another thousand miles to go and he would arrive in seventeen hours.

The bright lights of another truck stop were welcome after a further four hours of driving and he needed fuel, food, a shower and some clean clothes. The old guy was a similar size, just not in the belly but that belt he had whipped off would come in useful.

Pulling into the truck park he searched his pockets. He

remembered that he had one last wrap of drugs stashed away, and in the darkness of the parking lot he cooked it up before shooting it into his sore foot. The effects were instant and took away the pain in his body, allowing a few minutes of calm before he made his way inside to find the rest room area. A row of hot showers waited empty as he slipped into the furthest one in the line. A short time later black water ran down the drain as months of grime worked itself loose, and using a sachet of shampoo and a half filled shower gel that had either been discarded or left for this event, he scrubbed himself for twenty minutes. Tommy then threw his old clothes into a bin while pulling on the new.

The fit was poor but they were clean, the belt pulled to the maximum was hidden under a thick checked fleece top and with hot food in his stomach, he was ready to fill up and hit the road.

"Hey, you're not Bill, why the fuck are you in his cab?" A large black guy approached him, pulling out a knife. "Answer the question, mother fucker!"

"Bill is in hospital, he had a fall back in New Orleans and broke his leg so I need to get this load up there for him."

"Is that right, so why are you wearing his goddamn clothes?" Another two drivers appeared, "Everything okay Lloyd?"

"No, this fucker has taken Bill's truck, and his clothing. Phone the police, let's get them to sort this out."

Tommy tried to spring forwards towards the guy with the knife but the haze of drugs slowed his reaction and he was brutally taken down by a spanner to the back of his head. He hit the tarmac face down and lay there oblivious to his surroundings. A noise made him open one eye.

"What's your name boy?" Two police officers stood over him and Tommy could feel the handcuffs cutting in behind his back.

"And why is there a dead man in the back of the trailer? I think that you have some explaining to do son."

# CHAPTER NINE

Pat Hunter's phone rang. He checked his watch, it was late on a Monday evening and he didn't recognise the number but took the call anyway. He had been stuck in this Dallas hotel for the past few days and he would have gladly chatted to an insurance call centre if it relieved the boredom for a few seconds.

"Hi Pat, it's Melissa, we have a problem with the house and the evidence." Her distress made her skip any pleasantries and get straight to the point of her call.

"Have the FBI got back to you already? What do you mean by a problem?"

"It looks like someone wanted to destroy everything that I've done, they have burnt my house down Pat."

Pat got up off his bed as he realised this wasn't just a social call. "Wait, wait, just a minute, has this just happened?"

"No, it happened on Saturday night while we were out in the restaurant. The fire trucks we saw drive past, they were for me. Eric Bent thinks that someone broke in and started the fire deliberately but I think it was the police who broke in, they didn't want the truth to come out."

"Is there anything I can do to help out?"

"No, I just thought that you should know....all the hard work from the past few months putting the clues in place has gone up in smoke - we need to start again."

"I'm so sorry Melissa, you must be gutted but don't give up, let's keep on looking for the missing girls - remember I have a promise to keep." They ended the call and Pat stood staring at the phone, mentally digesting what Melissa had told him.

The FBI agents sat with Captain Eric Bent and his boss Deputy Police Chief, Shay Bennett. One of them opened the interview.

"Ok gentlemen, we have had an opportunity to review some of

the details provided but obviously we have lost a treasure trove of evidence held by Miss Jagger. Looking through the records, it's not pretty reading, Mr Bent. We have counted at least ten opportunities for you to interview Miss Jagger officially. By the testimony of your own staff, she was shown the door every time and we have seen five records of your staff using force to eject her - the mother of a missing girl thrown out of your station Mr Bent. How do you explain that action?"

Eric Bent opened his drawer and took out three folders. "Each of these files contains pleas for help from me to the Bureau. Do you want to see the replies from your management? You were not interested in helping. In fact, if you look at this document, you asked that I don't allow her into the building again and you offer assistance in prosecuting her. Now how do you explain your own actions?" They took the files and studied them before placing them back on the desk, looking slightly less comfortable with their interrogation of the police officers as one looked back up at Eric Bent.

"Ok, I think we have a big problem between us. You have obviously not interviewed any witnesses, including Mr Cookson who offered you evidence and that is not acceptable. However it would seem that our office could have handled your requests a little more sympathetically." Bent nodded.

"Agreed, so where do we go with this?"

"You need to conceal all evidence that we have mismanaged the investigation. There will simply be an agreement drawn up between us that Miss Jagger was provided with assistance throughout the missing person's investigation. We must be clear that at that time it was a missing persons report, nothing more than that." The agent pushed a file over towards the captain.

"Here is a full dossier we have made of every interaction you may have had with her. It's a comprehensive account of all meetings, of course we have used a little imagination in drafting the report, but we hope it will stand up to scrutiny." Bent looked through the paperwork.

"That's good, only the problem we now have is that Miss

Jagger has involved a newspaper and TV celebrity in a campaign against me. I can't make that vanish or deny having the conversation." The agent nodded.

"No, but we have built that into our dossier." Here, he pushed over another file.

"This covers the conversations you had on that day and the actions taken afterwards. It's their word against yours Captain, easy as that."

"What do you think Shay?" Eric looked at the deputy chief of police for support.

"I think that you have dropped the ball Eric, why didn't you bring this to my attention?" Bent looked at him in disbelief.

"Come on Shay, we discussed it a few times."

"Do you have copies of our meetings? I do, and I can't see one mention of Miss Jagger and her visits."

"You son of a bitch Shay, you would sell me down the river for this?"

"You just need to get your business in order, my position is coming up shortly Eric as I'm taking an early retirement. Get this right and my seat is yours. The assistant director of the FBI is going to be running for Senate in time for the next election and even a scent of poor leadership could blow her chances out of the water before she starts." Bent sat back in his chair shaking his head.

"Oh I get it, you are getting paid off for your silence while others within the department are trying to get their own person into power. Screw what has happened and how we have ignored a desperate mother. How do you sleep?"

"I just take the options presented to me." The agents nodded as Bennett spoke. "Look at the evidence Eric, this neglect spells prison time for all of us if it is uncovered, we disregarded all of her concerns. Whatever way you look at it, she was right. These girls are all dead somewhere and we all know it. The trouble is, we just shut our eyes and hoped it would burn itself out, same as we did with the Zodiac killer from the '70s; we couldn't find him, but he eventually stopped. At some point they either die or make a mistake."

Bent looked at him, resigned to the corruption. "Ok, I will sort my end out, we can't get in the way of politics for Christ's sake." He looked back at the two agents. "How about Washington and your promised investigation, is that even real?"

"We will do what we can do, but we don't have any spare staff, the President has seen to that. Our teams are dispersed everywhere trying to solve bullshit issues so Miss Jagger will just have to believe that we are pulling up trees behind the scenes. I do feel some sympathy for her, Eric, but we are in a self survival mode at the moment."

"So let's just get this right, we have a serial killer on the loose in the USA, he is in full attack mode by the looks of the similar style disappearances we're having reported to us, yet we are doing nothing about it." Eric was starting to get angry.

"Yep Eric, that's the long and short of it and unless we get a break and find some evidence, he will carry on until he decides to stop, dies or messes up. So far we have kept it from the public as best we can. We don't need to advertise that an individual is running rings around us."

Bent shook his head in despair. "God help us all. Ok, I will sort my department while you guys put the umbrellas up at your end. If Miss Jagger makes it rain, I don't want to get wet."

The others packed up their bags and left the building leaving Eric reflecting on the conversation. He would have to lie for the greater good, the major problem for him being that he would look as though he had an involvement in everything bad that was happening. If Melissa pushed for an investigation they were finished and so was the plan to have an FBI member within government. He was stuck between a rock and a hard place. He liked Melissa and he knew Mia as she had been to Jazz's birthday parties numerous times over the years. If Shay Bennett hadn't closed down his request to hold a complete investigation at the first time of asking they wouldn't have needed to lie. And now the bastard was denying it and burying him in politics. He didn't need Shay's offer of promotion; he needed someone to pay him off for silence, and Eric had just taken out a policy that would cover him when the crap started to fly his way. He had operated too long in this shady world to have missed a trick. In his thirty years of policing this was the first time he had been asked to be dishonest, and certainly the first time he had neglected his home town, none of which sat very well with him so he needed to be sure that when push came to shove he had the ammunition to fight his corner.

# CHAPTER TEN

The girl regained consciousness and tried to focus on the room she was being held in. Her head throbbed as though split in two, the hammer which had crashed down into it sat on top of a wooden pallet propped against the far wall. Squinting painfully through bloodshot eyes, she tried to spot any potential escape routes and thought that if only she could reach the window she could try and raise the alarm.

The room was large, maybe an old stable, the concrete floor so cold it was hurting her backside. It appeared that an old wooden pallet had been broken up, the wooden slats nailed against a glassless window frame forming tight bars. The light could hardly penetrate this barrier and the dust in the air could be seen dancing in the last of the pale beams which fought their way through.

The ceiling was high, possibly ten feet and made of concrete, the only way in and out being a large double wooden door which she assumed was bolted from the outside. She could see no daylight through the cracks and the room had the feeling of being part of a larger building.

Trying to get to her feet and feeling the tug of a rope, she looked down where it became clear that she was tied to a large metal ring fixed into the wall. The gag across her mouth bit into the sides making the area red raw and with cable ties holding her hands securely behind her back, she was going nowhere.

Straining her ears for ten minutes whilst controlling her breathing she continued to try to work out where she was held. There was nothing, the silence itself deafening. And then the sound of footsteps coming down concrete steps grabbed her attention - this wasn't a stable, she was in a cellar of some description.

She heard the bolt slipping across and a hooded man walked purposefully towards her. He didn't talk, just placed two dog bowls on the floor, one with water, one with food, before removing her gag. She waited until he was gone before twisting on to her knees and eating like an animal.

Sitting back against the wall the door opened again, she hadn't heard him approach this time so he must have been standing outside the door watching and waiting. What did he want? He stood motionless, dressed in a black boiler suit and wearing a balaclava, just watching her, unspeaking and oozing menace. After a minute of this intimidation he approached her, kicking the metal bowls to one side, any remaining water hitting the wall beside her. She thought she'd better try and talk herself out of her situation before he gagged her again.

"Ok I don't know what you want with me, my folks have no money, I only live with my mum and she cleans other people's houses to try to keep food on the table. You have made a big mistake, just let me go and I will keep quiet. I will tell my mum that I was with a guy I met and no one will ever know what you did."

"You aren't going anywhere until I get paid, then we will see."

"I just said, we haven't got a single cent to pay for anything, we can't pay you."

Picking up the bowls he looked down at her, cold eyes staring through the holes in the balaclava. "If I don't get paid you will starve to death, I can't keep feeding you for free." Shutting the door she heard him make his way back upstairs.

# CHAPTER ELEVEN

Pat's phone rang again as he was planning tonight's live show which he was filming from Dallas Zoo with the new Sumatran tiger. Donations from the show had help fund him bringing the tiger into the USA from a Russian zoo going broke. The public had fallen in love with the animal straight away, but tonight would be the first time that he had got up close and personal to her. He loved having the ability to get in with his tigers, play rough and gain their confidence - ideally he started when the tigers were cubs but tonight he was going in with a one year old. It would be a challenge, but this is what the people liked to watch.

"Hey Melissa, twice in one day, how are you doing?"

"Going well, just wondered if you could mention a girl who has just gone missing from a town called Pilot Point around an hour north of Dallas? I will send you some information and photographs over, she's been missing for two days…."

"Sure, I'll be going live at eight and there will be plenty of interest tonight – I'm getting in with a big tiger for the first time. Hope she's friendly!"

"I'll be watching, good luck and stay safe Pat. Brandon has stuck around for a couple more days so we will double the viewing figures," she laughed as she ended the call. There was a knock at her hotel room door, it was Brandon.

"When are the FBI guys planning on coming back?" he asked as she invited him in.

"Maybe next week, there wasn't much for them to study after the fire. Eric Bent just gave them a list of his files and they vanished as quickly as they came; probably another empty promise."

"Look at what I've just found…." he passed her his phone and she took a quick glance.

"Yep, a bunch of pictures of me working at my desk, what are you getting at?"

"Look at the walls behind you, I was just sending my mum some photos of you and I noticed it." Melissa stared intently at one of the photos, zooming in on the wall.

"Jesus Christ! The map and my written notes, you have caught it all on the camera."

"Didn't even think about it until just now, I can blow the pictures up and we can put it all back together."

"Brandon, you are a legend!" Melissa grabbed him in a hug before releasing him and looking again at the photos.

"Ok, no one must know we've got these photos. We can't lose them again."

"Shall I let Pat know?"

"No seriously, only you and I need know, the fewer the better. Tell Pat and he might let it slip on TV, then we are in danger." She looked at him, voicing her fear. "Someone burnt down my home to destroy what I have so they wouldn't think twice about hurting us to make sure that it's gone forever."

Pat spent the afternoon around the new tiger, he had to establish what trust he could build up between them and skewering a small piece of meat on a stick he pushed it through the bars. She walked straight over and took it, brushing herself on the bars like a domestic cat. He repeated the process another dozen times until she was looking at him for food. He felt he had built up a good initial rapport with the 170 pound cat who had returned to playing around the water and he now had to make a decision. It was just two hours until they would broadcast the show so he turned to his helper, talking to him quietly so as not to spook the tiger.

"Ok Conrad, I'm going in with her, you know what to do if she gets too excited."

"Sure Pat, I have a fire extinguisher and a stiff broom – I'll drag your half eaten ass out of there if needs be."

"Yep, but less of the half eaten if you don't mind."

Sliding open the gate, he walked two paces into the enclosure. She hid in the undergrowth at first, occasionally poking her head out to look before she became angry and agitated at him encroaching into her territory. She moved forwards five paces and crouched, eyeing him up, waiting for the opportunity. Pat understood the body language, she was waiting to attack him from behind if he turned around but was trying to build up the confidence to charge from the front. She couldn't and turned her own back on him instead. Pat spoke softly.

"See that Conrad? She has turned her back on me, I'm not a threat and she trusts me. We are making progress." Backing out of the enclosure and double checking the door, they high fived.

"I'm going in tonight, same routine and I think that we can give them a good show," he confirmed. He needed the viewers to name her tonight so wanted to give them enough of a thrill to motivate them into coming up with plenty of choices.

Bradley and Melissa sat online spellbound by the performance, almost holding their breath as the tiger moved to within touching distance as Pat whispered a commentary for the fans. On the left of the screen a long stream of names scrolled past and at least every third person was donating money or buying merchandise. They, like the tiger, were eating out of his hand and seemingly he knew every person who had joined his pack and had a story to tell about nearly every town and city he had visited.

"He is a force of nature Brandon," Melissa said, her eyes still glued to the screen, "look at the people who give him cash, it's incredible. He has promised to run an appeal for us tonight, for a young girl lost near Dallas. Tens of thousands of people will see it." As if hearing her, Pat then looked directly to camera.

"And lastly and on a far more serious note, you will have seen some of our appeals for help in finding missing people, something very close to my own heart as I have said before. This young lady has been reported missing from her home only one hour north of this zoo." A photo of a smiling girl filled the screen as he read out the details provided by Melissa.

"If anyone, anywhere knows anything or has seen something that is out of the ordinary or is difficult to explain, no matter how small, please contact the number below. Let's get her home safely."

Melissa's phone rang and picking it up, she realised it was two thirty in the morning.

"Hell Pat, do you know the time?"

"The police have just contacted me, they have had a tip off about the missing girl." Melissa was suddenly fully awake and sat up, turning her light on.

"What, Tanya from tonight?"

"Yes, Tanya. They're planning a raid on an abandoned farm - they are going in now."

"Where? How?" She tried to clear the sleep from her brain.

"How many girls are there? Is Mia there Pat?"

"They don't know, they are just acting on information. Someone has spotted a known drug addict going in and out of the house so they are going in to have a look. I will ring you back when I know."

Tanya tried to sleep but the cold air coming through the broken window was keeping her awake as she lay shivering. A noise outside caught her attention as the wooden panels barring the window were silently removed. The thud of two people jumping into the room filled her with terror before a flashlight shone into her face as two police officers stood in front of her.

"Tanya?" She nodded as a slim man spoke quietly into his radio.

"Got her, she's safe."

An explosion above their heads sent shock waves through the house followed by the sound of a dozen or more voices shouting.

"Police, get on the ground." And then silence.

Melissa's phone rang again but this time she was wide awake and sitting with Brandon who she had woken immediately after the first call from Pat.

"They have found the girl alive, she was the only girl there though," Pat told her, her phone on loud speaker so she and Brandon could both hear. "I'm sorry Melissa, I know you were hoping Mia would be there too. She is back with her mum and on the way to hospital. She has a nasty head injury but apart from that seems ok."

"Oh my God Pat, we did that! If she is alive others could be too. It's a good sign."

"The police are saying that it's a similar attack to the girl found dead, the weapon he used to abduct her is very similar to the one used on the girl in the trunk. They could be linked in which case we might have found our guy."

"He needs to tell us where the other girls are, I hope the FBI get their hands on him and get that bastard to talk." Melissa paced the room as she spoke, her excitement that they had moved a huge step forward in finding Mia palpable.

"They are conducting some forensic tests on the hammer as we speak so we should have an answer soon."

Twenty-three-year-old drug addict, John Booking, sat in the interview room sipping water from a plastic cup as two FBI agents sat watching him.

"Ok John, are you ready to talk to us yet? You have a damn lot of explaining to do."

"I will tell you all I know," his voice croaked as the need for heroin gripped his body.

"You are not looking too good there, do you want the doctor?"

"No, let's get this done so I can go home."

"Ok, when we are done here we can discuss that issue. Why were you in that old farm building John?"

"You know why I was in that place, I was looking after the girl."

"Looking after her? She has a cracked skull and the medics have placed her in a self induced coma. The poor girl has a bleed on the brain, she is dehydrated and suffering from hypothermia

- that's not what I call looking after someone."

"I was paid to keep her there, a guy contacted me on my phone and offered me five thousand dollars to take her and keep her in the house until he showed up."

"Do you have a record of the message?"

"No, I had to leave my phone at a drop off point in Dallas and he took it after I left."

"Why did you do that?"

"He left drugs there; he said that he would return the phone along with the cash and more drugs when the job was done. He is coming to the place tonight to pay me."

"You expect us to believe that bullshit? You received a message on your phone from a stranger, you gave him your phone and half killed an innocent girl for free? What planet are you on boy?"

"Look, I have just got into town and in case you haven't noticed I don't have anywhere to live. I have been making my way around this country trying to get a break and I've been set up, someone is using me."

"And how have you travelled around the country with no money?"

"I stole cars, vans, whatever I needed, mostly beaten up old things. I can tell you where I have been if I can see a doctor....I need the doctor now, I don't feel too good."

"Your prints are all over the hammer, you smashed her head open, or was that someone else as well?"

"I want a lawyer." The agent leading the interview stared at him, thinking this was just the break they needed in solving the case of these missing girls and saving everyone's ass.

"You are going to need the best one John, the hammer you used to smash that young girl's skull into pieces also killed a young girl a few days ago. It also had particles from other people's skin and bone embedded in that wooden handle. What do you have to say about that?"

"I am saying nothing." John Booking sat there shaking, both with a need for his next heroin fix and also from the realisation that he was in well over his head.

They stopped recording before one of them knocked the cup out of his hand, the water spilling over his stained white t-shirt.

"You made her eat and drink from a dog bowl you Goddamn piece of shit. I am going to push for you to be investigated for every missing girl in this country and by the time I have finished with you, you will be begging me for the death sentence."

Banging the table the agent shouted, "Get this bastard into his cell, he can rot in there while he waits for an attorney." Two police officers entered and took him handcuffed into a grim, barren cell where a plastic bowl of dog food had been placed on the floor.

"Ring your bell when you are done, I will take you for walkies and throw you a ball."

"I need a doctor," he repeated as they slammed and locked the barred door.

"No man, you need a fucking vet, now shut up boy and eat up." He could hear the laughter as they walked off down the passage way leaving him alone.

The two FBI investigators sat in the interview room mulling over what he had told them.

"What do you think Brad, have you ever heard such a poor explanation?"

"He did it, we just need to find out how many more he has killed. That bastard is holding far too many secrets, he has travelled all across the country and the car used to take the girl found in the woods was a battered old stolen car, just as he explained. He was caught red handed at the scene with the murder weapon and he has admitted it. His whole profile fits what we are looking for, all we need is a full confession and the deal is done." A bang on the door stopped the conversation and a police officer poked his head in.

"Yes Officer, what is it?"

"Sir, we have a problem, the suspect has just sliced his throat open. He has bled out and we couldn't stop it - the ambulance is on its way but I think he's dead sir."

"How the hell?"

"He used broken plastic from smashing the dog bowl we put in there for a joke, we didn't think he could do it."

"You provided him with a weapon? What sort of law enforcement officers are you? You have allowed a serial killer to end his own life before we could even get him into a court room - that is dumb even by your standards, Holy crap, Washington are going to drop bombs all over this building, and I for one don't want to sit here and wait for it."

Melissa's phone rang, this time she recognised the number of the police captain, Eric Bent.

"Hey, I need to talk to you about the guy taken in for questioning in Dallas."

"Yes Eric, what's happened?"

"He's taken his own life in the police cell. I guess the evidence we had on him for the murder and kidnapping was so strong that he couldn't cope."

"Why, what evidence did you have?"

"We linked him to a number of crime scenes from right across the country. We have DNA on a number of people and we want to identify some of the potential victims. I know this is a difficult request Melissa but do you have Mia's hairbrush? We need her DNA."

"You think this man killed her?"

"We think he was involved but I am not saying that she is dead Melissa."

She began to sob. "Where have you found DNA on this guy? What did he have?"

"It was a weapon Melissa, a hammer. I'm sorry but I need to tell you the truth as it's going to be on National TV this evening. They are calling him a serial killer."

"She's dead isn't she Eric?"

"It looks that way, I am so sorry."

Hanging up in a total daze, she looked at the bare hotel walls, picturing the face of her beautiful daughter and the vision of a filthy man with a hammer standing over her. With a broken heart, she picked up her phone and dialled.

"Pat?"

"Hi Melissa, I have only got a few minutes, lucky I saw the call. Any news?"

"They caught the right guy, they have evidence to link him to a lot of the girls – he's a serial killer Pat and you know what that means?"

"Yes, but let's not give up hope. I have promised you and my sister so don't give up."

"The main stations are going to tell the country tonight that the serial killer has been caught and has killed himself."

"Wait just a second. What the hell do you mean? I thought the police had taken him into custody."

"Yep, they did, but he still killed himself, couldn't live with the guilt apparently."

"Jesus, ok keep me informed, I have a live show from the zoo in two days time but I won't mention it until you give me clearance. I have this show to run for the next few weeks but I'll get down to you when I can, maybe at the weekend?"


The man lay on his hotel bed listening to the six o'clock news. It was incredible, a year's work and numerous killings, all attributed to one young junkie. It was almost an insult - was his work not perfect enough to get the recognition it truly deserved? Every single mission that he had undertaken had been meticulously planned. How dare they blame an imbecile.

But blame him they had, just as he had planned - a drug hungry bum who would do anything for cash and try any scam. He had spotted him straight away, hustling on the street, feeding a habit and it had taken seconds to get his number.

"Hey. I need three guys to clear a garden, one afternoon's work, fifty bucks. Give me your number if you want some fast cash...." The rest had been simple; a fictional promise of five thousand and the guy would have done anything, in fact he did everything. He had cleared his life score and he was reset back to squeaky clean .... what a comfortable position, and what a brilliant mind. He lay, hands behind his head, contemplating his future... *No more killings and I will never now be caught. Can you promise yourself that? No, I thought not ......*

# CHAPTER TWELVE

The slam of the iron gate in some God forsaken prison in an unknown state didn't resonate with Tommy. He thought that his body was operating normally in his haze but a drug addicted homeless normal was not something that most people would recognise. He had been whisked through some type of reception process, not understanding anything that was going on around him, unable to focus on anything except the call of heroin ringing in his ears again. Tommy hadn't even realised that he had left the more gentle setting of the police building before entering the harsher glare of the county jail until a gruff voice asked him if he had any drug or alcohol issues.

"Yeah, I have a heap of drug problems and the police officer has got my stuff. Why, what have you got?" The officer looked at him with no empathy, he only saw another useless junky.

"I have a cell with a locked door, that's where you are going son. I call it cold turkey, not sure what you're going to call it in twenty-four hours. I don't know what planet you're on boy, but those police officers don't give a shit about your drugs, you're mine now."

"Where am I?"

"Tennessee, in prison son and it looks like you'll be with us for some time."

Tommy crashed onto a bunk, vaguely aware of another person lying in the bed above him. The man leaned over the edge of his bunk, staring down at him.

"Hey, you ok? I'm Jess."

" Tommy …. what the fuck is going on?

"You're in trouble, that's what's going on, and I think that in a few hours you will be in bigger trouble. Do you need anything?"

"I always need something."

"I can get whatever you want, no problems. No cold turkey in this cell man, we party twenty-four seven."

"I need to stop taking that crap, it's killing me. How do I get help to quit?"

"Never tried Tommy, no point, we are all stuck in this hell hole so why wouldn't you want to dream of outside a little?"

Slipping into a light sleep Tommy had fitful dreams as the drugs from the truck park ran through his blood stream. The clang of his cell door opening brought him back round to reality.

"Cookson, come with me." He followed, not understanding where he was heading until he reached a sterile looking office where a woman in her fifties sat behind a desk. He was pushed into a seat in front of her, his hands in cuffs.

"Do you have drug or alcohol issues Cookson?"

"Yes, I take a lot of drugs, mainly heroin."

"When was the last time that you used?"

"Yesterday, half an hour before my arrest."

"Are you ready to stop?"

"Sure, how does that work?"

"In here that's easy, the warden makes you stop without any medication, he thinks that it should be down to willpower. I can put you into a cell by yourself if that helps?"

"No point, if I want it, I will find it - doesn't matter which cell I'm in."

"Ok, well, if you need some spiritual support, just ask, we have a good guy here. He will call round and see you at some point anyway." Looking up and nodding, the woman signalled the officer to take Tommy back to his cell.

Jess lay there smiling, knowing where he had just been.

"See brother, you have just found out the hard way, there isn't any help for us poor drug users - oh yeah - apart from God, you'll find out all about that motherfucker as well this morning." He waved a small bag; "Whenever you are ready my friend, easy rates to pay..." Tommy rolled over on his side, facing the wall.

"Keep it, I'm good thanks."

"Cookson!" a voice shouted from outside his cell an hour or so later. "You have a visitor." The officer carried on walking down the landing while Tommy pulled on his shoes before looking through the bars.

"No one knows that I'm here," he said. A Catholic priest stood there smiling.

"Sorry Tommy, God knows that you are here. My name is Father Bell. Pleased to meet you."

One month later

Tommy sat in the legal visits room in the court house, his orange jump suit the only source of any colour in the drab looking room. His hands and feet were shackled as he sat behind the cheap wooden table. The door opened and a smartly dressed guy walked in, placing a folder on the table. "Hi Tommy, my name is Justin. I'm your attorney for the trial." Tommy looked at the guy in front of him who seemed too young to be out of short trousers.

"Great, you are the third new attorney I've seen, I guess they don't give me much chance of winning if the last few have dropped me?"

"Nope, I think that's a fair assessment, but this is the first time that you have been lucid enough to tell your story. In case it slipped your brain, you threw the first two out of the room because they tried to take a deal. I'm new, I know that, but I'm good - if I can find a fault in the case I will spot it, I always do. I'm Harvard trained and they make us pretty good out there."

"Ok Justin, you've sold yourself well, what are we looking at?"

"At the moment, first degree murder for which they will give you a few hundred years with no hope of parole, or the death penalty."

"Great, and what do you think?"

"It's what I know Tommy. Like I said, I'm good. I have found ten people who have come forward since the killing to testify to our firm that they were attacked or raped by the same man. He was a monster Tommy."

"Fuck, you have discovered that already?"

"And more, he had a previous prison sentence for sexual offences against children." Tommy smiled for the first time since his attorney had entered the room.

"Glad I killed the old bastard then."

"Well, here's a theory. You can disagree whenever you chose. You were high on drugs, you were desperate to get to New York to kick the addiction - I already have a copy of the phone call to the help line. The guy made you sleep in the back of the van and tried to sexually assault you as you slept - he had a knife on him."

"Did he?"

"Yes, the police found it beside his body. Anyway, you woke up, panicked and fought back .... you broke his neck in the struggle."

"And why was I wearing his clothing and spending his money?"

"He had already given you a change of clothes, yours were full of lice. I have your original clothing - it stinks Tommy, and yes it is full of bugs." Tommy smiled for a second time.

"I guess that's what happens to us homeless Vets."

"You were hungry and thought that nothing could get worse for you so you took his cash to buy food and fuel to try and run away. That's not a big deal Tommy and it's not a hundred years or death."

"Will that wash with the jury?"

"When I show them who you really are it will. The people you saved in action - I have them here and they are all testifying to your character and bravery. The Marine Corps have sent a representative to help us as well so we have a frickin' army out there rooting for you man. What jury on earth is going to point the finger at you?"

"You did this for me? Why did you take the trouble? I would have just slid back into jail life and disappeared forever."

"Like I said, I'm Harvard and we don't let our heroes down. Now, are you ready to kick butt Sergeant Tommy Cookson?"

"Let's do this."

"Ladies and gentlemen of the jury, have you reached a decision on which you all agree?"

"We have, your Honour."

"On the case of first degree murder, do you find the accused guilty or not guilty?"

"Not Guilty."

The court room erupted with celebration and even the prosecution raised a smile. The judge looked over towards their table.

"Thomas Cookson, you have been found not guilty by this court and you are free to leave." Emotions whizzed through his head as Justin led him out into the public area where they took a seat in a small, discreet office.

"Ok Tommy, I took the liberty of bringing you a fresh set of clothing, I thought that we might need them." There was a knock at the door and a uniformed Marine Officer stepped inside. Tommy stood instantly.

"At ease. You have done your duty Tommy, I'm Major Rik Edmonton, and I'm here with gifts." He passed an envelope across the desk.

"This is twelve thousand dollars in cash, it's what we owe you for the payments due into your bank. We have also set up a bank account for you, all further payments of fifteen hundred dollars each month will be paid into that account directly. Please sign here." He put the necessary paperwork on the table in front of Tommy who signed, and started to laugh.

"I was a bum a month ago and I couldn't buy a fucking conversation." The major looked at him sadly.

"You were never a bum, we just couldn't find you. You are a Goddamn hero son, welcome back." He held out his hand.

"Thank you sir, I am happy to have served." Tommy stood, took the hand and shook it warmly. "I'm also happy to be back." The smile left Rik's face and a more concerned look engulfed his features as he held out a typed letter.

"Tommy, the hostel in New York has held a place open for you - I have the details here. It may be a good idea to get up there and get yourself prepared for the world, it could be a few weeks well spent."

"Yeah, think you're right but I might fly this time, seems safer." Rik reached into his bag.

"Thought you might say that too," he said, passing him another envelope. "Here are the tickets, you fly out this evening."

Seven Weeks Later

Melissa sat in her newly rented apartment, it was smaller than the house but until the insurance company agreed to pay for the rebuilding of the family place it was all she had. Plus it was a thousand times better than sitting in a cheap hotel room. Brandon had long since returned to work and apart from the weekly online chats, she had not seen him for a while and she was missing the inane conversations that seemed to spring from fresh air.

The doorbell rang, the harsh tone making her flinch as it was the first time anyone had bothered to call in on her since she had moved in. Opening the door she was confronted by a large man, possibly in his thirties, who looked at her with sorrow in his watery eyes. It took no more than a second for the penny to drop.

"Tommy Cookson! What the hell has happened to you? You look a different man."

"Thank you, I admit I was off the rails for a bit, but I knew I needed to catch up with you, mainly to apologise for the way I treated you, but also to share information with you, and I don't want money this time. That will haunt me forever …. I'm so sorry."

Giving him a quick hug she looked at him quizzically as she led him through into the lounge.

"You know that they caught the guy don't you?"

"I saw it on TV up in New York and that's what I need to talk about. I saw Mia getting dragged into a van Melissa and I couldn't stop it, I was too far away. But I did get around five seconds of it on film, which I kept on my phone."

"Do you still have it?"

"No, I sent it to the journalist up in Chicago, a guy called Brandon. He tried to interview me up there a few months ago."

"Yeah, I'm good friends with him, and I heard that you left him standing on the street with a McDonalds in his cold pink hands. When did you send that?"

"Maybe two months, possibly three, I forget. I posted it up to his office."

"Wait one minute," she said and taking her phone, she made a call.

"Brandon, guess who I have with me? Tommy! He has sent you a package around three months ago, it's a phone with a video of the guy taking Mia – I'll put him on."

"Hi Brandon, Tommy. Sorry about the interview man, I was in a bad way. I sent my phone to you in a white envelope - I addressed it to your office. It has a recording on it."

"I haven't got it, let me check my drawer." There was a pause where Tommy heard papers rustling as Brandon searched before his voice came back on the line. "Nothing Tommy, I don't have it." Tommy banged his forehead with the palm of his hand in frustration.

"Brandon, you must have it, I sent it to you. Check again please."

"Tommy, I'll go and ask around but I haven't seen it."

"It's important that you find it Brandon, the man who took Mia is not the same guy who killed himself. The dead prison guy is a lot shorter than the man I saw, he was at least six-three, the guy they arrested was five-nine on a good day."

Melissa gasped, this was the first time she had heard this news. "Can you be sure Tommy? You were really high."

He held the phone to one side while he spoke to Melissa.

"I know what I saw." He returned to the call, "Brandon, do your best man."

Putting the phone back on the table Melissa considered the possible options.

"Ok so maybe there were two of them, we may never know. What evidence can you give to the police?"

"Without the phone, nothing. Any court room would laugh my evidence out of the door; as you have pointed out, I was out of my brain. But I know what I saw, the guy I saw grabbing Mia banged his head on the top of the van, a five-nine guy would need to jump to do that."

"What was Mia doing?" Melissa pleaded, frantic for information.

"She looked out cold, I thought that she was dead."

"Was she dead Tommy? Was she fucking dead in that parking lot?" He shrugged his massive shoulders. "I can't say. She wasn't moving."

"Fuck Tommy! I didn't need this shit. If what you are saying is right, the killer is still out there and they arrested the wrong man."

"Sorry, I just felt that I needed to say something. Up until now, no one has listened - I tried to report it to Captain Bent at the time but he didn't listen either, he just threw me out."

Lost in the enormity of listening to the testimony of Mia's last seconds of freedom, Melissa drifted off into self preservation mode. She didn't want to hear that her little baby was killed in clear view of the public and in a busy parking lot. Why didn't anyone stop him? She snapped back into the present.

"Thanks Tommy, leave me your number... can I phone you back when I sort my head out? We need to find that phone." Nodding, he realised that this had been too much for her to comprehend. Should he have given her the news in a softer manner? It wasn't how he was trained to deal with things so he quickly left, closing the door behind himself on the way out. Not sure if he had done the right thing or not, he had unburdened himself of the guilt he felt, but had just heaped a load more on Melissa.

As soon as he had left Melissa picked her phone back up and dialled.

"Pat, it's Melissa, we need to chat, are you busy?"

"No, I'm back in the hotel, just getting ready to film the last episode of the show. I will be picking my new helper tonight."

"I'm guessing it's the young blonde one who keeps flirting?"

"You'll have to wait and watch. Anyway, what's up?"

"It's strange; a witness to Mia's kidnapping, Tommy, just showed up at my door, says he has a video on his phone of her being taken."

"What? That's amazing, just a shame that the scumbag killed himself before the court could do it for him. Is Tommy the homeless guy?"

"He was, but not anymore; he looked like a Marine again."

"So he has shown you the film?"

"No, he hasn't got it on him, but it's more serious than that, the kid isn't the killer."

"How do you know that?"

"Tommy saw everything, the killer is a big guy, maybe six-three or taller. John Booking was a lot shorter."

"He must have made a mistake, they have all the evidence in the world to convict him, he was our guy for sure."

"I'm not so sure Pat, I'm waiting to see the film. The phone was posted to Brandon up in Chicago but at the moment it has been lost somewhere. He's looking for it now so hopefully he'll find it."

"This Tommy guy needs to go to the police with his evidence; does he have anything else?"

"Nope, and no one believes him because he was a drug addicted bum."

"That's the problem Melissa so let's just wait. Do you have Tommy's address or contact details if I need to chat to him?"

"You don't need to talk to him, that will make it complicated - leave it to me."

"No problem, I'll come down this weekend, I have some things

93

to discuss with you. Ask Tommy to come along and we can have a meal."

"Ok Pat, I'll see you on Saturday."

Looking up at her wall she studied the maps and clues she had started to collate again since the fire. *Cincinnati, Memphis, New York, Utah, San Diego, Omaha, Philadelphia, Rio Grande, Oklahoma, Denver and Dallas. What did they have in common? Who would travel to these individual places just to take young girls, and why in clusters? He must stay around in town for a week or so. It doesn't make any sense.* Picking up the phone, she contacted Eric Bent again.

"Hi Eric, it's Melissa. What if I told you that I didn't think John Booking was the killer?"

"I would say that you're crazy. We have rock solid evidence that he did it, we even have the weapon with his DNA on and that of lots of the girls. He was our guy, case closed."

"We have some new evidence, a video on a phone showing someone else taking Mia."

"Hang on, is this that homeless guy? He tried to sell me the phone for a thousand bucks back then and wouldn't show me shit. He's bluffing Melissa, he's just after your money."

"He's back in town Eric, cleaned up and sober offering it for free."

"Bring it down then and I will have a look at it."

"We don't have it, it's currently lost." Melissa could hear Captain Bent's sigh down the phone.

"Surprise, surprise. The case is shut Melissa, I'm sorry that this bum has opened up old wounds and my advice is don't get involved with him. He's just killed a guy in a truck and walked free from court. Hero my ass, avoid him at all costs." The line went dead.

Brandon finished writing his article. The few days he'd had with Melissa had proved to be profitable and he had a heart breaking story to tell the readers; lost kids leaving heartbroken parents, and a young drug addicted killer wandering the nation who selected victims and showed no mercy.

He also had an invitation to spend a lot of time with Pat; this would lead to TV work and a promised book deal when it was over. On top of this, he had developed a love interest with Jazz Bent and they had stayed in touch since he returned to Chicago. Brandon counted the days until he would be able to go back down and spend a weekend.

Submitting the article he felt a flush of pride, his first major piece, guaranteed to catch the attention of the reader. Almost as soon as he'd pressed send on his screen, his phone rang.

"Brandon, come to my office. This article is brilliant and I have a proposal for you that I think that you might like, but I'm not sure about your mum." Bounding up the stairs two at a time to the office, he entered, breathless.

"Yes Mr Grayson, what did you have in mind?"

"This is a good piece of work Brandon, how about we let you loose for a whole year with the tiger guy, follow him around the country, and write a monthly article? I have spoken to Mr Hunter and he's agreed to split your salary fifty-fifty. At the end of the trip, you come back to work for us. How does that sound?"

"I'd like to do that Sir, it sounds like a dream."

"Ok, well, there's a few things to sign that I've had drawn up ready....I was pretty sure you'd go for this opportunity. Don't let us down cowboy and keep in touch. And just in case you find yourself having too good a time, if you miss a deadline you will come right back to us. Understood?" Grayson pushed some papers across his desk towards Brandon.

"Sure, what am I signing?"

"It says that if you don't return to this newspaper at the end of the twelve months, you will owe us fifty percent of the salary you have been paid." Brandon had a quick read through and took the pen Mr Grayson held out to him.

"When do I start?" he asked as he signed the last page of the document.

"Next week, it will give you a bit of time to sort your shit out. We'll see you next year."

Floating out of the office a thought banged into his brain - *the phone*. For the fourth time that week he went into the mail room office where the secretary looked at him with despair.

"Are you are coming about that parcel again? What is it with you? It isn't here, I've told you…check for yourself." Brandon walked into the back office, a meticulously organised room and saw his pigeon hole was empty as usual. He returned to the desk.

"Jane, what am I going to do? It was a really important letter with a phone in it."

"Why didn't you say it was a phone that you were waiting for? We've had an old battered phone sitting on the desk for weeks, no one knew where it came from so I think someone threw it out Honey." Brandon stared at her in disbelief.

"Why would anyone throw it out?"

"It was a piece of shit, cracked screen and no battery life, just sat there waiting for someone to collect it. What do you want me to do?"

"If it turns up again it's mine, please keep it safe."

"If I find it I will phone you sweetheart, just don't hold your breath."

Riding his bike back home through the busy traffic gave Brandon the chance to think. He had gained the respect of Mr Grayson and was definitely the golden boy of the moment. He had stumbled over the story of the year and also had the chance to have a brilliant adventure and make a few bucks from a book. At just eighteen, life was looking good.

"Hi Mum," he called as he entered the house. The smell coming from the kitchen was delicious so he made his way straight there and looked through the glass of the oven where he could see the crunchiest roast potatoes cooking away next to a rib of beef.

"Mum, this looks fantastic, what's the occasion?" He laughed as he said it; normally she was too tired to lift her head off the couch when he arrived home.

"Well, I just had a call from Mr Grayson, it seems my boy is going to become a man this year. Thought that I had better feed you up before you go out into that big, bad world."

"I was just about to tell you Mum, are you ok with it all?"

"Well, I managed when your dad walked out on us so I guess I can cope for a few months without you." Brandon walked over to where she was putting mats on the table and put his arms around her in a big hug.

"I'll come back some weekends, and as you say, it's not forever. If I get this right, the paper will give me a longer contract. It's my chance."

"I say go for it, now have a shower and dinner will be ready in thirty minutes."

His phone rang the minute he started to undress. Melissa.

"Hi, Melissa, what's up?"

"Two things," her voice was slightly agitated. "Did you manage to locate the phone?"

"No, one of the girls thinks that they threw the phone out as it had been sitting on the desk for a while and they thought it was junk. But they will keep looking – I'm sorry."

"Threw it out? Jesus fucking Christ!" This did nothing to improve Melissa's growing temper and she carried on with her tirade of complaints. "And secondly, I've just been sent the article you have written for your paper."

"And that's good isn't it?" Brandon asked, feeling from the tone of her voice that he wasn't going to get a positive response.

"Brandon, I shared my home with you, I treated you like goddamn family. So where was Mia's name in your report? Where was any glimmer of hope for all the parents waiting for the next phone call or knock on the door? You talk about serial killers and police raids, you talk about blood stained hammers and DNA evidence. You even talk about fucking plastic dog bowls. How am I supposed to feel Brandon, because at the moment I just feel used?"

"It wasn't like that Melissa, I just wrote what the editor wanted in the story. I had included Mia and the other girls in the first draft but he said that I didn't have the column space for everything. Sorry, I didn't mean to upset you." Melissa gave a big sigh, knowing she was taking her frustrations out on him.

"Just make yourself useful and find the phone. I'll see you Saturday when you have a lot of apologising to do. There'll be quite a group of us here and we're all going out for a meal, me, you, Jazz, Pat and Tommy." This was great news to Brandon.

"Is Tommy back together again? The last time I saw him he was a mess."

"A hundred percent beef cake again Brandon, he could take any girl's heart with those looks."

"What, better than me?" he quipped, feeling Melissa's mood had lightened.

"Oh no sweetheart, no one is better than you," she laughed. "Your little boy lost looks have won over Jazz."

"You know it, see you on Saturday." Brandon hung up with a big smile on his face.

# CHAPTER THIRTEEN

The camera rolled as Pat spoke to the lens, the roar of a tiger and the chattering of monkeys behind him telling the waiting audience exactly where they were. Bronx Zoo, New York.

"Good evening everyone, we are reaching a peak point of the series. Let's have a recap of where we are with our last few contestants. We lost Justin four weeks ago when he failed to sell any merchandise to members of the public. All of his prices were double that of the other competitors, his thoughts of profit distracted him from making any money at all while the other contestants sold out their entire quota and showed a good profit for the charity." A shot of Justin leaving the hotel in the back of a tiger striped pick-up was shown.

"Three weeks ago we had a double eviction, both Jenny and Rachel falling into a dispute while booking VIP guests for our charity gala. Who would have thought that we would have had such an explosive ending to the show?" A clip came on screen showing the two women fighting over a phone call.

"And then who could forget the literal fall of Zade?" A shot of a man falling into a pile of animal dung was shown to howls of laughter from the crew.

"It seems like cleaning up after the big cats wasn't for him." An interview with a smiling Zade followed in which he gave his reasons for quitting the show.

"And then last week we lost Ali in a close run contest, neck and neck with Beth all week until the remaining three had to give the conservation presentations. Ali fell to pieces in front of the world's leading experts, while Lilly-Ann and Beth powered through to tonight's final. And what an exciting ending we are in for. Before I tell you all what is going to happen, let's hear a word from our sponsors......"

The hotel bed creaked as he rolled off. It had been a while, the dreams had started again and the blood lust was building. His work had been busy and had involved a lot of travelling from state to state. Colleagues didn't have any idea what he was thinking but they were starting to bore him and were getting in the way of what he needed to do. He must hunt, but the memories of the close call in the woods had taught him the lesson of patience. He had watched the police officer vomit on the muddy path before slipping away while he dissolved in panic. A more composed response from the officer and he could have been caught before making good his escape. So many things were in his favour that night, a young mother who stopped to give him a lift on her way into the office in the early morning light had been a life saver, she never made it but her body certainly wouldn't be left in the trunk of a car for discovery, she was going the same way as the others went - it was necessary for the mission. And with all the rumpus over little John Booking, that one left in the trunk would probably go down to him as well, poor thing.

The biting temperatures helped him move around without the eyes of CCTV picking up every movement; a large woolly hat pulled low, a heavy jacket with the collar up protecting exposed flesh and a large black umbrella shielding everything made it so easy.

And so she appeared, an attractive young woman, maybe twenty years old with a smart leather bag, heading to an appointment from the property rental offices. Showing clients around unoccupied buildings and stores, all on her own, one hour of personal time with each high-end client, what could possibly go wrong for her? He brushed passed her as she left her office and noticed her name badge, Sophie Harper. The office phone rang five hours later.

"Good afternoon, Silverstone Agencies, Sophie speaking. How

can I help you?"

"Hi, my name is Trevor Steele, I was wondering if the large factory unit on the edge of town was still available to rent? I just had a look at the outside and it seems to fit in with my requirements for my expanding business. Can I book an appointment with you to see it please?"

"Sure Mr Steele, when would you be available?"

"I'm in meetings all day tomorrow, but I'm free late in the afternoon; when is the latest I can go out there with you?"

"With me? I'm fully booked tomorrow but I can put you onto another colleague?"

"No, my friend dealt with you last year and he recommended you for the job. If you're not available I can wait."

"One moment, Sir." He waited while there was a short pause before her voice came back on the line. "I can fit you in at five thirty tomorrow, it will be dark but if you have seen the outside already that won't be a problem. The building still has full electricity and has only been on the market for two weeks. Shall I book you in?"

"Yes please, I'll meet you over there as I'm working on that side of town so it will save me a thirty minute drive in and back again."

"Sure, I'll meet you by the reception door, it's the blue one opposite the gate."

"Yes I saw that earlier. OK, see you tomorrow Sophie." And that was how easy it was to ambush your prey…set the bait and sit and wait.

Sophie looked up at the rain-filled night sky before climbing into her car. She had been running the business single handed for a couple of days while the owner and his wife had a Vegas two day trip, probably gambling away her next month's bonus. Due back tomorrow she had busted a gut to get everything ready for them as she wanted them happy, but also needed a pay rise.

This factory rental could be the cherry on the cake if it was taken as the firm stood to get ten thousand easy bucks a month for not a lot in return. The contract was tight with all repairs and building works being the company's responsibility and a condition of the contract was that the building must be handed back at the end of the rental period in the same condition it was rented out in. All Silverstone Letting Agencies had to do was count the cash - or in this case count the cost.

Soon exiting the town, she turned onto the industrial site, a plot of three large, newly built warehouse buildings and at the end of the road an older building previously used for meat processing and distribution. She had looked around the site once and didn't like it; although spotlessly clean, an odour still clung in the air where the smell of butchered meat was ingrained. Leaving the lights of the warehouses she turned into the darkness of the yard where a small car was facing her and gave her a reassuring blink of the headlights. A tall man exited his car at the same time as her and they met at the door to the building.

"Hello Mr Steele, what a dreadful night to be looking around this place...shall we go straight in?" She opened the door and flicked on the internal lights as they entered. While he gazed around the space, she opened her briefcase, withdrawing some documents.

"Here are the important details which you will need before making your decision," she told him as she pointed out the square yardage of the building along with all the facilities available. "It was previously a meat processing factory and is still set up as such so it can be ready to go within a very short space of time." Her perfume wafted into his nose, a tantalising odour as she continued to discuss the previous use of the place in blissful ignorance.

"I have to be honest Mr Steele, the place does creep me out a little, especially as I'm a vegan," she laughed.

"Oh that's ok, I'm a full on carnivore. Can I use the rest room here? I've just come from a two hour meeting."

"Sure, everything still works, let me show you where they are."

Sophie looked at him as he entered the room, he was a big guy and maybe if he were ten years younger she could go for him she

thought as she noticed how
the back pack he wore emphasised his broad chest and v-shaped back. She paced the factory floor for another few minutes before she heard a call.

"Sophie, the cubicle door is locked shut and I can't get out. I need a little help or we could be here all night."

"Ok, I don't know what I can do but here I come." Pushing the door to the rest room open, she laughed. "This is a first." The knife slipped straight into her throat as she stared into his laughing eyes before collapsing onto the thick plastic on the floor, looking up in terror as a figure dressed all in white continued to smile.

"Don't fight it honey or there is a lot more pain where that came from." The knife thrust in and out another five times like a piston, blood spurting over the evidence suit, his smile vaporising into a menacing sneer as multiple blood speckles covered his face.

"Just thank me for bringing the plastic over last night, think of the mess."

Wandering the building, now in darkness to avoid any unwelcome interruptions, he picked his way around from room to room. He didn't need anything, he had come fully prepared but it felt like a home from home as he explored the past evidence of butchering.

The smell coming from Sophie was so familiar as she had done what nearly every one of his miserable victims had done in the seconds before life slipped away. Hanging from the meat hook, she looked elegant in the beam of his head torch, as if she were flying through the night sky and it reminded him of an old film he had seen once where Peter Pan flew through the darkness. He pushed her slumping body and the chain gave a rhythmical creak.

"Let's get to work young lady, we have a busy night, and someone is dying to meet you."

It was so much easier working with the tools he was used too, the girl he butchered in the woods had been difficult and he had felt clumsy and unfulfilled; this time he had the feeling of an artist as the knife glided through the flesh effortlessly.

"Now let's have a cleanup and we can all go home Sophie. Would you like that?"

He lay back on the hotel bed, it was nearly 5.30am and he had been up all night with his work. Tonight's lesson was to bring a fold up bike the next time he killed someone who had a car. Getting rid of the little stolen piece of crap that he had been driving around before taking hers to dump had taken far too long and it was another risk he would avoid the next time. Perfection was a hard thing to find. The hot shower which awaited him however, felt like a great end to a truly marvellous night and as the water cascaded over his tired body, as was his routine he considered every action he had taken during the hunt and kill. Did he make any mistakes or leave any clues? Her belongings had been burnt with the car and her appointment diary was destroyed. There was only one thing that he couldn't be sure about, if she had left any notes in her office. But that was fine, the phone call was made from a public phone and he had been so heavily dressed that any CCTV would not be able to identify him.

This latest quest would of course alert that busy body woman, Melissa Jagger who never seemed to give up writing and campaigning. He had never taken a mother and daughter, but there was a first time for everything and it was definitely a thought.

Drying himself down he inspected his face for blood before shaving. He then took out the laptop and logged on, sending a private message.

*Hi sweetheart, up early and ready for work, didn't want to wake you with a call so chat when I get back tonight, love you all x*

The toast popped up out of the toaster with a noisy spring and slapping on some peanut butter, Melissa considered what to do for the day. She needed to find a job as since that creep John Booking had been caught, her online site had fallen silent and so had the donations. People hadn't moved on, they had just accepted the inevitable, everyone that was, except her. Whatever had occurred she needed closure. Mia was almost certainly dead, Tommy had seen as much but closure couldn't come until she could bury Mia's body or the filthy bastard who took her shared his secrets before his execution.....which she was determined would come one day. She phoned Brandon.

"Hey, are we still good?"

"Sure Melissa, at least I hope so. I was planning to stay at yours this weekend."

"No problem. It's only Thursday today so can you do me a favour?"

"Sure, I've been put out to grass up here for the rest of the week so what can I do?"

"Is there any way we can do checks on that guy Booking? You know, where he travelled, where he stayed....he stole so many vehicles he must have been arrested at least once."

"I can try, I have access to a good data base of court cases around the country so as long as he used a real name I may get a result."

"Just try and let me know what you have when you come down to see me."

She rang off and turned on the TV, where the face of a pretty young woman flashed up on the screen. Increasing the volume she watched the report in disbelief.

*'Sophie Harper, aged nineteen, has not been seen since leaving her office at 17.12 yesterday late afternoon, when CCTV shows her locking up the office before driving away in her black Chevrolet Spark. Police were alerted by her worried parents in the early hours of the morning after she failed to show up for a family birthday celebration. Dallas Police have asked for anyone with any information to phone the number below. There appears to be no reason for her to want to lose contact with her family. Her father has made an appeal for her to get in touch, he states that all the family need is for her to make contact.'*

It was like a cold wind smashing against Melissa's face and slumping back into the chair and dropping her toast she mumbled, *"He's still fucking out there and he's still taking girls."*

Grabbing the phone in anger she punched out the numbers.

"Mr Bent, what did I try warn you about? That girl Sophie Harper who has been taken, who the fuck do you think did that? And let me give you a clue, he hasn't risen from the fucking dead you bastard."

"She's been missing for less than twenty hours Melissa, we don't know anything yet."

"Déjà vu Mr Bent, you know it and I know it. We have an inconvenient truth that you are going to have to face, you got the wrong guy." Slamming the phone down she cursed again. "I knew it, I just knew it." She picked the phone back up still livid and dialled again.

"Tommy, it's Melissa, you were right, it isn't our guy. Can you come over? We need to chat."

An hour later he knocked at her door, still wearing his gym clothing. "Sorry, I was in the middle of my workout, good for my mental health apparently."

"And by the looks of it pretty good for the body too," Melissa replied, giving him an appreciative look.

"You're only human Melissa, who can resist a Marine?"

"Very funny," she replied, leading him through to the kitchen and putting the kettle on. "Did you catch the news this morning?"

"I don't have a TV in my room, what's going on?"

"Another girl's been taken half an hour out of the city."

"I wondered how long he would take to start up again; there will be plenty more if we don't find him."

"How do we do that?"

"He must have left a clue somewhere....in the car park with Mia, the guy's face wasn't covered, I just wasn't in a good state to focus but if we had found the phone we could at least put a photograph out there. Someone would know who he is, he must have family or work friends. No one is invisible."

"You did a good job of invisibility for a while."

"Yep, but even I had to come up for air at some point"

"I spoke to the Captain about you, he told me some things…."

"What, like I'm a bum and I was in prison?"

"He told me that you killed a guy."

"I have killed plenty, twenty in one sitting back in Afghanistan.

"That was different and you know it. You were fighting for your life."

"What do you think was happening in the back of that guy's truck? He was trying to put his dick in my ass hoping that I wouldn't mind."

"And you killed him in a fight?"

"Yep, he never said please before he tried."

"Seriously, you are that cold about it?"

"No, it was just one of those dangerous situations that homeless, drug addicted people put themselves in and it happens to someone every single day. If you don't fight back you are screwed, sorry for the pun." She looked at him, sympathy in her eyes.

"You must promise me that you will never get back into that state again."

He let out a grunt. "Didn't plan on it the first time, just thought that I would be like the guy in the books, the former soldier who walks the wilderness and saves the helpless. Trouble is, I became one of the helpless. Life doesn't follow a book narrative unfortunately." Melissa passed him a cup of coffee and sat at the breakfast bar cradling her own cup.

"Tommy, what's happened to my Mia? What do you think he has done with her?"

"Do you want me to tell you the truth?"

"She's dead isn't she?"

"Yep, certainly, possibly even before you knew that she was missing. No one has survived this animal."

"I hoped upon hope that when the girl was found alive with John Booking that the others were hidden in a remote place somewhere."

"Nope, that was a set up to throw the police off the scent. Shows us one thing though Melissa...." He looked at her and noticed the tears running down her face.

"What does it show us Tommy?"

"It shows us that he's worried about you and the group so you must have been closing in on him."

"How would he know?"

"He's probably watching every move you make on line. How many people have signed up for your group?"

"We have over a million followers and growing."

"Well, he's undoubtedly one of those people."

"Fuck, you're on to something, someone burnt down my house and someone tried to frame John Booking. He really is intimidated by us."

"He was, but not any more by the looks of it. We need to take care." Melissa got up and took her mug over to the sink, rinsing it under the tap.

"Let's continue this conversation on Saturday when we're all going out for a meal, just the inner circle of people I trust. We need a strategy to flush this bastard out into the open, maybe set a trap for him."

"Look at the evidence before you start going private detective on this shit. The man is an expert at killing and he leaves no clues. That tells me that he plans everything down to the last single detail. He is a cold and calculated killer so you're not going to find it easy to trap this guy. He could even be former police or military as he's forensically aware...and where the hell are the bodies? These things just can't be hidden forever; someone, somewhere will be walking a dog, hunting or going running and they will see something. I don't want to upset you but when I buried my old dog in his favourite field a few years ago, animals dug him up within two weeks." He stopped when he saw Melissa's face, "I'm sorry, I wasn't thinking."

"Tact isn't a strong point Tommy is it?"

"Engaging brain before opening mouth? No, never got the

hang of that one." He tried to start another explanation before Melissa cut him off.

"Tommy, shut the fuck up! I get it, I have realised it for weeks, Mia is gone but let's try and find her to give her a decent burial at least."

The Chicago flight touched down five minutes early and Brandon came through the gates in a rush, quickly spotting Melissa and giving her a big hug. "I've found some things out, I'll tell you in the car," he said as they walked towards the exit. Melissa nodded as she inserted her parking ticket in the machine and paid.

"Yep, a lot has happened since you left town. Now on another note, Jazz is excited to see you.....what do you think of her? Is love in the air?"

"Yeah, she's very cool and we get on well. Let's see where it goes." Melissa unlocked the doors and they climbed in the car before she turned towards him.

"Really, an eighteen-year-old seeing where it goes? I think that you possibly just put it where it goes..." Brandon felt the blush rise up over his face and pretended to look for something in his rucksack before turning towards her, a more serious look on his face.

"Stop it Melissa! Changing the subject, I've managed to track our guy down as he'd had a few run-ins with the law - two vehicle thefts, two robberies and a couple of drug offences. Get this though, when Mia was taken he was in prison; he served six months and was released three weeks before he killed himself.
He would have busted the charges with any attorney representing him, his alibi was one hundred percent cast iron solid. Can you imagine the pressure they put on him to confess?"

Melissa nodded. "But he still took the girl and kept her in the old farm. He was looking at a big sentence and I guess he couldn't handle going back inside."

"Just means that we can go to the Captain with this information, get the case reopened and find Mia." He looked at the expression on her face.

"Melissa, are you ok?"

"I'm fine, it's just that I had a moment of clarity when I was chatting with Tommy earlier, we aren't finding any of those girls alive. I always knew it deep in my heart but I'm a mom and I can't let go of my baby. He killed every last one of them Brandon. Let's not tiptoe around it anymore, we need to nail the bastard."

The restaurant was buzzing as the five of them sat around the table, each and every one of them fit to bust with the amount of food eaten.

Pat pushed his card into the reader brought over by the waitress.

"This one's on me, another great night out so thank you all." Melissa stood up, pulling her jacket from the back of her chair.

"It's been brilliant, however we haven't discussed the main business. If you two are going out to watch a movie," she looked at Brandon and Jazz, "we'll go back to my place and talk. Is that ok?"

"That's fine with me," replied Pat, "just remember Brandon, you're on my team from Monday morning so be at Dallas Zoo by ten. Ok?"

"Who won the show?" everyone asked in unison.

"I'm revealing the winner at ten thirty on Monday. Brandon, you'll be helping me."

"Me, on live TV?"

"Yep, so look smart, the public will love your little schoolboy face," he laughed as he patted him on the back.

"Let's get this done then Melissa. Tommy, after you my friend."

Sitting around the kitchen table a short while later, they considered their options, Melissa keen to give the men her thoughts.

"We can press the police to reopen the case, obviously the compelling evidence is that their star suspect was in prison at the time of the offences. They will have to comply, the court will make them if we push it." Pat took a sip of his coffee.

"True, but they were next to hopeless the last time round."

"That's true Pat but we have one big advantage now. They have admitted the crimes are linked and they have already involved the FBI so would have no other choice."

"Good thinking."

"The second and more dangerous plan is that we go looking for him ourselves; we know where he is operating from and it's always in these clusters," she pointed to the map. "Eleven hubs and all the crimes have taken place within an hour of a hub. We also know that he is watching us through the website."

Pat took another sip of his coffee, lost in concentration before speaking. "How the hell do we know that? And I thought we had lost all of this evidence?"

"Brandon had taken photos of everything on the wall before the fire and he's worked out that we have clusters of offending areas. He also suspects that it's almost an inside job as the guy is aware of our own investigations and is trying to throw us of the scent. He is either a policeman, which I doubt because of the different areas of the country he takes his victims from, or he is watching your live appeals and our online work. He's got to be one of our followers Pat." He nodded before draining the last of the cup.

"Can we get a list of subscribers and followers from the IT server?"

"We could, but there are over a million names just with my account...how many followers do you have Pat?"

"Good point, what do you suggest then?"

"We hire our own private investigation firm - I have some cash left in the campaign funds, and we may really make some headway."

"And who do you have in mind?"

"Tommy knows some guys he worked with in the Marines. They were special investigators tracking down war criminals around the world. They have set up their own investigation business in New York, mainly tracking people smugglers and finding the missing. They've said that they can help." Pat turned to Tommy who had sat quietly up till now.

"Tommy, you've been doing some homework - sounds great. What do they charge?" He pushed a sheet of paper over to Pat. "Not cheap, but this is a discounted rate."

"A thousand a day? That's not bad if they can provide a good service. Can we speak to them?"

"Sure, I'll set up a Zoom meeting for us all. How about on Tuesday some point in the evening after your filming Pat?"

"Anytime after six, Brandon and I will be together then and he needs to be involved." Pat stood up and took his mug over to the sink before slipping his jacket on.

"Ok everyone, good work. I need to get back to the zoo this evening, we have a new tiger coming into another zoo next week and I need to sort out the paperwork. Good to meet you Tommy, hope to see you again soon buddy. And one more thing Melissa, I made a tidy profit from the TV show, the phone lines went wild and I had a slice of that action so I'll pay the investigators for a three month period."

"My God Pat, that's so generous!" Melissa hugged him.

"Don't thank me, thank the great American viewer. Anyway, I still need to find my niece as whatever happened, my sister can't rest until it's over."

"Amen to that Pat," agreed Melissa and closing the door she beamed at Tommy. "The guy has just given us a blank check to find this bastard, I told you that he would come good."

"You know he has a soft spot for you Melissa?"

"He's a married guy with a kid, but if he was single though, I must admit I'd be interested."

"I'm single Melissa."

"Tommy, I think that you've had one too many beers!"

"Stone cold sober, so when the time is right for you, it sure will be right for me, you are a beautiful woman. Anyway, just putting that out there, sorry if I have embarrassed you."

"Embarrassed? No way, just that it's not a good time Tommy. Not saying never though…."

"Ok then, didn't crash and burn?"
"No Tommy, you live to fight another day."

# CHAPTER FOURTEEN

"Morning Brandon, welcome to my world, good to see that you are nice and early." Pat and Brandon stood outside the tiger enclosure, well before the zoo's opening time.

"First time that I've been in a zoo without members of the public getting in the way; it's cool," Brandon replied, looking around the space in awe as the sounds of a multitude of animals awakening from their night slumber assaulted his ears. Pat laughed.

"Just wait until you come in at night time, my family come alive in the dark. They are ambush predators and they hunt and eat at night time normally. They are not built for speed and endurance so they creep up and attack from behind whenever they can, and when they do, they aim for the head and throat. It's usually a lethal attack in the wild."

Just then a large tiger wandered over to the fence, brushing its cheek against the bars as it left its scent. The size and power of the animal was hypnotic to Brandon who had only seen these animals on TV, and now in the flesh its pure might and grace was magnificent. "I get why you care so much Pat, I never realised how beautiful they are."

"You just wait, when they see me in the middle of the night they know that I'm going to feed them so they go crazy. One zoo in a city has actually banned me from feeding at night time as the tigers roaring was keeping everyone awake." He laughed. "The local kids were scared stiff so I agreed."

"What do you want me to do when the filming starts? I've never been in front of a camera before."

"Just chill, I'll do the talking, you just need to say *hi*. When I bring in the competition winner they will do a piece to the camera and then we're done. I'll then show you around and tell you how things work."

Two young women then appeared wearing Pat's branded clothing, both looking more nervous than Brandon. Pat turned to them with a welcoming smile.

"Morning ladies, not long now. We'll do a short introduction, show some of your best bits from the show and then announce the winner. If it's not you please keep your composure, it's a game show and I'm sorry that there can only be one winner. Brandon, meet Beth and Lilly-Anne, one of these young ladies will follow us around the country for the next year organising the crap out of us."

"Cool, good luck," Brandon said with a smile, giving the girls a half wave in welcome.

A smartly dressed member of the film crew then appeared and took control. Pat listened as they gave him his instructions and he practised reading the autocue for a minute before nodding that he was happy.

The production assistant took the contestants to one side. Debbie had worked on a number of these types of shows and was well aware of the disappointment one would face in a moment so was keen to pre-empt any problems.

"Listen in ladies, I don't know the result but just remember, this is live TV so no swearing and no meltdowns. You have both seen and understood your contracts? They nodded and she continued. "The runner up will still receive five thousand bucks but mess up and start going crazy on daytime TV and that offer is taken away. OK?" Again they nodded, both seemingly mute with nerves.

"You have entertained us for six weeks girls so keep it going for another few minutes. Breathe, relax and don't forget to be yourselves." She finished just as the clapper board was raised and the show began.

"Five, four, three, two, one and action."

Standing to the left hand side of Pat, Brendon could not help but be impressed with the ease he spoke into the lens. Faultless and nerveless he nailed the introduction before turning to the two girls standing to his right and smiling.

"Ok, here we go, let's have a recap from the show. In week one, the contestants designed a new range of merchandise for the charity, Lilly-Anne came out as the winner with the famous leather-hatted tiger cub toys. Who could ever forget the head falling off the prototype in front of the watching children?

Week two took a twist with the charity event organisation round. Beth managed to persuade Bruno Mars to give a half hour show free of charge for the guests, raising an amazing thirty thousand dollars before running out the clear winner.

Week three saw both finalists fail magnificently in the *design a zoo* game, Zac Edwards stunning the judges with his new look enclosures while Lilly-Anne and Beth both finished eighth and ninth respectively.

Week four saw a return to form for both our finalists in the school education rounds, both Lilly-Anne and Beth scoring maximum marks with our judging panel and sharing first place.

Week five saw the courage of all of the surviving contestants tested to the full with the tiger walk challenge. Walking through the enclosure with Pat proved to be a step too far for most, but Lilly-Anne breezed through, even having time to pet the big boy Lupa on her way to victory. Zade didn't cope too well with his early bath in tiger dung.

The final week, week six, saw a number of tests for the two remaining contestants, Lilly-Anne and Beth, supported by their previous challengers. They were asked to present their plans for the development of tiger conservation around the world. Three hundred experts from all continents attended and gave their approval to who delivered the more impressive proposals.

I now stand here with the results for the Pat Hunter, Tiger Apprentice Challenge." There were a few seconds pause while the cameras flicked from face to face.

"The winner for the Tiger Apprentice is...... Lilly-Anne." A shower of sparkles came down upon her head as Beth stood still smiling weakly.

"Well done Lilly-Anne and commiserations Beth - it was a tight run thing. Let's see the best bits from both of our finalists."

The camera stopped rolling while the people at home watched two minutes of clips.

Meanwhile Beth sidled up to Pat and hissed at him. "You bastard, you promised me the job, you told me that if I shared my bed with you I would win."

"In five, four, three, two, one, action." Pat turned back towards the cameras as though he hadn't heard her.

"Well it's been a fantastic show, a big thanks to our sponsors because without you this could never have happened, and thanks to all our Tiger Cubs for watching and phoning in. You are making a massive difference to tiger conservation and saving the tiger's habitat. Keep tuned for our live broadcasts Monday, Wednesday and Fridays and we will see you all soon."

The cameras were turned off and were being packed away, Lilly Anne was on her victory lap hugging the production staff while Beth confronted Pat again.

"We had a deal but it's your loss Hunter. I hope that you get found out for the phoney that you are." Pat looked over towards the production assistant.

"Get her out of here Debbie, and stop her payment. She has broken the contract." Zoo security staff took her by the arm and gently led her towards the exit as she shouted over her shoulder. "This isn't over, I'm going to the press."

Debbie joined her. "You mutter one word to anyone and it appears anywhere in print, we will take you to court. That home your parents have worked so hard for all their lives will belong to Mr Hunter. Do you want the money or not? It's your shout."

Beth looked at her; she had nowhere to go with the argument and she knew it.

"Yes please, I'm sorry, please don't go after my parents. What he did was wrong, but I promise to keep quiet. We need that money, my dad needs a medical procedure and this money will cover some of it. "

"Honey, you're not the first person to fall for his charms and you sure as hell won't be the last. Chalk it down to experience." Handing her the cheque she smiled. "You're a nice person Beth, too nice for this type of work," she said before turning and walking back to the ongoing party.

Brandon who had heard some of the exchange stood looking puzzled.

"What was that about Pat? She was so angry with you. Did you promise her something?"

"No Brandon, she made it clear last night that she wanted to win and offered me all sorts of promises. It happens a lot in this world. I turned her down and said it would be a fair competition. She obviously got the wrong idea so it's lucky she's gone. Come meet Lilly-Anne, you'll like her, you're the same age."

Lilly-Anne stood looking into the enclosure. Slim and standing at around five ten, she had the aura of a screen idol already with long blonde hair touching her shoulders, a stunning figure and a face that mesmerised you for a second longer than you felt that you should look. She had built up a strong fan base during the show where her razor sharp brain and figure-hugging outfits were the perfect combination. She also had the back story to match. Her parents were killed in a boating accident when she was seven years old so she was taken in by grand-parents who adored her. She was doing well at high school until she was diagnosed with a brain tumour at fifteen years old. She fought the disease with the help of her local church and was operated on by the best surgeon in the country free of charge.

Lilly-Anne was the TV company's ideal contestant; everyone loved her and wanted her to get through and have a break. She had over seventy percent of the viewers' votes from home and if she hadn't been picked by Pat there would have been a major ratings slump in future broadcasts. He had no choice other than to select her, it was an order, and if he failed to pick Lilly-Anne the media plug would be removed. Welcome to prime time TV!

Brandon held out his hand.

"Hey Lilly-Anne, congratulations." She took his hand and smiled.

"Thanks Brandon, we both have a busy year in front of us." Her hand felt soft, warm and gentle and he found he didn't want to let go.

"We sure do, what are you going to be doing?"

"What, you haven't been watching the show? Shame on you!" Brandon shrugged, a bit embarrassed that he didn't know.

"My mum didn't want to miss *'Suits'*, it was on at the same time." She looked at him and smiled again before explaining what half of the country had been watching.

"P.A. to Pat, so I guess a bit of everything. Keeping him organised, making sure the show stays on the road, just a full on twenty four hour a day position. How about you?"

"Media stuff, I work for a paper. I'll be writing articles for the newspaper, keeping the online focus going for the conservation work and maintaining a blog so everyone can keep in touch with us. And of course whatever else I'm asked to do. My mum is worried sick about the whole thing, she thinks that I'm going to be eaten by a tiger or run away with the circus. How about you, are your parents going to miss you?" Lilly-Anne stared at him.

"You really haven't watched any of the show have you? I was raised by my grandparents, and no, they are happy for me to get the chance. They think that I may get signed up by a production company or something afterwards....wishful thinking on their part."

"I'm sure that you will leave someone staying at home with a broken heart for the next year?" Brandon questioned.

"You are asking me if I have a boyfriend already?"

"No, not like that...yes, just like that. Sorry!"

"I don't have a boyfriend at the moment, we broke up during the show. He didn't want me to go away for a year so we put things on hold. How about you?"

"No, I don't have a boyfriend either." They both started to laugh.

"I have a girl that I have dated a couple of times, but that's all, nothing serious."

"Well, looks like neither of us is going to miss our old lives too much then Brandon."

Pat walked over and placed his arms around the both of them.

"Let's get to the office and get this show on the road. New York City tomorrow so let's go."

He took Brandon to one side, "I just need to chat with Melissa before we set off. Do you want to come, or stay here with Lilly-Anne?"

"I'll stay here if that's ok Pat, we need to get to know each other. Is it ok to walk around the zoo until you get back?"

"Knock yourselves out, I should be back in a few hours."

Melissa was in the process of making dinner when her phone rang,

"Hi Melissa, I'm in town for a couple of hours and I have a proposition for you. Can I come around?"

"Sure Pat, shall I set you a place for dinner?"

"Sounds great, see you in half an hour."

Ringing the door bell Pat could already smell the aroma coming from the kitchen but when the door opened, it wasn't what Pat was expecting.

"Hi Tommy, I didn't realise that you were going to be here."

"Nope, I wasn't expecting to be here either. Melissa phoned me earlier and gave me an invite, she thinks that I need feeding up." Her head appeared around the door. "All of you men need feeding. Come on in Pat, it's nearly ready."

Tommy helped himself to a beer from the fridge. "Beer Pat?"

"Not for me; you're looking very at home here Tommy."

"Melissa has been very good to me, I don't know how I can ever pay her back," Tommy replied, opening his beer and taking a long glug.

"I guess by not returning to being a drug addicted hobo would be the best way," Pat said, tapping Tommy on the shoulder. Tommy batted it off, he had heard worse a million times.

"Ouch Pat, that was cutting; those days are gone, I can assure you."

"Come and get it," Melissa gave the call for dinner.

They sat down to eat, Tommy still wondering why Pat was verbally aggressive towards him, it was almost as if he were in the way of something. Melissa placed the bowls of food on the table.

"What did you want to discuss with me Pat? I'm intrigued."

"Well I know that the insurance company haven't paid up yet, and I also know that this place is costing a small fortune. I have a house just outside of town on long term rental. I haven't used it much this year due to the filming commitments, but it's handy when I'm in this part of the world. I spoke to the letting company an hour ago and they have agreed that you can move in. It will be free as I've paid in advance for the year. When your place is finished, move out and go back home. What do you say?"

She sat stunned for a moment. "Is this a joke or am I right in thinking that you are offering me a house for free until my place is rebuilt? Oh my God Pat, thank you so much." She stood and hugged him. "You have no idea how worried I have been about money."

"Well, worry no more, glad I can help a friend."

Tommy finished eating. "There is no end to your generosity Pat." He turned to Melissa. "I need to go so can I skip the dishes today? I have a friend calling me in an hour and I need to be on my laptop. I'll see you all later." He gave Pat a slap on the shoulder that felt just a little too hard. As the front door closed behind him, Melissa turned to Pat.

"Is everything OK between you and Tommy, Pat? He seemed a little frosty towards you."

"Hope it's ok, he was a bit put out about me turning up. Maybe he is a little jealous of our friendship?"

"Makes sense, he came onto me earlier, not in a bad way. I told him I wasn't ready. He might be brooding on that…"

"Yeah, just be a bit careful of the guy, we don't really know him yet."

"I will be, don't worry. Now, getting back to your kind offer, when can I see it?" asked Melissa, slapping the palms of her hands onto her legs excitedly. Pat laughed, seeing the young girl in her bubbling out.

"How about now? It's only just out of town." Before his words had left his mouth Melissa was up and standing by the door ready to go.

"Ok, I guess it's now then," he laughed.

His car pulled up on a small, single track road leading up to a gorgeous white wooden house set in a few acres of land.

"Nearest neighbour is four hundred yards that way," he pointed towards a distant plume of smoke coming from a chimney, "so apart from the deer who regularly come to pay you a visit, you'll be left alone." Opening the door, Melissa could see that it was as nice inside as it looked on the outside.

Pat followed her inside. "It's fully furnished although you will need your own bedding. The barn is locked, it only has my old stuff inside so there's no need to go in there. Everything else is yours."

"Oh my God, this is perfect," Melissa exclaimed as she tried to take it all in. Pat nodded, liking her approval of his taste.

"I've just been so busy with my schedule going crazy this year that I didn't get the chance to use it. The zoos and TV studio have taken up all my time. Makes sense for it to be used by someone."

"I'll bring my things over next week, maybe Tommy can help me."

"Good idea, just one thing….the place is for you to live in, not a crash place for Tommy." She looked at him, "Sure, no problems."

Tommy walked the twenty minutes to his single bed apartment, deep in thought about what Pat had said to him earlier. Was that how people still viewed him? Mud sticks and if a friend speaks to you like that, what chance did he ever have of moving forwards? Or maybe Pat was just jealous, perhaps he had a thing for Melissa and was playing the long game, Mister nice guy with loads of cash burning a friggin' great hole in his well-pressed trouser pockets.

*Might as well check my mail box, maybe Uncle Pat has dropped a fat cheque into my account,* he muttered to himself. For once his mail box wasn't empty, with a white, blank envelope sitting at the bottom.

*What the fuck? Good old Uncle Pat,* he continue to mutter to himself as he opened his front door, and tossing the envelope onto his sofa he grabbed a beer from the fridge, half draining it in one massive gulp.

*If this is the woman downstairs complaining about my music again,* he continued his one way conversation and took another gulp from the bottle, *Fuck them, I'll read it in the morning, it's too late to start a fight now.*

# CHAPTER FIFTEEN

New York City on a bright Tuesday afternoon seemed like a magical place to be as Pat, Lilly-Anne and Brandon walked through the gates of the Bronx Zoo, Pat explaining to his young team what they were going to do whilst there.

"We've just purchased a new tiger for this place, he is young so hopefully I'll be able to use him for the breeding programme. Tonight we're going to go live at eight o'clock, so the public can witness the first time we work together." He turned to his new apprentice.

"Lilly-Anne, who has confirmed attendance to the unveiling of the tiger?" Lilly-Anne flicked open her notebook before replying.

"The Mayor and his officials are all coming, Mr Trump is currently in the city and has stated that he will come, but he wants to make a statement speech. I have given him two minutes and he's accepted. Everyone else who you mentioned is attending so it's all in order."

"Excellent, let's have a walk around, see the boy for ourselves and then get back to the hotel to unpack and prepare ourselves for tonight."

A roar greeted them as they approached the enclosure. Pat turned to them, the customary gleam in his eye he had when with his beloved tigers. "Hear that you two? That's why the city banned me from coming in here at night time, that bellow carries for miles." The tiger now lay motionless on its side by the pond in the centre of its enclosure. As they stared in at the magnificent beast, the head keeper approached. "Hey Mr Hunter, how are you doing? It's been a while since I last saw you." Pat shook the man by the hand.

"Too long Tim, how is he settling in?"

"Perfect, he's a calm boy, no signs of aggression towards any of the keepers."

"Have you been in with him?"

"Every day, just as you asked. He's a pussycat Pat, a lovely natured animal."

"Fantastic! Brandon my boy, tonight you and I are going into that enclosure. Lilly-Anne did it on the show so tonight it's your turn. Lilly-Anne laughed. "It was one of the scariest things I have ever done, you can see the dominance in the tigers' eyes which they never take off you, always looking for your weakness. So awesome." Brandon's face was a picture as he looked at the two of them.

"Really Pat, day one and I'm in with a man eater?"

"Your mum will be proud, we won't film it live but it will go onto the site. OK?"

"If you say so," he agreed but inside he bubbled with excitement. This was the life he had hoped for, danger and gut tingling experiences. It really was like running away with the circus.

Lilly-Anne started talking to Tim, the head keeper while Pat pulled Brandon aside. His demeanour had changed for a second and Brandon felt its chill.

"We need to have a chat Brandon, I'm worried."

"About what?" Brandon asked in confusion, "I've only been with you for one day."

"It's not you, it's Tommy."

"What's the problem?" he asked, relieved he hadn't already blotted his copybook in some way, "I thought he seemed a good guy Pat, you got on well with him on Saturday."

"I'm trying to work him out, you know. He's just turned up out of the blue and I'm still not quite sure why."

"What worries you about him?"

"A few things...he has travelled all over the country, he has killed a guy in a truck, he knew where Melissa lived and he just turned up and tried to get money from her. He has this mystery video of the attacker and surprisingly he gives a description of someone his build and height. The phone has been lost - if it ever existed - and he was a drug addict, same as the guy who went to jail and claimed he was framed. Maybe it's a coincidence or maybe he met him through drugs.

He was the last person to have seen Mia but did nothing to stop the attack. Ask yourself a question, if you were a war hero kick ass marine, would you film a girl being abducted or run over and try help?" Brandon shrugged but had no time to give a reply before Pat continued listing his misgivings.

"And now he's all over Melissa, with her every day, wanting to know what's going on. When we suggest Private Investigators, guess what, he has a friend who owns a firm. How convenient again. I'm not sure what I should do, the last thing I want is to scare Melissa, but if I tell her, she may think that I'm over reacting to Tommy getting upset with me on Monday when I showed up for dinner. But a key point for me is that all this trouble started after he left the military. While he was busy in Afghanistan and Iraq, we had no cases like this but since he went on a drug-fuelled tour of the US, twenty six or twenty seven girls are missing - I have lost count."

"Why was he upset on Monday?"

"He made it very clear that he didn't want me around, luckily for me Melissa heard me talking and invited me in. He was then very cold with me all evening, ask Melissa, she will tell you."

"Leave it with me, I'll have a word with her when I phone."

"Don't mention me. You need to promise, I don't want any bad feelings between us."

"I'm a reporter Pat, I'm used to making stuff up. I will sort it."

Brandon sat alone in the small office behind the tiger enclosure at the zoo. He had thought about the conversation he was about to have all afternoon and his initial bravado was wearing thin. This was not going to be such an easy subject to raise. Taking a deep breath he picked up the phone.

"Hey Melissa, it's your boy speaking from the big apple."

"Hello lover boy, hope that Pat is taking care of you?"

"Yeah he is but I've just been thinking about what's going on back there and it may be nothing but something is making me feel anxious." His heart thumped and he could feel the stress levels rising as he spoke.

"Shoot, let's see if we can work this out," Melissa answered. She sat listening while Brandon relayed the story about Tommy, taking care not to mention Pat.

"And you thought of this all by yourself?"

"I had some thinking time while we flew up here. It may be nothing, but it's worth considering. You know, this all started after Tommy came home. Do you think it's a coincidence?"

"How about I go over and see him, ask him for an explanation, see what he says? If it's all crap then we will have a beer and talk about it, I don't want to spoil a friendship." Her voice sounded a little frosty but it was lost on Brandon.

"Whatever you think is best, just be aware that it may be dangerous, if it's true then he may panic and hurt you."

The sarcasm dripped from her voice as she answered, she was sick of mistrust, and what did a young kid know about the world?

"I'll tell you what, I'll phone the police anonymously and let them ask the questions. Then we will clear it up. That way we are all safe and I don't have to ask the embarrassing questions." It was the only way she could think of to shut Brandon up - the guy was in fantasy land and what's more, she could almost hear Pat's voice in the words he spoke. Brandon sensed that the conversation was beginning to slide towards a disagreement so quickly changing course he added. "It was just a thought. Anyway, I'm in with a new tiger this evening. Pat thinks that it's a good idea and you'll be able to watch it online tomorrow."

"Oh my God, be careful. I will set an alarm on my laptop to remind me to watch. Speak soon....and thanks for the concern Brandon."

She sat down to continue watching a show on the television, Brandon's words spiralling in her head. *Why didn't he help? If he had the time to film it, why not shout or do something, he could have saved her. Why didn't he save my girl?*

Picking up the phone she made the call to the police. "I want to report a suspicious person."

The alarm on the laptop sounded, a reminder for her to log on. It would be Brandon's first broadcast from the Bronx Zoo and she was excited as the opening credits rolled up.

*'Do not replicate anything that you may see in this broadcast, it could result in serious injury or death. Pat Hunter is a professional and surrounds himself with professionals. All of the things which you are about to witness are carried out with the safety of the tigers, crew and general public in mind at all times.'*

And there he was, standing beside Pat outside a brightly lit tiger enclosure. Brandon and Lilly-Anne were busting with excitement as they spoke to the camera as Pat watched on like a proud parent before joining in the commentary.

"Ok you tiger cubs, we have a treat for you this evening. I haven't been fully introduced to our new boy just behind me," he pointed to the tiger who prowled ten feet away from the crew, watching every move, "but I'm getting in there in a moment to introduce myself. Now Brandon here thought that he was going to have a little stroll around in there tonight after filming, but no, we're going to do it right now, get rid of his nerves and introduce him to the big boy. You ready Brandon?" Melissa looked at the screen and yelled at the television. "WTF Pat, be careful with my boy!"

Nodding, Brandon followed Pat to the enclosure door.

"Everyone is watching at home Brandon, they think that you are going to be eaten. How does that feel?" Brandon looked straight at the camera before answering.

"Scary, if Mum's watching turn away now."

The door slid open and they stood in a sterile space, just one door away from the waiting tiger. A pungent aroma crept into Brandon's nostrils, tugging away on his reserve of courage by the second. The warm scent made things very real, not the type of fear a child would have if they thought something was hiding under the bed as they lay, trying to sleep, it was the fear they would have if they checked, and saw two big brown eyes staring back at them.

Pat squeezed his arm and whispered out of range of the microphone, "This one is a pussy cat Brandon, just follow my instructions."

The second door slowly slid open and they walked into the enclosure. The first thing to hit Brandon was the sheer size of the animal as it stretched up and clawed at the tree in front of them before crouching down, facing them, it's body a tight coil waiting to spring. Brandon's stomach flipped and he suddenly wanted another nervous toilet break. Pat whispered to Brandon and to the listening public, not taking his eyes from those of the tiger.

"Ok, he is sizing us up right now, trying to figure out why we are in his garden."

The tiger growled and showed his teeth while fixing an unblinking gaze upon them.

"This is not so good, he is feeling confident and is saying to us, "You come one step further into here and I will attack you. We are just going to stand our ground and see what he wants to do." The tiger backed away into the undergrowth, a gentle snarling coming from the dense cover of the bushes.

"You may think that he has gone away, but he hasn't. He is setting an ambush for us. If we move past that scrub line he will attack us for sure. Brandon, we need to get out of here fast. Back away to the door while I cover you." Melissa was spell bound mumbling to Brandon on the television as though he could hear her. "Get out, quickly…."

Pat placed his hands up, making himself look larger. "Get behind me Brandon and head slowly for the door. Do not turn your back, keep your eyes on the tiger."

Two feet away Brandon was sweating heavily and he had lost control of his breathing. Only Pat could hear his panic. The tiger's head slowly came through the leaves as it crouched, fixated by the two humans within its territory. The enclosure door opened with a mechanical groan, seeming to take an age and Brandon bent down and scrambled through, quickly followed by Pat as the door closed a little quicker than it had opened. A blur of colour and speed followed as the door was secured, the tiger hitting the fence inches from where Bradley stood. He jumped, swearing out loud to the amusement of Pat.

"Hopefully we can edit that reaction out Brandon." The tiger was left pacing the fence line, eying up another attack but it wasn't his night tonight.

Pat spoke to camera, unmoved and composed.

"So, there you all see the unpredictable nature of working with tigers. This guy has been passive for a week or so, offering no problem to the handlers, yet tonight he would have killed us both in a heartbeat."

The team ended the fifteen minute show reading comments made from viewers; some were angry with Pat for creating an incident but he laughed them off, others were worried that Brandon was going to be eaten. He put on a brave face when Pat asked him on air how it had felt.

"It felt good, I trusted Pat and the team and knew that they would keep me safe. I can't wait to do it again."

The other questions were about Lilly-Anne. The public loved her and Pat was asked to promise not to put her in with the tigers.

"Can't promise that one, what do you think Lilly-Anne?"

"I'd love it, I will give anything a try." This led to another hundred plus messages which couldn't be shared with the public and the moderator was in tears of laughter as the show wrapped up. "Lilly-Anne, I think it's fair to say you have some new fans," he told her, still laughing at the suggestive comments.

After filming Pat spoke to them both.

"Tonight was excellent, a bit scary but still safe....well, we got out of there with a second to spare to be honest. The public love you so next time we'll be asking for some money for another big tiger for a zoo possibly on the west coast this time. I think that with you two on board we'll smash the record of twenty thousand dollars. We'll wrap things up here and in a couple of days we're travelling back to Dallas."

It took another hour before Melissa was calm enough to go to bed. If this was a taste of things to come her nerves would be frayed beyond repair. Brandon's poor mother must be petrified. Turning the light out she sighed, two of her favourite guys in the world nearly eaten on live TV. *It could only happen to me*, she thought, drifting off into a tiger filled dream.

A knock on her door woke her, and looking at the clock she saw it was just past two in the morning. Who the hell knocks on a door at that time? She hurriedly threw on a dressing gown before approaching the front door.

"Who is it?"

"Austin Police Miss Jagger, could we have a quick word with you please? Sorry for the late hour." Opening the door, she checked the ID of the two waiting officers before inviting them in to the hallway.

"What can I do for you?"

"We have just conducted a search of a house close by. We have found this and wondered if you could identify it please?" She was handed a plastic evidence bag. Melissa looked at the gold object, shining through the bag at her and felt a sudden coldness creep over her.

"It's Mia's necklace, I gave it to her for her sixteenth birthday. Where the hell did you find it?"

"We just conducted a search of a house lived in by a man named Tommy Cookson. We found it there. Do you know him?"

"Yes I do, he was here earlier." She looked at the evidence bag again and checked the inscription on the back of the pendant. "Yes, it's hers, look." She held it up to the light, the inscription on the back clear. *Mia, love always Mum.*

"Where is he? Have you arrested him?" she asked, still not able to believe this was anything to do with Tommy.

"He's in a cell down town refusing to answer any questions. The only thing he has told us is that he has never seen the necklace before." She shrugged, exasperated.

"But it was in his house?"

"Yes Ms Jagger, he had it in his lounge, not even hidden, as though he had been looking at it tonight." She felt as though she could vomit, before the feeling turned to rage.

"Sick son of a bitch! He turned up at my house offering to help me, he even tried to date me. All the time he knew where my little girl was."

"He won't be dating anyone for a long time, ma'am, he has just escaped a murder charge in another state but this time we will make it stick. I promise you that. We are charging him with murder tonight, possibly with another twenty-five cases to follow. This bastard is going to fry."

The man lay on his creaky hotel bed watching the news. The third item made him stop eating his takeaway burger and chips.

*'The Austin City Police have arrested a former Marine Corps Sergeant who had been decorated for bravery. Thomas Cookson was arrested in his home at 01.30 this morning after an anonymous phone call to the police. It is believed that items belonging to the missing girls have been removed and taken away for analysis. A police source informed us that he will be charged with one murder with possibly more charges to follow. We will keep you informed as the story develops.'*

He laughed, wiping his greasy fingers on a paper napkin as he spoke to the photo of former Sergeant Thomas Cookson now plastered across the television screen.

"Well good for you Tommy Cookson, you have been a busy little bee on my behalf. I think that you could have a table booked in hell shortly. So sorry that I will not be joining you." He took a large drink of the takeaway cola. "Hopefully this time that damn woman will stop looking for me. If she doesn't I may have to pay her a visit in the dead of night. Ohhh yes, now that sounds exciting."

Throwing the burger wrapper in the bin, he washed his hands again. "No more girls, promise yourself that one thing and you are free." Cleaning his white teeth and checking them in the mirror, he looked himself in the eyes. "Or maybe just one more when the timing is right. Slaughtering Melissa Jagger, what a great way to end my journey."

# CHAPTER SIXTEEN

The cell door swung open, Tommy was lying on the bed trying to make himself as comfortable as possible.

"Cookson, we're taking you somewhere special where you will have your first taste of maximum security. It's 04.30 so we might make it in time for breakfast."

He stood up and stepped towards the police officer who was speaking to him before another two large guys stopped him in his tracks.

"You are enjoying this aren't you?" he said before lunging forwards again. Immediately grabbed by the two larger officers, his head was smashed into the cell wall as he was restrained. It seemed like they were taking no risks with him.

"I've done nothing wrong, it's a set up. I'm innocent and you know it."

"Of course you are buttercup. You know how often we have heard that?" Blood trickled from Tommy's lip as he spat out.

"Fuck you!"

"Get this gentleman into the van, he has a date to keep," the police officer said.

The clang of the cell door in the armoured van rang around his head, the flash of multiple police car lights and the rattle of a helicopter overhead spelt out the truth. He was in a world of trouble and had no one to get him out of it. No alibis for any dates they cared to shoot at him, no witnesses to towns and cities he visited and no pot of endless money for an attorney. His past history was biting him firmly on the ass. He could prove he was in Chicago for sure, trouble was that he had told Brandon that he had seen people taken and killed. And sure as eggs are eggs Brandon would be a star witness against him. His mind flicking through every different scenario, in the same way as it did while patrolling the mountain areas in Afghanistan.

Who was the enemy, and who could he say was trying to set him up? Could he put enough doubt into a jury's mind again? He needed to use every underhand trick he knew to find out. He knew he had enemies everywhere, the family of the guy he killed and the dealers he still owed thousands to for drugs. But then it clicked, the police who had put him away for the murder of the trucker and the looks on their faces as he had left the court a free man. And suddenly, bingo! Here they were with evidence from out of nowhere. A jury could buy into that and maybe believe that they had set him up. This was the year for discrediting the police after all with cities on fire over allegations of police brutality, but it was still a long shot.

But Mia's necklace, how did they know about that? How did they find out it was in his apartment and could he explain how it got there? That was an impossible thing to argue to a jury as he had only seen Mia once and she was in the process of being murdered at the time. But he was there watching and he had admitted that to everyone. All he cared about at that time was money for dope, he didn't contemplate the seriousness and consequences of being at a murder scene. It appeared he was in checkmate with no more moves.

The line of flashing blue lights led the way into Travis State Jail, and glancing through the van window, he could see a mob of reporters, obviously tipped off about his arrival. Flashlights burnt into his eyes dazzling him for a second until he was driven through the gate area and into the relative calm that comes once inside the fortress of a maximum security prison. But this calm didn't last for very long.

"Get him off the van, we're going into the STGMU," he heard ordered from outside the vehicle.

"What the hell does that mean?" Tommy asked the guard who had travelled in the back with him.

"That means Security Threat Group Management Units. It also means that you are going to see no one nor talk to anyone until we say so. You're in our world now. You think that you can wander around Texas and do what you like, fuck no boy. You're going to die here."

The chains on his feet and hands rattled as he shuffled along, armed guards wearing protective clothing with invisible faces covering every step he took.

"Keep moving, don't look around, look straight in front." The constant instructions reminded him of when they took prisoners in Iraq. Dominate them and don't give them time to think.

"If you do anything dumb son, we will shoot you dead," he was told just to reassure him they meant business.

Reaching the unit, a group of staff dressed in the same protective clothing waited at the entrance.

"Stop!" He did so without hesitation. They took him into a sterile room out of sight from the cells.

"We are going to remove your clothes, you then have fresh clothing to put on. If you fail to comply with any order we will use force. Do you understand?"

"I get it." The restraints were removed and the staff stepped back.

"Remove your shoes and socks and put them in the bin to your left." Silently he followed the process until he was standing naked in front of the staff.

"Put on the other clothes." Again he complied.

"Sit on the chair." The chair scanned his body for hidden objects while the staff stood in silence. This was not the petty chatter from the police officers, this was professional. They knew what they were doing and they did it well.

"Ok, step off and get into your cell. Do not turn your head and go directly to the back of the room." The door closed as he did so with a meaty clump. A face then appeared at the cell hatch. It was the warden in charge who addressed him through the small opening.

"I don't care what you have or haven't done, every man in this unit is treated in the same manner. Comply with the regulations and it will be fine. Act aggressively to the staff and we will take you down. Somehow I don't think that will be necessary."

"Nope, it won't, I just want to phone a friend of mine to tell them what has happened."

"That will not be allowed. You will give us the numbers of the people you would like to call. I will then tell you who you can contact. For the next week it will be nobody. Is that clear?"

"Crystal."

"Do you understand why you are on this unit?"

"The crimes that I am being charged with but it's a bullshit charge."

"Let's not get into that, you are mine because you are thought to be a potential problem to the smooth running of this jail. That is why I had to get out of my bed at an ungodly hour to process you. Prove otherwise and we will get along just fine." The hatch closed leaving him sitting alone.

Taking a breath he composed himself, he had given up once before in his life and it had led to a year of drug addiction and pain. He would fight the charges with every last breath he had. If he won, he would walk free again, if he lost he was dead. His mind drifted to the meal and conversation he had the night before. Melissa would be aware of the charges against him by now and she would have formed her own opinion. She would hate him and want him to die for what he had done, but most of all she would want the details of what really happened to Mia. To get that sort of information she would need to remain calm, as if not, she would believe that he would clam up and die with his secrets. Melissa would have to make contact at some point so he would just have to wait.

He lay on the hard bed, knowing the next few weeks would be tough. Prisoners would know of his alleged crimes and would try to take some kind of revenge, and the guards would certainly dislike him. Some of the girls were from this local area and might have been known to staff.

A breakfast pack was passed through his door flap, a sign that the place was starting to wake up, and a hum began circulating around the ten cells in the unit telling him they knew he was there. An old prisoner looked through the cell hatch, watching intently as Tommy picked up the plastic bag of cereals.

"I hear you killed twenty five girls at least…."

"You heard wrong, it's a set up, I haven't killed anyone."

"How about the truck driver, you saying you didn't do that one?"

"Nope, not denying that. I killed him stone dead, he was asking for that one. I need to get a message out of here if I want to prove I'm innocent – how do I do that?"

"No chance my friend, you aren't chatting to anyone for a week or so, they are the rules. Break them and they break you."

"This detective agency in New York is my only hope, Frontline Investigations. Former marine buddies of mine, if someone could just tell them where I am…."

A stern voice cried out, "Move away from the door, you are only out to empty the trash can," and the prisoner moved away quickly, muttering to himself. Slumping back on the bed, another face appeared in the hatch but this time it was a guard.

"You try that shit once more and see where it gets you."

# CHAPTER SEVENTEEN

The house was all Melissa had dreamt of, space to think, an office the size of her old bedroom and all the appliances brand new. But the dark cloud of Tommy's arrest had shrouded her in depression and she had not stopped crying all day. She phoned Pat, needing to discuss it with someone.

"This place is more than I deserve, she thanked him before continuing with her real reason for phoning. I guess that you have heard about Tommy?"

"Yep, someone just showed me a newspaper. Do you believe it?"

"They have strong evidence on him, he had Mia's necklace. How the hell has he got hold of that if he wasn't right there at the time? He must have taken it from my girl's dead neck Pat, it all seems to make sense. I hear he's been charged and taken to jail but I want to kill the bastard myself. Brandon was right to phone. Did you know he was going to warn me?"

"He was worried all day, he likes you and he trusts you so it made sense for him to call. It was his choice."

"I'm still not putting my evidence away, there are unanswered questions that I need to look into. I have to understand why his killings have followed such a deliberate pattern. If the prosecutors want it, I will hand it over, otherwise I will carry on. What about the private investigators?"

"Don't worry, I've phoned them already and cancelled the contract. They were shocked that their friend is a killer but they understood." There were a couple of seconds of silence while Pat thought about what else he should do.

"Do you want me to ask them to find out what happened? Maybe Tommy will tell them some details."

She sighed, "Do you think that he will, you know, tell them

about Mia?"

"Possibly, if they work with the police. They will be able to piece it together if they want to. They may be able to find the resting places of the girls....I guess that they are close to the original crime scenes. I'm not an expert but it must be dangerous driving around with someone in the trunk of your car."

She nodded to herself, "That's what I think; if Tommy gives us locations, the dogs can do the rest."

"We're coming down tomorrow, can we come over and stay at the weekend?"

"It's your house, come down when you like. Is Lilly-Anne coming with you?"

"Her and Brandon are a tight team, where he goes, she goes."

"Oh dear, that may upset Jazz."

"I think that Jazz is consigned to history, Brandon and Lilly-Anne certainly have something going on already."

# CHAPTER EIGHTEEN

The man studied the updated website for Melissa's campaign. A shiny photo had taken pride of place, her new house, a lovely white building, friendly and welcoming. Let's see about that he thought as he clicked on a couple of links.

Facebook could do the work of two detectives in a few seconds and sure enough every description of the place was given if you cared to look. And he certainly cared, it was always amusing how many secrets people gave away on social media. He already knew the area, he had previously stalked a young woman for two weeks before aborting the mission but it seemed that the preparation had not been in vain.

Standing in the darkness of the white house he felt power surge through his body. She was going to die tonight, in such a horrific way that it couldn't be linked to anything he had previously done. The violence would be long and brutal, she would also be subjected to the most sickening sexual assault he could dream of. This was his swan song, a crime that would be talked about in hushed tones for all of the town's history; a crime so bad that the house would need to pulled down to erase the memories of what had happened within those beautifully painted walls. Everything he longed for, he would always be a shadow of absolute terror and never forgotten, and it was only moments away.

Melissa sat watching television, sipping the last of a nice bottle of red she had bought to celebrate the move. There were a few things she would like to do to the place, but only after chatting to Pat on Saturday. A deer barking in the forest behind the house startled her - she was still getting used to the noises of the countryside.

A light drizzle tip-tapped on the dormer windows in the

lounge, whilst inside the crackling wood fire threw out a comfortable warmth. She got up and went to the log basket to place another log on the fire, TV was good tonight and she had no intention of missing her favourite program.

"*Damn, out of logs,*" she muttered to herself, and considering watching TV in the cold or braving the rain to bring in a more wood, she made a decision.

"*Jacket on, let's go.*"

The intruder light sprang on as she left the kitchen door open to go to the wood store; it was only twenty yards away and she'd be out and back in within two minutes. A little trickle of anxiety crept into her stomach as the forest seemed to creep closer to the house in the darkness, shadows jumping from branch to branch in the harsh glare of the light. A brief movement by the barn caught her eye but it was gone as quick as it arrived.

Holding the logs close to her chest, she kicked the kitchen door shut again on the way back in, dumping the logs and going back to lock the door before letting out a sigh of relief. Thirty-five and still afraid of the dark, she gave herself a mental talking to before returning to the lounge.

"*All done, now where were we?*" she asked herself as she sat down in to watch her program.

The man sat at the top of the stairs, woollen hat wet from the rain, his heart pounding from the excitement of what he was about to do. Creeping into the spare bedroom, he carefully put the plastic sheeting over the floor, every slight noise sounding like an alarm going off. A row of different tools sat on the bed, and he knew out here in the middle of nowhere he could take as long as he liked and start when he liked. There were so many forms of punishment and he had a multitude of choices.

Melissa sat downstairs laughing as the action unfolded on the television. The doorbell rang and looking at the clock she was surprised to see that it was only eight thirty.

*Oh crap, who the hell?* she thought, thinking she was now going to miss the end of the show.

She called through the door and was delighted when Brandon

answered. Opening it excitedly, she was surprised to see two people waiting to come in.

"Hi Melissa, I hope we're not disturbing you?" Brandon asked as he gave her a hug before introducing Lilly-Anne. Melissa returned the hug before smiling at Lilly-Anne.

"No, come on in, although my favourite show is on so you might have to watch it with me. Do you watch this Lilly-Anne?" she asked, leading them both into the lounge.

"Do I? I missed it last week, so am very happy to catch up on the plot."

The man sat listening, he could hear the conversation and silently prayed for them to leave as he had work to do. The music signalling the end of the show played and he heard Melissa's voice.

"Can I show you around?" The man backed away from the door, looking for an easy escape route. *Fuck, this was going to get messy, he would need to kill all three. That wasn't in the plan.* He moved back into the room softly closing the door, and picking up a large boning knife, he sat on the bed, waiting to spring forwards, controlling his breathing, calming the excitement building up within him. He would kill the man, and rape and kill the two women, the only dilemma being which order would be best. It felt like selecting his favourite chocolate from the box. He then heard the male voice answer her.

"We could have a look around but I thought that maybe we could all go out and have a bite to eat first, before it gets too late."

"That's a great idea, I need to go shopping in the morning as I don't have a lot in the fridge at the moment. Let me pay though." Lilly-Anne stepped forwards.

"Not a chance, it's on us tonight." Melissa pulled on her wet jacket and checked the doors before turning the lights off, leaving the lounge illuminated by the crackling log fire left to heat up an empty house. She climbed into the backseat of the car and looked up at her home, not noticing the figure standing in the darkness of the upstairs window, watching them leave. She put her hands on Lilly-Anne's shoulders, as she sat in front of her, next to Brandon who was driving.

"I can't wait to hear your stories already."

The man packed his bag back up, livid with rage and unsatisfied violence. She had given him free access into the house, which was the perfect scenario but luck had just been on her side tonight. However, she had to stay lucky for twenty four hours a day, seven days a week but he only needed to be lucky for one minute.

# CHAPTER NINETEEN

Pat checked the Saturday sports schedule before heading off to see Melissa. As she welcomed him in, he tried to flatter her. "It was a toss up between going to watch the soccer in Dallas or seeing you guys here…. no contest really."

"You think that I'm dumb Pat? Dallas are away in Miami this weekend so we're the only show in town." No one could catch Melissa out with a sports question and Pat laughed, admitting that she'd seen through him.

"Ok, you win! By *we*, I take it Brandon and Lilly-Anne are already here?"

"Yes, they arrived last night out of the blue. Just what I needed after the whole Tommy thing, it's cast a shadow over everything," Melissa replied as she walked through to her office, Pat following.

"Damn right, I didn't see that one coming, although it makes sense, the way he appeared on the scene from nowhere. Let's just leave it up to the authorities to resolve now. Sorry to hear about the necklace though, that was a horrible thing to happen."

"Yeah, I just can't believe that the guy sat at my table making plans for how we could catch the killer, when all the time it was him. He saw my pain but went home and looked at his trophies. What a bastard Pat, how could anyone do that?"

"Well thinking about the offences he's charged with, he's got to be a psychopath. Thank God he didn't come for any of us, I guess young girls are his thing so he wasn't interested in us."

"He would have a shock if he had come for me," Melissa said as she opened the desk drawer and produced a pistol. "I would have plugged the fucker right between the eyes."

"Easy tiger," Pat exclaimed, holding his hands up, "put that thing right back in the drawer. Is it even loaded?"

"There's no point in having a gun if you can't use it. It's loaded and ready to go, what's more I'm a good shot," Melissa told him as she put the gun away just as Brandon and Lilly-Anne came down the stairs. Pat hugged them both.

"Hey you two. You beat me to it, hope you haven't taken the best room?" Brandon gave him a slap on the shoulder. "Snooze you lose Pat. We were thinking, how about I go shopping with Lilly-Anne and buy some groceries and cook for us all tonight? Our treat." Melissa gave a thumbs up.

"I say that's a great idea, we can play some games, have a few drinks and relax for once." She smiled at them both, "I think that you two make a good couple. Nice matchmaking Pat."

"Out of my hands, they just need to stay focused on the jobs I've given them, no little butterflies and birds floating around their brains otherwise we could all be eaten."

They all laughed as the two of them got in the car and disappeared off towards the town. Pat and Melissa headed for the kitchen where she made them both a coffee. Pat stood looking out at the garden through the kitchen window.

"Are you settling in ok Melissa? It can be a bit lonely out here, it's pretty remote."

"I love it, just gives me space to breath. Thanks again Pat for helping out, the insurance company phoned yesterday, they have agreed to rebuild the old house. They think it will take around ten months. Is that still alright?"

"Ten months sounds perfect, we'll be near the end of the twelve month contract by then." Melissa handed him his coffee and they sat down at the table. "Have the police released any more information about Tommy?" Pat asked.

"Yes, they sent a young officer around to talk with me so I could give a statement. He's denying everything apparently but has no alibi at all. He's being held in a secure unit inside Travis jail, I've told the investigation company where he is."

"Why have you done that?"

"So they didn't waste time trying to find out what prison he's in, they'll need to talk to him at some point."

"True, good thinking. Did they have a plan?"

"They were talking about hiring a New York attorney to represent him. They don't believe that he can be capable of what the police are charging him with, but I don't know how they can afford that expense." Pat grunted his agreement.

"Good luck to them with finding a good attorney, you need deep pockets for good advice." He glanced towards the open office door.

"Glad to see that the operations room is up and running again. I was convinced it was Eric Bent and his team who tried to close us down."

"Who knows - it could have been Tommy as well, they both had good reason to destroy the evidence."

A short while later, the front door burst open and Brandon and Lilly-Anne came in clutching takeaway bags. "We ditched the shopping and headed for the Chinese, hope you don't mind," Brandon explained as they emptied the bags out on the table

"Trust you two, no I think Pat and I can manage that," Melissa laughed as she put the plates out and everyone delved into the food. A good while later Pat sat back and let out a notch on his belt with a contented sigh.

"Thanks for that guys, I need to get back to Dallas this evening as I'm meeting a guy about another new tiger for the west coast zoos, not sure which yet. We just need to get the money together from our supporters on Monday. You two need to be on good form, I'm relying on you."

Kissing Melissa on the cheek he left, the roar of his sports car sounding like it had one of his tigers under the bonnet.

As they cleared away the debris from the meal, Melissa took the opportunity to find out how things were going in the tiger camp. "How's it shaping out working for Pat? He always seems full on." Lilly-Anne answered before Brandon had considered what to say.

"It's a fantastic experience, he looks busy all the time and he is, but he's also kind and gentle. The way he cares for his fans is incredible. He heard of one fan who had been taken to hospital with no health insurance. Pat visited and paid the medical bills in full on the understanding that she wasn't allowed to tell anyone. That's the sort of man he is." Brandon looked up from scraping spare rib bones into the bin. "I didn't know that, that was an amazing thing to do."

"I wasn't allowed to say, don't tell him that you know, he might sack me," Lilly-Anne pleaded, suddenly worried she shouldn't have said anything. Melissa gave her a quick hug. "Don't worry, neither Brandon nor I will say anything but it's a shame more people don't know what a generous man he is."

# CHAPTER TWENTY

"Ok everyone, we are going live in ten seconds, and remember, we need the money to fund this project so let's beat our record."

Lilly-Anne worked the viewers like a professional and after the thirty minute show they had seventy thousand dollars pledged from around the world. Brandon wrote a heartfelt message for the website along with a photo of the young tiger they wanted to buy which further boosted on-line donations.

As usual Pat gave a short appeal for help in finding a missing girl. Sophie had been missing from her letting agency office for some time and Pat showed a photo of a beautiful smiling girl to the camera.

Brandon checked the live messages, where as usual Lilly-Anne's fan club was growing, but one thing caught his eye, a private e-mail to Pat. He read it through and it chilled him to the bone.

*'I helped Tommy Cookson take the girls. You seem keen to have me caught. If you give me $20000 I will tell you everything and stop the torment. Meet me on the Harry S Moss trail at 06.00 Tuesday morning. Walk along the path and I will find you. Bring the money and do not tell anyone else about our arrangement. Fail to come and I will kill Lilly-Anne sometime over the next month.'* He took the laptop straight into Pat's office. "Have you seen this?"

"Yes, I've just opened it. We can't be blackmailed into giving our money away, it's a shakedown Brandon, no more, no less. I have already called the police and they're on their way. Don't tell Lilly-Anne, she doesn't need this pressure at the moment."

Within the hour, two plain clothed officers dressed as zoo workers came into the office. After reading the message, they reassured Pat that they were taking this very seriously.

"We're going to catch this creep Mr Hunter, tell him that you'll be there with the money and we'll do the rest." Pat was happy to oblige.

"I've been thinking about it. I know the area pretty well and my guess is the guy will be on a bike so he can come and go quickly." The policemen nodded in unison, one of them explaining their plan.

"I think that you're right but we'll have a tracker in with the cash so we'll get him. Set up the meeting."

Pat opened up the e-mail and replied. *'Agreed, I will be on the trail at 06.30. I will have a black sports bag containing the money. Please tell me where the girls are.'* A response came back within 30 seconds.

*'Money first Mr Hunter.'*

The police officer's phone rang and after listening for a few seconds, he hung up.

"We can't trace the source of the message. He's using a sophisticated device to hide his location."

Pat continued to stare at the screen somehow hoping that more information would appear but nothing else came. The senior police officer tapped Pat on the back, bringing him away from the blank screen.

"Ok Mr Hunter, this is the bag you will use," he held out a sports bag. "The tracker is in the handle. We will place a listening device in your jacket and we will also have you under surveillance at all times. Stay on the track and do not under any circumstances leave our sight. We will brief you again in the morning before you leave your hotel room."

Pat had a sleepless night, thoughts of the next morning whizzing around in his head but he'd managed a few moments of dozing between confused thoughts. When his alarm eventually rang, raising him from a light slumber, he felt exhausted as he stepped into the shower. A knock on the hotel door hurried him as he dried his hair.

"Room service sir." Pat opened the door to be greeted by the policeman now wearing the hotel uniform.

"Breakfast sir. Shall I put it on the table?" The door closed behind them while the policeman checked the sports bag and ensured the tracker was on and working. "Ok Mr Hunter. It's down to you. Stay calm, do not leave the pathway, and follow all the instructions given to you. Any questions?" Pat had none, he just wanted to get this done.

The cold air blowing over the park chilled Pat; he was nervous and walked slowly along the track holding the bag, the sun still fighting to make its way over the tree line.

A push bike sped up behind him, tyres crunching on the hard ground. Holding his breath and waiting for the bag to be taken, a soft voice sounded in his ear piece. "Stand By." It was reassuring to know they were watching him…tiger enclosures were dangerous places, but compared to an unseen killer they were small change. The bike sped past, the rider not giving Pat a second glance. He continued to walk as the sun broke cover and startled ducks flapped their way across the water.

A text pinged onto his screen and standing still, he read it.

"Everything OK Mr Hunter?" the voice in his ear sounded concerned.

"I've just had a text from the killer." He read it out aloud.

*'You have betrayed me and called the police. I have seen them in their cars. Something you love will now be taken away from you. The deal is off.'*

"Shit, he's going after Lilly-Anne, get over there and protect her."

The voice came back reassuringly in his ear. "Relax Mr Hunter, we're on it. Come back in and let's chat. He will be back in touch, he has twenty thousand reasons to talk again."

Sitting in the back of a police car, Pat shivered as he took off the listening devices. "What went wrong?"

"We don't know, it wasn't the guy on the bike, we stopped him and checked his phone, he's just an office cleaner. He must have been watching, maybe a marine buddy of Cookson's, he could have been hiding anywhere. Those guys are experts in setting up covert observation points."

"He's said he will kill Lilly-Anne."

"We are with her, she'll be safe."

"For how long? You can't stay with us forever."

"We're in touch with our local FBI field office and it can do whatever it wants to do. This isn't just about you, it's about all the missing girls so we'll do what is needed."


The tiger keeper came into the Bronx Zoo at five thirty in the morning, ready to check on his charges. A cold mist was drifting across the pond in the enclosure but through it he saw something which stopped him in his tracks.

"Holy shit! Oh fucking no!"

The young male tiger lay dead near the door of his sleeping quarters, a pile of vomit on the ground around his head. He phoned the park vet, Rex Wade, hands shaking with panic. This boy was the start of the breeding program and in the course of the night a perfectly healthy tiger had died. It was incomprehensible.

Unpacking his bag next to the lifeless body, the vet struggled to hold back a tear. "I just can't understand what's happened, I gave him a complete health check just two weeks ago after quarantine. He was a perfect specimen." He looked around the enclosure for any clues as to what might have killed this beautiful beast.

"Jim, since when have we given food to the tigers in the sleeping area?" Jim, the keeper looked at him in confusion.

"We don't Rex."

"Someone has, look over there, a bone that hasn't been eaten. Don't touch it and phone the police, I think this boy has been poisoned."


"And live in 5,4,3,2,1, action!"

A tearful Pat Hunter spoke to camera, trying to contain his emotions as he stuttered through his opening line before composing himself.

"I have some dreadful news to share with you this morning. I have just come from a phone call with the Bronx Zoo in New York City. Someone has poisoned our beautiful new tiger who was found dead at 5.30 this morning. Whoever did this despicable act knew what they were doing and disabled the CCTV before giving him meat contaminated with a deadly substance.

After the show on Monday, a person made a threat to me that they were going to take away something I loved if I didn't pay them $20000. I don't have that sort of money, we are a charity which is why we ask you guys to help us out from time to time." He took a deep breath.

"There is a chance that the killer is watching live right now. What I will say is, take this out on me, not the tigers. If you want to hurt me, message me in the same way as Monday. I will meet you anywhere in the country. Just don't hurt the animals please. They don't deserve to die in agony. Thank you." A film of the tiger playing in his enclosure followed for a few minutes before cutting back to Pat.

"On a brighter note, if there can be one on what is the saddest moment of my career, your donations have enabled us to buy another tiger. I can announce that this girl is going to San Diego zoo and will be there in a month or so, once the vet has given her the all clear. Thanks for watching today's shorter show, we will be back to our normal routine on Friday."

Brandon stopped filming. "Well done Pat, that was a tough show. Can't understand why anyone would want to hurt our boy. What happens now?"

"Luckily we have insurance against attack; if it was just bad luck and he died of an illness we would be in trouble, however the insurance company will pay back the money we spent. It means that eventually we can replace him."

"That's not what I am asking - the attack was aimed at you. What do we need to do to keep safe?"

"Let's leave that to the FBI, they are going to hang around for a while. I'll tell you more later Brandon, now is not the time as I have some arrangements to make. We're heading West on Monday so bring your 'A' game - we'll be meeting some of Hollywood's finest if Lilly-Anne has sorted out the details."

Closing the office door he slumped into his seat and took a deep breath just as his phone rang.

"Pat, this is serious, the police are all over the zoo. What happens when they start asking questions?"

"You tell them what happened Rex, you're the vet. You received a call for assistance, you came in and found the tiger dead. You are conducting an autopsy later which will find out the cat was poisoned."

"But what if they find the cancer?"

"Don't let them find it. It will cost us a lot of money, plus you'll go to prison for giving the tiger the poison. Keep cool and no one need ever find out."

"But what if someone saw me unplug the CCTV?"

"You need to chill the fuck out, you got us into this mess by not spotting the animal was dying when we bought it. What sort of vet misses a brain tumour? No wonder he was an unpredictable animal, he almost killed us last week. It's your fault, but my solution. Keep your composure for a few days and it's over. I had to go through a whole drama with the police on a bike path and I didn't melt down." He was getting frustrated but trying to keep his voice down as he continued. "We are the only two people who know. Everyone else thinks that I have been threatened. Mess up and we both go to prison so just keep calm." He placed the phone down as Brandon walked in.

"We're definitely meeting some 'A' list stars Pat, can I phone my mum and tell her, or is it a secret?"

"Brandon my boy, welcome to the Pat Hunter circus where you'll meet all sorts of people from film and music stars to giants in the world of power and politics. Of course you can phone your mum, tell her that you'll say hi to Will Harris and Heston Brash for her. They're promoting a movie called 'Tiger Beach', so they'll be on good form.

"Cool, this is going to read well in Chicago too. I'm writing about the new tiger as well - where did we get her from?"

"A private collector in Atlanta. A guy named Mark Cooke, a good guy but a bit crazy. He used to sleep with her until she got too big and he couldn't cope with her anymore so phoned me. Google him, there's a lot of information about him on line."

Brandon went back to the office he shared with Lilly-Anne, who had just finished making another phone call and was looking somewhat frazzled. She sat back in her chair, puffing out her cheeks in a big sigh.

"Jeez, the agents for these guys are a nightmare, everything needs to be just so. If I can't have everything perfect they say they're pulling the plug. I even have to promise to have a tiger behind their shot at all times....hell, we'll have to tie them down!" Brandon bent down and gave her a quick kiss. "If anyone can organise it, you can....I'm pretty sure even the tigers will do as you ask."

He sat at his laptop and looked up Mark Cooke which made for hilarious entertainment. The guy was an eccentric lotto winner who surrounded himself in exotic animals, apparently preferring them to people. Finding an email address, he sent a request, asking if he could have a one minute interview for the tiger website and the paper. The answer came back thirty seconds later, with a resounding NO. However he did enclose a few lines which Brandon had permission to use.

'I respect Patrick Hunter immensely, the work which he conducts to protect these beautiful creatures is at the forefront of my thoughts. This is why I was happy to donate my own tiger to the zoo enclosure free of charge. I know that she will be happier in the space you can offer and she will receive the highest level of care available.' He read it twice. "This can't be right," he mumbled, "the guy is a nut job."

"What's that?" Lilly-Anne half listening to him suddenly took interest.

"The guy who owned the tiger, he doesn't even know what day it is by the looks of things." Printing out the email, he took it straight to Pat's office.

"The guy is crazy Pat, I'm going to have to reword his statement." Pat laughed, "Told you...what has he said now?"

"He's claiming that the tiger was given to us for free but we know different, he wanted twenty thousand dollars for her. I'll just put that we raised money through our fans to pay for her." Pat looked a little uncomfortable, "Well, hold on to that one for a little while."

"Why? I want to get it out for the press release to coincide with Monday."

"We didn't exactly pay for her Brandon, she was donated as he said." Brandon looked at him in disbelief.

"Where has the money gone to then? People paid in good faith and we sold this as an appeal for the tiger. What's going on Pat?"

"Who do you think is paying for you and lover girl out there? We need money to continue but the public would rather donate to pay for a tiger than for the admin costs of the company."

"But that's fraud, surely we're breaking the law?"

"Technically, maybe. But the money is for ongoing costs. It will all be used for the associated costs of the tigers."

"What, you mean like on a new car and a house in the country that you don't even use?" Pat stood up, using his full height to intimidate Brandon.

"Brandon, be careful with what you say. Don't challenge me, just trust me. I'm not spending the money on myself, it's used for insurance, for food, for wages and bills. I'm investing in the brand as a whole. If you go chatting to anyone about this, remember, it was you and your girlfriend who prised the money from their tight fists. I will just remind people of your fundraising abilities and we can all be branded as conmen together, or, you can allow me to keep feeding my tigers. Your choice."

"Ok, Pat, have it your own way. But we will not be asking the public for donations again." Brandon told him standing his ground although trembling with anger.

"Suit yourself, you might want the animals to starve or not have vet checkups, but I would look at the books before you accuse me of fraud the next time. Everything adds up, all I take is a salary, and that's not very much considering the hours I put in." He dialled a number and held his phone out towards Brandon.

"Would you like to speak to the accountant? I have her waiting."

"No, sorry. I didn't understand. Sorry Pat." He left red faced and flustered, returning to his own desk where Lilly-Anne looked at him in consternation as he flung himself onto his chair.

"I made an enormous mistake Lilly-Anne. Bloody hell, I was nearly fired!"

"What did you do?"

"Read the figures wrong and thought Pat was stealing money from the public." Lilly-Anne shook her head.

"You idiot, don't mess this up. We're having a great time so think before you speak. He's a great guy, he never puts his own needs before the animal's."

"Yup, I've learnt that lesson. So, are we going live tonight?"

"Yep, but not in the enclosure, just some feeding shots and Pat has got some really cool stuff from a UK park where they are feeding the tigers differently. The public will love it."

"Going live in 5-4-3-2-1 and action."

"Welcome to our enclosure where we have Tammy, one of the big girls out tonight. She's hungry and if you listen to her roar, she is asking where her dinner is." The camera panned around, showing Tammy pacing backwards and forwards in her enclosure as Pat continued.

"We have a surprise for everyone tonight, Brandon and I are going in to feed her which we don't normally do, but this girl has been left alone for too long and she needs a bit of loving. But before we do that, I want to show you how our friends in the UK are feeding their boys and girls. Over to you UK." A five minute clip of a wildlife park in the UK showed tigers climbing trees and searching for food which had been hidden in nooks and crannies.

"Pat, we're not supposed to be in there tonight, she's really feisty and we can all see that she is not feeling friendly." Brandon was starting to panic again.

"She's not the only one who is not feeling friendly Brandon, are you coming in or not? As I said earlier, it's your choice."

"Oh, I see, you're teaching me a lesson for questioning you. It was a mistake Pat, I said that I was sorry."

"In or out?"

"In." Lilly-Anne appeared, catching the end of their exchange. "You two are going in there tonight? When is it my turn?" Pat turned to her and gave her shoulder a squeeze.

"You're going in next week, you will love it, we'll have two cubs to play with."

"Cute, ok be careful. Are you filming from inside Brandon, or am I taking shots from outside?"

"You better do this one, I need to keep my eyes on that girl." Another growl came from the undergrowth as a wheelbarrow of meat was pushed up to the door. Pat turned to Brandon who was looking increasingly worried.

"It'll be fine, she wants to eat so the last thing that she wants to do is chase us away. She doesn't bite the hand who feeds her Brandon," he reassured him as the door to the enclosure slipped open and Pat walked in pushing the barrow full of a butchered wild pig. He tossed a lump near to a rustling bush and the tiger came out and sniffed around the raw meat before grabbing it and taking it back under cover. Pat quietly explained her behaviour as the two of them moved forwards, Brandon suddenly feeling very vulnerable. He was twenty feet from the escape door, the furthest he had moved inside an enclosure yet.

"You're looking a bit white young Brandon, everything ok?" Pat observed.

"I guess so Pat, I mean, you know what you're doing don't you?"

Tossing another joint of meat towards the bushes, the tiger came out a little quicker this time, eating the meat where it dropped. She finished, looking up expectantly and Brandon's heart thumped as she moved forwards towards them. Jumping up and banging her paws onto Pat's shoulders, she licked his face as he laughed and rubbed her back.

"You soppy old girl! Phew, that's a strong case of bad breath," he laughed as he pulled her ears. "Come here Brandon, I want you to meet my girlfriend."

Brandon moved across as the tiger watched his every move before leaving Pat and brushing her head against Brandon's legs, her sheer power nudging him backwards. Leaning down, he rubbed her head as she continued to purr.

"My God Pat, I had no idea how gentle they could be."

"She could kill you in one second, she just doesn't feel like it today." He took the third lump of meat and fed it directly to her. "Gently," he said as she took it with the very tips of her lips.

"Good girl. Let's go Brandon, we have pushed our luck enough today. Don't show her your back or she will attack. Walk slowly backwards with me." The door slid shut behind them and Brandon spun round towards Pat.

"Jesus Pat, that is the most exciting thing I have ever done," he exclaimed, his eyes blazing with the excitement. Pat smiled at his enthusiasm.

"And just take the lesson, I would never do anything to harm you. Trust me."

# CHAPTER TWENTY-ONE

Melissa sat in the large courtroom. She had waited two months for this moment when Tommy Cookson would walk through the single door to her left and sit behind the table, where he would see Melissa and remember what he did to her daughter and also to the other innocent young girls who he had taken and murdered without remorse. He would have to listen to the evidence piling up against him, while the jury also listened intently, privately horrified by what this monster had done and the terror he had presented all over the country.

Since his imprisonment no girls had been reported missing from his personal killing fields. The violence had ended and all he needed to do now was reveal where the girls lay hidden.

The door opened and a group of security staff entered. In the centre of them Tommy Cookson shuffled forwards as he looked over at the public sitting expectantly. Seeing Melissa he shouted over, "I didn't do it, I've been set up." She looked away disgustedly but couldn't drown out his pleas.

"Sit down Mr Cookson and keep silent. Any more outbursts like that and I will have you removed." Judge Searle looked at him unsmiling and unapologetic as he continued. "Do you understand?"

The attorney stood, "Yes, he fully understands, Judge."

"Excellent, then we will begin." The list of offences were read out, the courtroom in absolute silence as each grain of information was scattered for the jury to digest. At the end of the list, the judge again turned to Tommy.

"How do you plead to the charges?"

"Not guilty," he replied, staring at Melissa.

The prosecution and defence attorneys then presented their opening speeches before the defence took to the floor.

"I would like to call the first of our defence witnesses, these next five men will vouch that Tommy Cookson could not have been in the area of Dallas, Austin or even Texas at the time of the offences."

Called in one at a time, the men gave evidence to support that they had been with Tommy nearly twenty-four hours a day so he could not have left Florida to commit these crimes. They were all happy to testify this under oath.

Then the final of the five men took the stand, looking uncomfortable as he was sworn in. He presented his story, almost word for word what the other four had said. He finished his evidence with the following statement. "Tommy was with us all the time, he is a war hero and he did not go to Dallas to commit these crimes."

The prosecution attorney was quick to stand and begin his first detailed cross examination.

"You are saying that Mr Cookson was with you at all times?"

"Yes, lived and slept together."

"Did he go to Texas at any point during the time you knew him?"

"No."

"When Mia Jagger was taken, was he still with you?"

"Yes."

"How do you know? How can you be sure?"

"Because it was in all the papers and we talked about it."

"What, even Mr Cookson? Did he discuss the crime with you?"

"Yes, he was angry that no one had helped."

"So if I was to tell you that Mr Cookson was at the scene of the crime, what would you say?"

"Impossible, he was with us."

"So you have said. But Mr Cookson was at the scene, he has told us he was there. Please read his statement." He passed the witness a piece of paper. He read it in silence before looking up at Tommy.

"Sorry Tommy, we were just trying to help."

"So you didn't see Mr Cookson?" The prosecution attorney

insisted.

"We did, but only for a week. I'm sorry."

"So why are you here lying under oath?"

"They put us up in a hotel and gave us food and money. We thought that they would give us more if we told this story."

"And why are the stories all the same?"

"They told us what to say," the witness replied, again looking over towards Tommy's team.

"So the defence attorney told you to lie and gave you the script?"

"Yes. As I said, I'm sorry."

"No further questions."

The judge looked up. "These are serious allegations, the jury will ignore the evidence given from this morning's witnesses. I am halting the trial based on the evidence presented in regard to perjury. The allegations against the defence attorney Mr Campbell are serious and could lead to a prison sentence. Officers, please arrest Mr Campbell on a charge of perjury and bring him to my office."

The mumbling around the room raised its level as loud conversations broke out everywhere.

"Silence!" The judge banged his gavel on his desk before turning to Tommy.

"You will need a new attorney; Mr Campbell will no longer be acting on your behalf. If you have no funds, we can give you a representative. Is that clear?" Tommy stood in shock as he saw any chance of a defence come crashing down around his ears.

"Yes sir, I have no funds and I will need help."

"We will provide someone but they will need to be up to speed by tomorrow, I am not stopping the case. All of your witnesses have been called and discredited and your attorney has gone the same way. We shall recommence in the morning."

"All rise." He stood and left, leaving Tommy watching as his only hope to freedom was led to the cells ahead of him.

"It's fair to say the morning has not gone in your favour son."

An older disinterested looking man in a wrinkled suit sat in front of him in the cells area of the court.

"My name is Mike Dobbin, your new court appointed attorney. I have looked through your papers, and to be honest, you have nothing in your favour. We can try fighting the evidence which they are going to present but honestly, I don't know how. The victim's necklace was in your apartment with only your DNA on it, but everyone knows that." He flicked through the documents. "We can try and rescue the deal that was offered through your previous attorney, for life in custody rather than the death penalty?"

"How does it look to you?"

"In my opinion you have no hope, they're going to send you to death row. My suggestion is that you try for a mistrial on the basis of having no time to prepare."

"Will that work?"

"You have no defence but it's your only hope. Then they will have another trial and find you guilty, unless this mysterious phone appears…and I don't think that is very likely Mr Cookson." Tommy shook his head despondently.

"Doesn't look like it. I'm innocent Mr Dobbin and I need you to believe me."

"Mr Campbell did all he could to fight your case; presently he's in the process of being charged for perjury and suspended from practicing law until after his hearing. I can assure you that I will not be trying his tricks. If you are innocent, I feel sorry for you but everything I've looked at points to guilty. Do you want me to try for a deal?" Tommy looked up at him, this time with a determined look in his eyes.

"I want you to get me out, no deals."

"Ok, just don't expect miracles. I've got to see the judge shortly and he will ask me if I'm ready for tomorrow. If I say yes then we meet here again in the morning, if I say no, we get another month. Your shout."

"We might find the phone in the next four weeks so tell him we need more time. And there's another angle to look at; Mr

Campbell was looking into the fact that while I was fighting a war for our country there were five other cases of abductions in the relevant areas." Dobbin flicked through the case notes again until he came to the relevant page which he read before shaking his head and answering.

"The reason he hasn't raised it is that for at least three of those cases you were on leave from your unit. They say that you returned to the USA for those periods of time so it's not a good defence, in fact it works out better for the prosecution. Let's keep that one hidden for now." He closed the file and got up to leave.

"See you in four weeks Mr Dobbin, please find the phone, it must be in that Chicago newspaper office somewhere." The attorney shrugged his shoulders, a couple of years from retirement, he didn't need this crap.

"We've tried twice and it's not there. They say that it was thrown into the trash months ago. It simply isn't going to turn up." Tommy banged his fist onto the dirty table top and a pen rolled onto the floor.

"Well, I didn't know that, it's difficult to speak to anyone while I am sat in the unit. Fuck it, let's just get it done. I'll see you tomorrow."

"As I said, it's your call. I'll see you in the cells in the morning and in the meantime I'll try to work on some form of defence."

Tommy sat in his single cell back at the courtroom. He hadn't slept the previous night as the events of the day had played through his mind. A fresh faced guard appeared. "Mr Dobbin is here to see you. Are you ready?"

"Sure." Mike Dobbin entered and wasted no time in filling Tommy in on what he had discovered over night.

"Hi Tommy, we've got a tough day today ahead of us; they have a couple of witnesses they're calling, one of them being Brandon who is going to give evidence about your claims to being at the scene. Apparently you told him that you had seen other murders too. Did you say that?"

"I did, I saw the killer but never got a good look at him, he was in some heavy clothes, big jacket, hat, that sort of thing."

"Holy shit! So you were at the scene of a few killings?"

"I was high when I spoke to him, I was hungry and needed some cash. I said too much to Brandon and I lied…I only saw one killing. I was trying to get money from the papers."

"But you said that you were there for a number."

"I did, but I swear that I wasn't." Tommy slumped in his chair in despair. "It doesn't look good does it?"

"No, it just proves that you tell lies for your own gain. Shit!" Dobbin shook his head as he flicked through the evidence again.

"They're also calling Pat Hunter. Apparently he has a text from your accomplice admitting to the killings."

"That's bullshit. One, I didn't do it and two, if I had done it. I wouldn't have anyone helping me."

"Well let's not say that to the court, we will dispute the text as a hoax, as someone trying to gain money from him. He didn't want to come here, the police forced him to testify. He claims that you two were friends."

"We knew each other, not really friends though."

"And then they are calling Melissa to identify the necklace which you had in your home."

"It had been stuck in my mail box," Tommy told him resignedly, "I didn't just happen to have it in my house."

"We can't prove that but they can prove you had it. They win."

"Ok, so what do I do today?"

"Nothing, if we put you on the stand they will rip you to shreds. Just go with the flow and say nothing to anyone. All of the evidence will be heard by lunchtime so the jury may well be out this afternoon. Let's wait and see."

The morning passed in a blur as the weight of evidence stacked up against him. The only victory seemingly was Pat's evidence, there was no proof that the sender of the text was associated with Tommy and even Pat confirmed that he doubted its authenticity. Regardless, it had been a poor day. Dobbin asked Judge Martin Searle if he could approach the bar as the jury filed out to decide the verdict.

"Judge, we have heard everything and although it doesn't look good can I ask that the deal for life imprisonment be put back on the table in place of the death penalty?"

"No Mr Dobbin, you can't. Your client is a danger to anyone who comes into his path, God knows how many people he has killed. Maybe one day he will tell us."

Once more Tommy walked slowly out of the court room, this time avoiding the stares from the public. The weight of evidence was enormous and even he was starting to doubt his own innocence. This time he wasn't placed in a cell but instead led to the legal visit room where Dobbin pushed a brown bag over the table towards him. "You might as well eat something while we wait, son."

Eating a dog-eared sandwich, Tommy made small talk with Dobbin, despondency pressing down on him like a vice.

"So what did you say to the judge? Don't tell me that you were trying to cut a deal?"

"I tried Tommy, they're going to find you guilty so the best we can hope for is life for each of the missing youngsters they can link to you. In reality the jury will decide it's death, I can't paint it any better." Tommy got to his feet, pacing around the small room.

"Fuck them, I am innocent and you need to believe that. They're going to execute an innocent man."

"I will appeal straight after the verdict, it will give us some more time to try find the phone. It's our only hope."

"If I hadn't been so stoned I might even have seen who it was at the van with Mia, but I could hardly even see the van. I just remember a guy carrying a girl, he was a big, strong guy as he picked her up with one arm. I just couldn't see who it was and every time I dream, I see the same thing. A faceless person carrying a body. I try to call out but no sound will come. The dream always wakes me up, even when I was on the streets."

"Maybe the video will tell us, if it turns up. Without it we are screwed."

A shout came through the door. "Mr Dobbin, the jury are

coming back in." Dobbin looked at Tommy, his face saying it all.

"Shit, they have only been out forty-five minutes, that's not a good sign. See you up there and good luck."

The verdict was read out slowly and clearly for each of the charges. Thomas Cookson was found guilty for the murder of twenty-five girls with another twelve cases left on file for future investigation. The vote was unanimous and the jury had expressed their wish for the death penalty.

A cheer erupted within the room where the families of so many of the missing girls sat hugging and crying. One voice shouted out from amongst the group.

"Tell us where they are you bastard!" before court security closed him down.

"Mr Cookson," Judge Searle scowled, "I have considered the facts presented along with your absolute lack of remorse for the crimes you committed, or for the feelings of the grieving families sitting in this court room. I do not say this lightly but on this occasion there is absolutely no hope that you will ever be a better person after a lengthy period of imprisonment. You are evil beyond belief, the worst example of humanity disguised in the story of a war hero. You are no hero sir, you are a cold hearted killer and it therefore gives me pleasure to sign this certificate for the sentence of death. May God have mercy upon you."

# CHAPTER TWENTY-TWO

Taken away to a high security prison cell, Tommy considered each and every option. He didn't want to rot in prison after taking a deal for a crime he didn't commit, nor did he want to die in front of a selection of grieving families who all thought their torment was going to stop along with his heart. Sure the killings had stopped in the short term but they would continue as whoever was responsible was just too cunning to allow this opportunity to get away with it to slip through his fingers. An innocent man taking the heat for his actions, Tommy knew the type and also knew it wouldn't take long after his own death for this maggot to come out looking for fresh meat. He had to get a message out to Melissa, she had to believe him and keep looking for the phone.

Taking his chance as the prisoner delivering books for the library entered the unit, he showed him the envelope he had cadged from another prisoner.

"What will it take for you to post me this letter out?" he hurriedly whispered to the man. The small, elderly, shrivelled up white guy hissed back.

"What have you got?" Tommy pushed over a small pouch of illegal tobacco.

"It's all I have." The man took it and handed over a book. "Put it in here and before I leave, tell a guard that you have taken the wrong book and need to swap it. Don't mess up or I will lose my position."

It was small, but it felt like his first victory in a long time and breathing a large sigh, he collapsed back onto his bed to read his new book. Surely Melissa would understand, all she needed to do was read the letter where he explained everything a lot better than his attorney had ever managed.

The spring flowers were budding all over the lawn as Melissa pulled out weeds from the flower beds along the border. The post van pulled up and the usual whistling man jumped out and wished her good morning.

"I hope it's only good news this morning Tony, no bills please," Melissa smiled at him.

"No, not this morning, just one letter for you Melissa and it looks personal so you're in luck. See you tomorrow."

As he drove off, she wiped her hands on her work jeans before tearing open the envelope. She almost guessed the sender before she had read the signature at the bottom. *'Tommy, how the hell did he get a letter out to me?'* she mumbled to herself. *'You callous bastard, can't even leave me to grieve in peace,'* she added, staring at the paper in horror but not reading a word before tearing it into a dozen bits and throwing it onto the small bonfire she had made for her weeds. *'Fuck you, you bastard,'* she spat, the words disappearing into the air like the paper smoke from the fire. *'Let's see how he likes this,'* she said to herself as going back inside, she picked up her phone.

His cell door burst open and a search team entered. "Turn and face the wall," he was ordered as restraints were placed on his arms and legs. A guard stepped into the cell.

"How dare you try intimidating the mother of the girl you slaughtered. You think that we won't find out, you think that your little library friend is going to keep his mouth shut when all hope of parole is taken away from him? You have just cost him another ten years in this prison. You happy boy?" Pulling him out of the unit, the guard almost spat in Tommy face as the ferocity of his message rang out in the empty walkway.

"You are going to taste solitary conditions for a long, long time boy. And then you are going to die. You just don't get it do you? In here you are nothing, hot shot; I am the lord, I am the almighty and I alone decide on your fate. And today boy, is your day of repentance."

Rushed through a series of corridors and clanging gates

Tommy arrived in the most desolate area he had ever seen, so bereft of life and colour that the faces staring from cell doors with wild unblinking eyes looked as though their souls had been taken already.

"Welcome to my world where you will only speak when you are spoken to. You'll get fifteen minutes out of this cell everyday when you will be alone and you will not communicate with anyone. If you break these rules, I will fucking break you into a million pieces before that lethal injection pumps poison through your sick brain."

The door slammed shut behind him, leaving him in the filthy cell, blood and other bodily secretions smeared on the walls where messages of hate were written. There was no furniture aside from a solid plastic bed that looked as though a previous occupant had tried to destroy it, luckily for Tommy unsuccessfully. A filthy metal toilet sat in the corner, no signs of having been cleaned since it was installed. Before he could take in any more of his bleak surroundings, three guards came back and opened the door, all wearing protective clothing.

"You don't know me," a voice came from behind the helmet of the lead man, "but you met my niece when you killed her twelve months ago. I have dreamt of the time that I would stand facing you, and here we are." Smashing his baton against the top of Tommy's arm, the bone fragmented in blistering pain. The other two joined in with the beating, smashing his nose and mouth with their heavy boots as he tried to cover himself on the floor.

"You are ours, say anything and you get worse next time. Not one single person in this place likes you Cookson, everyone knows that you are a heartless, gutless, bastard." Managing to kneel and with the searing pain in his arm, he knew it was pointless trying to defend himself as another boot smashed into his eye, blood hitting the back wall before the door closed once again.

Staggering back onto his bed, he tried to move the shattered arm, the pain almost blinding him before the door opened again. It was a hard faced woman wearing the same protective uniform.

"I see that you have just fallen over. I told you to stop trying to jump up and smash your night light. Do you want to see a doctor?"

"Yes please."

"And what are you going to say?"

"I fell."

"Good, I will be with you at all times to ensure that you remember this. Just a word of warning, the doctor has been told about you and he already hates you. Keep your mouth shut, understand?"

Tommy winced in pain, barely able to speak.

"I do."

A short time later, a medical team arrived at the door, the doctor entering first. If Tommy had expected a good bedside manner, he was quickly disillusioned.

"Ok Cookson, the guard has told me that you fell, and I can see that you have a bone sticking out through your skin. You're going to need an operation to fix it but we can't do that here so we're going to take you out for the day. Don't get any smart arsed ideas." He moved towards Tommy, whose pain intensified as he tried to sit up.

"I'm going to give you an injection to numb the pain. You are a filthy, girl-killing son of a bitch, and I shouldn't care about your discomfort but unfortunately for me, I am bound by an oath. Even animals like you get my professional treatment. Hold out your arm boy." The needle slid in to his vein easily and the relief was almost instant.

"Don't get too comfy," the doctor warned him, "we're going now and you'll be back in this cell before you know what has happened."

An eruption of noise from police sirens and overhead helicopters drowned out any other noises as the escort rushed itself the two miles to the hospital where hushed whispers and aggressive stares followed him along a private corridor towards the operating theatre. A tall, black porter opened the door as he was wheeled through and he spat into Tommy's face, phlegm dripping onto his chin as the guards laughed. "Hope that you die on the table, you filthy animal," he snarled as a doctor appeared and wiped Tommy's face before looking at the porter with a frown. "I will take it from here."

The sharp stab of the anaesthetic needle entering the back of his hand took all the misery away and he managed to count to three before darkness overcame him.

He awoke suddenly, his head pounding. Glancing around for a second, he realised that he was lying back in his cell with the damaged arm in plaster, emitting a constant throbbing which seemed to take over half his body. Life couldn't seem to be any worse; even on the streets he had felt safer, and what could the best outcome possibly be now? He was pretty certain this wasn't going to be the last beating and Dobbin had lost all contact - he wasn't even sure an appeal had been made. Fucking hell, if he had just kept his mouth shut, the last unit was torturous but it was a better shit hole than this place. He was now just waiting for death and for him in this cell life was far worse than death. He had no one; if anyone even gave a flying hoot about him then things might feel a bit better, but they didn't.

Managing to slide the bandage from the sling around the corner of the door, he tugged on it, finding it held firm. Tying the other end around his neck, he tugged one more time before allowing his body to slump. The knot tightened around his throat and cut off the air supply as he drifted away, fighting the urge to save himself before the darkness once more smothered him.

"Wake up you selfish bastard," he heard in the distance as the defib machine punched his chest for the third time. His eye flickered open, as he heard the words closer this time, "He's back." A blur of activity surrounded him as he tried to make sense of what was happening.

"Stay where you are, don't try to move," he was ordered as a trolley was pushed into the cell across the debris of litter torn from medical equipment.

"It's your lucky day, if we hadn't heard you gasping like an asthmatic horse, you would be dead now boy."

"I want to be dead, let me die, please."

"What, and rob the poor families of justice? No boy, you're going to face them when the time is right, not when you feel like it."

He felt himself drifting off and some time later, opening his eyes again, Tommy saw the fat bored guard sitting outside of the gated door to his cell, empty drink cans and sandwich wrappers lying under his chair. He spoke huskily as his damaged throat felt bruised and sore.

"What time is it please?"

"Six thirty in the morning, half an hour and I'm home to bed."

"How long am I staying in this room?"

"Depends on you son. Once you stop trying to kill yourself you can go back to your unit. Until then, I have a duty to keep you alive - that is until they kill you."

"Am I going back to solitary?"

"Doubt it, I think that you are done in there, you didn't like that place much then? No one does, they're cruel bastards down there."

"They broke my arm and gave me a beating, that's all I know."

"I don't want to hear that stuff, you probably deserved some of it anyway." Tommy was awake now. This was the first guard who had spoken to him decently and it gave him an instant of hope and of feeling human again.

"Can I tell you something?"

"Tell me whatever you like for the next thirty minutes, then you can finish the story tonight. Listen son, whatever you are in here for I'm not judging you. That has already been done, and the good lord will do it again later. Do you have any faith in Jesus Christ?"

"No, not for a long time."

"Well you better damn well find some. Father Peter Bell is coming to see you at ten o'clock sharp and if he tells me that you have refused to talk to him after all my efforts to get him to come into the jail today, I'll be pissed off, and I promise that me and you are going to have a very silent night, understand?"

"Peter Bell? I think that I knew him in another prison." Tommy searched his sluggish brain for an answer, he was sure he had heard the name before. The guard nodded.

"He's a good man, he has only worked in this place for a couple of months, but he told me that he knew you in Tennessee when he worked in one of their jails."

"Yeah, something like that, that's right. He only saw me twice; why is he interested in me?"

"Who knows son? Obviously he liked you." He checked his watch as another overweight guard waddled towards the chair.

"Ten minutes early, God bless you Jimmy, I'll make that up to you tonight." Picking up his rubbish, he sorted out his bag before writing a last note onto his clipboard.

"See you tonight son and remember what I said," and he was gone, leaving a far harsher face looking in on him.

"Don't even try speak to me you evil son of a bitch," the new guard warned him before burying his head in a book.

Tommy woke up some time later and lifting his head from the thin, hard pillow he could see two figures at the gate. One was the guard, the other was a much younger, more athletic man.

"Morning Tommy, I hope that you remember me. Father Peter Bell, I guess you were told that I was coming to see you?"

"Yes Father, sorry, I was a bit out of it back in Tennessee, thanks for the help. You just weren't the type of religious guy I expected to see back then."

"The number of times that I'm told that; people seem to think that a cranky, retired Irishman is going to appear and beat them into confession. I didn't much like that last prison either, religion has it's place but so has a rehab unit. The warden wanted me to be both I think." Looking into Tommy's eyes he continued. "I was the Padre for a Parachute Battalion in the UK for five years where they insisted that I should do what they do. Luckily I could, and still try to keep fit, just no jumping out of balloons and planes now." Tommy sat himself up, with some difficulty, trying not to put any weight on his arm as he did so.

"I didn't realise you were military, you haven't told me that before. Why did you move all the way over to Texas?"

"Well this is my new parish; life moves in mysterious ways, or so they say. We have some common ground Tommy. I spent a long time in Helmand Province Afghanistan, the same as you and I've seen some bad things also. If we can't offer each other support as humans, what else do we have left? I spoke to the warden yesterday and she explained your situation to me." Father Bell looked down at the uninterested guard sitting in his chair, still reading. "If you would like a thirty minute break I can stay out here and chat for a bit." The man heaved himself out of his chair, not needing to be asked twice, relieved to have a break from the monotony of a constant watch.

"No problem Father, give me a call when you've finished, I'll be in the office."

Peter Bell watched him waddle away before turning back to Tommy.

"What's going on then Tommy? I understand your desperation but why try kill yourself now, when you were under such close supervision in segregation?" He looked at the bruises on Tommy's face and the broken arm.

"Ah, I get it, another man who has fallen in his cell. Let me guess, you were trying to break the night light. Those things are dangerous, I have seen so many examples in lots of prisons. The guards really are bastards in that type of unit."

"I guess they didn't like me staying with them, one of the guys was a relative of a missing girl."

"Nasty, what are you going to do about it?"

"Nothing, this place is too small. They'll get me again for sure."

"I can ask for you to be moved?"

"As I said, the prison is a small place. I can't hide and until I can prove my innocence, I'm a target."

"And how can you prove that?"

They chatted for an age, Tommy slowly going through his story since leaving the military, the day he watched Mia go missing, the hope he found with Melissa and the rest of the group and how he felt that the police had set him up in revenge. Peter sat in the chair and listened, hardly needing to speak as the story flooded out, sometimes with tears, sometimes a rage rising and falling as he spoke, but never stopping. The first chance that this dam had been given to burst and it came in a torrent of foaming, angry water. Once Tommy had finished his story the chaplain spoke.

"We have talked for over an hour Tommy and I think that you've got a lot off your chest. How do you feel?"

Tommy sat on his bed looking drained. "How do I feel?" He considered his emotions before replying. "Listened to, maybe even believed. Either way, it feels good."

"If I said that I wanted to help you, would you trust me?" Peter Bell then asked.

"Help? In what way can you help, apart from listening?"

"I think that you're innocent Tommy and I'm going to help prove it."

It was as if a sledgehammer had hit him in the chest, a gentle sentence delivered at a whisper from a smiling face, but the impact of these words carried such force. He cried as if he would never stop, kneeling at the gate of the cell while the chaplain stroked his hair as though he were a small child.

"I believe you Tommy, and I think God believes you as well. Together we will find the truth." Tommy looked up with red, sore eyes. "You have no idea what those words mean to me Father. Thank you so much."

"I have enough information to be getting on with, so let me see what I can find out and I'll see you again in a week. Guard!" The man waddled back out of the office and plonked himself back in his chair. "Thank you Father, it was good to have a break away from the gate."

"No problem Officer." He turned back to Tommy. "See you soon and stay positive." The sound of his footsteps faded as the guard put down his book.

"I don't know what he said to you son, but let's get one thing clear, despite whatever God has said, you are still a piece of shit."

Lying back down on the hard bed, Tommy closed his eyes and considered hope for the first time in months.

# CHAPTER TWENTY-THREE

Pat's phone rang again; he'd already had three missed calls from the same number, Rex Wade, the Bronx zoo vet.

"Yes Rex, what can I do for you this morning?" Pat's voice had a hint of irritation springing from it.

"The insurance company have phoned, they want me to preserve the dead tiger as they're not paying us until they conduct their own investigation. They need all the organs, including the brain." His voice had raised an octave and Pat could tell that he was in full panic mode. He tried to keep his own voice calm while inside he was seething with the guy's lack of courage.

"And where is the body?"

"Still in the chiller, I'm not allowed to dispose of him until the government say so."

"Ok, calm down and let's think this through. Apart from the tumour in his brain that you failed to spot, are there any other signs which will point to health issues rather than poison?"

"I don't know, I would doubt it and I've covered my tracks with the poison. Any tests will show contamination because it's true."

"Exactly Rex. Now, if the brain is missing, let's just say the tumour is removed and all they have is sections pre-sliced, will they be suspicious?"

"Yes, I'll have to tell them I was checking for health issues and they won't be happy. It'll just be a hatchet job."

"Well I don't care if they question your workmanship, so long as they pay up."

"But what if they question me? I'm not telling lies under oath. This is a lot of money and they're suspicious. They will have investigators asking questions Pat."

"Well you have two options, you either lie and keep with our plan, or you can tell them that you killed the tiger with poison you obtained illegally, unplugged the CCTV to cover your crime, tampered with evidence, committed fraud and broke all the rules required to be a vet. Which will it be? I need to know." There was a brief silence before the vet responded.

"I could tell them that you told me to do it." Pat let out a sigh, he had been waiting for this tactic to emerge.

"And what proof do you have of that?"

"This recorded conversation. If you don't get up here and help clean up this mess, I will let the police listen and we can both go to jail."

Pat's brain whirled as he considered the options but he had confronted enough danger to realise that these threats were just a weak bluff.

"I'm not coming up, I have work to do down here. Deal with it, stop flapping and let me know when it's sorted." He ended the call.

A San Diego sunrise in summer was a beautiful place to be, and even at six thirty in the morning a small crowd had still managed to gather around the new tiger enclosure, a barrier keeping them far enough from the VIPs to stop unwanted contact. A bank of lights and trailers took over the nearby car park before the actors arrived in separate golf buggies, looking every inch as though they wanted to be seen as normal, everyday people after spending an hour in makeup. Rattling through pre-rehearsed banter to try and sell the film, the two stars were met face to face by Pat who outshone them both as they clamoured for air time and a killer line to make the audience love them a little more. His very presence and charisma seeped through every TV set in the country, seemingly without effort.

"Man you're good," blustered Will Harris, rattling off a few more well practiced lines before the cameras cut away as the actors ignored the public and vanished back into their Hollywood bubble.

Brandon and Lilly-Anne watched from the side of the small stage, glowing with pride at being part of this team. With the guests long gone, they approached as Pat sat typing something into his phone. He looked serious as he glanced up at them both.

"Guys, we need to talk."

"Sure Pat, what's up?" Brandon asked as Lilly-Anne looked concerned.

"I need to fly up to the Bronx Zoo today, the vet is going into a meltdown and can't handle a simple insurance company interview. I need to give him a bit of moral support as we can't afford to lose twenty thousand dollars for a breeding tiger. It's only seven o'clock so if I get a flight soon, I can make the late afternoon meeting and return here for tomorrow morning's filming."

"Sure, we have enough work to do here anyway, we have that full documentary to edit," Brandon reassured him.

"Great, Lilly-Anne, book me return flights and I'll meet you both back here for breakfast tomorrow."

Pat woke with a jolt as the plane touched down In New York. He had slept solidly for the entire trip, and with the fortune of having empty seats beside him, he'd had no disturbances. He hailed a cab from outside the terminal, the driver recognising him instantly. "Hey Tiger man, I guess it's the zoo for you today?" Pat laughed; his profile was certainly growing since the TV show.

"The tigers always come first. It's great to be back up here," he told him. He liked the Bronx Zoo, it had a vibrant atmosphere and was the place he preferred to work from. Rex almost broke down in tears of relief as Pat barged through his door.

"Ok Rex, I'm here after a five hour flight to help bail you out so let's get to work. Show me the body."

The animal was pulled out on a shelf from a large fridge unit, still looking magnificent, even in death. "What a shame," Pat commented, stroking his head. "He would have been a fantastic boy in stud." Rex patted the animal's side.

"I agree."

"Where are the organs?"

Rex pointed towards a door on the other side of the room. "In the laboratory, the tumour has been incinerated."

"And what time are the insurance company arriving?"

Rex looked at his watch. "Ten minutes, you've just made it so we'd better get over there."

Making their way down the corridor to the boardroom, Pat stopped walking suddenly and grabbed Rex by the shoulder. It was the only blind spot from the other offices in the area and he had picked it well. His anger with Rex had been building for a few days.

"If you fuck this up, it's all on you. Do you understand?" Rex glared at him, his own fury showing in his eyes.

"No way, I'm not taking the rap. You forget our conversation earlier, we're both involved." Pat held out Rex's phone in front of his eyes. "What, the conversation we had on this phone?" Rex made a grab for it but Pat caught his arm and twisted it behind his back.

"You son of a bitch, you have just taken that from my jacket pocket," he panted through the pain of his twisted arm.

"As I said Rex, you have no proof," Pat insisted as he released his arm and pushed him away. Rex looked flustered; Pat had never laid hands on him before and straightening his shirt, they both continued down the hall and entered the boardroom.

Pat went into celebrity mode instantly.

"Good afternoon ladies and gentlemen," he greeted the three insurance investigators who were already waiting and sitting patiently. Pat and Rex sat opposite them on the other side of the boardroom table as Pat initiated the discussion.

"I understand that you have doubts about the work of one of New York's finest vets, in fact the only vet licensed to work with tigers in this state?" A middle aged, suited man answered him with a tight smile.

"We do indeed, twenty thousand dollars is a hefty cheque to write out for our firm so we need to conduct our own tests."

"And do you have anyone even approaching Rex Wade's credentials, because I am not allowing a butcher to cut my boy into ribbons for your bottom line?"

"No, but we have a vet who is willing to give a second opinion, and the tiger is already dead, Mr Hunter."

"Not good enough, anyone touching my animals, alive or dead needs to be a complete professional in tiger work. A regular vet doesn't cut it, if you excuse the pun. Now, as I see it, you have two choices, pay what you owe or we will go to court and I swear to you, it will cost you a lot more than twenty thousand dollars. You have until six this evening to put that cheque in my hand. Now get out of my zoo and do your job." Pat stood, glaring down at the three inspectors, waiting for a response which wasn't long in coming.

"We don't mean to be casting any doubts at Mr Wade's competence, it's just our policy to follow up on large claims."

"Well how about this for policy, we pay tens of thousands each month to you in order to look after our animals across the entire country and we tell our massive fan base what good guys you all are. It is not a small investment for us but the moment we come to you with a significant bereavement, the loss of possibly a future fifty tigers which would eventually have been released into the wild, you cause us a problem and insist your general vet is more qualified than one of the world's leading experts. My viewers helped fund that tiger and you are trying to steal their cash. What if they all doubted your integrity? What happens if the millions who follow me and my work start to question your morals while dealing with claims? Do you think those losses of potential business would amount to less than twenty thousand dollars?"

"I would doubt it Mr Hunter," the man again replied, seeming to shrink into his seat.

"Then why don't you pay the money, settle the claim and we buy a new tiger and carry on with our conservation work and our positive promotion of your company? We are not going to be bullied by you to do things that are not needed." Pat stared them down for a second before adding, "So who makes the decisions?" The woman sitting in the centre of the three opened up her laptop and checked on her notes, looking a little flustered as she did so. Normally these three put the heat on others but today was a different type of meeting and it felt as though they had gone to a gun fight with a butter knife.

"I think we can agree to settle the claim without further delay. You will have the money transferred into the account by close of play. I'm sorry for this misunderstanding." She closed her laptop and stood up. Pat held out a meaty hand towards her which she meekly shook while avoiding eye contact.

"Apology accepted, and if you will excuse me I have a meeting with the mayor this evening. I'm glad that you are now not the topic of discussion." The CEO of the zoo came in as Pat finished speaking, looking hassled. "Sorry I missed the start of the meeting, where are we?"

"I think that we've reached a satisfactory conclusion, with reimbursement for the tiger due by end of play today," Pat told him, "unless you have anything which you would like to add?"

"No, not at all. Would you like to follow me, I will show you the quickest way out of the park," he smiled at the investigators.

Pat and Rex remained seated in the conference room until the people were out of sight. Rex looked at Pat in admiration.

"How do you do that Pat? You destroyed them."

"I had no choice, you had crumbled. Treat people like tigers Rex, look big and powerful, hide your fear and never show vulnerability. They didn't want to fight me because they thought that I was too strong for them. They are bullies who feed on the weak but I am strong, I am the king of the bloody jungle today!"

"Jesus, I thought that we were going to get found out but you were brilliant."

"I needed to be, as you already told me, you would have sold me down the river. Don't you ever make threats to me again, do I make myself clear?" Rex held his hands up in submission.

"Perfectly clear, can I have my phone back please?" Pat scrolled through the contents, pressing delete on the recordings.

"And if you ever try a trick like that again I will break you," he promised, throwing the phone down on the table as he stood up. Leaving no time for Rex to answer, he left and headed back to

San Diego.

# CHAPTER TWENTY-FOUR

Peter Bell stood in the office of the prison warden, Miss Tracy Bull, a fierce looking woman in her mid fifties, the size of her neck living up to her surname. A former Olympian weight lifter for the US team, years of throwing heavy weights above her head and ingesting industrial amounts of steroids in the early eighties had left its legacy as she limped back behind her desk with a cold glass of water.

"Ooh Peter, not a good knee day today, I need them both replacing but my bank manager thinks differently."

"I feel your pain Tracy, how can I help you today?" Peter asked as he took a seat opposite her.

"One of my managers came to see me yesterday, they thought that you were making promises to a prisoner. Mr Tommy Cookson. Do you know him?" She took a drink, along with a couple of pain killers.

"Yes, I went to see him a few days ago, he had been beaten up Tracy, and your guards left him with a nasty open fracture of his arm." She rolled her eyes at the news.

"Holy shit, not another. OK, leave that with me, those guys in that unit are running rogue."

"Thank you, I can ask for no more." She made a note on her pad, Peter making out the word *'investigation'* before she placed it in her drawer. Of all the people that he worked with across the world, she seemed to be the most compassionate of managers. Tracy picked up a pen and twiddled it in her fingers as she fixed her eyes on the chaplain.

"I have been told that you think that he's innocent, what's more I'm told that you're going to investigate the evidence in your own time. Is that true?" Peter held up his hands in mock submission.

"Yes it is, I believe what he is telling me but I wouldn't call it investigating, I'm just looking at his version of events." Pushing her pen to one side she looked at him above her glasses.

"Normally in a case like this I would be telling you to stay away from it. However, what you do in your own time is your business, and to be honest I'm not convinced that the court hearing was conducted properly either - the whole case took less than two days to hear. How can that be fair? I want you to take a couple of week's unpaid holiday and see what you can find out. That way, I can deny that I had anything to do with this matter. Is that okay with you?"

"Seeing that you don't pay me anything anyway, I think that it sounds very fair. I just need one more quick visit with Tommy and I'll be on my way."

She stood and clasped his shoulder to show her support and feeling a true warmth, he smiled before she added, "Knock them out Peter, and Tommy will be moved out of harm's way while I look at the problem. I'll have him taken to a unit near Huntsville."

A prison guard opened Tommy's cell, and looking disinterested, he grunted in the direction of the bed. "Father Bell is here to see you." Peter Bell stepped into the foul smelling room before turning to the guard. "Do you think that we can use one of the empty offices on the unit? I need some privacy."

Sitting together in the small interview room Tommy listened to what Peter Bell had planned. He needed to speak with both Pat and Brandon in San Diego tomorrow afternoon where they had a live show from the zoo and would certainly be around there for most of the day. He then intended to speak to Melissa before flying to New York to speak to his former colleague running the investigation firm. His last stop over would be in Chicago where he had arranged an on-air interview on a prime time radio station to discuss his work in prisons with death row inmates and the possibility that some of these men were pleading innocence and could show compelling proof to support their case. He intended to use Tommy's case as an example.

Most of all he needed to clarify for sure if the newspaper office had turned up the phone. Tommy sat silently, unbelieving that anyone would do this for him.

"Thank you Father, that sounds incredible," he said, his voice croaky through lack of use.

"Maybe nothing will come from it Tommy, but I certainly plan to rattle some cages during the trip."

"I can't ask any more from you Father Peter, thank you for believing in me." Peter shrugged his shoulders in modesty.

"It's nothing; to be honest, I'm looking forwards to the challenge. On another point I might have mentioned to the warden that the guards had been heavy handed with you."

"Oh shit, that could cause me problems," Tommy replied, dismay on his face.

"I don't think so, the warden is moving you to another facility near Huntsville, Texas this afternoon while she has those guards investigated." Tommy's face fell even further.

"You know what that place is Father don't you?"

"No, I don't, I just know that you'll be away from these people."

"It's death row, they're moving me over for execution."

# CHAPTER TWENTY-FIVE

The crowd cheered as the tiger leapt more than twelve feet to snatch the hanging leg of a wild pig from a platform in the enclosure, the power and grace evident as he tore the meat down before ripping off the flesh and cracking the bones with effortless ease. Brandon leant over and whispered.

"Lilly-Anne, when we edit this video we must put that part in as slow motion to emphasise the speed and athleticism of a five hundred pound animal. And we need the part where it leapt the entire pond when it saw the food for the first time." She nodded and looked up at him.

"Got it, Brandon. Are you going to get in there and stroke this boy?" She laughed at the horror on his face at the suggestion. Pat overheard the joke and joined in. "He won't even go near the enclosure, just in case it growls at him. No he is not going in with Timba, you are Lilly-Anne." Her beautiful smile vanished momentary.

"Is that for real Pat?"

He nodded. "Last week I said that you were next so go get changed, we are getting in there in ten minutes. It will be announced by Brandon to the public in a second."

No sooner had the words left his mouth than Brandon grabbed the microphone and made the announcement. People raced towards the tiger enclosure, as Lilly-Anne walked through the excited crowds, all of whom were unaware that she was due to be the main attraction today. Pushing open the creaky wooden door to the office, she got changed in a small staff room, where, through the open window, she could hear the excited chatter from the public. One child shouted to his dad, "Are we going to see the lady eaten by the tiger Daddy?"

"You never know son," came the reply, "you saw what it did to that pig, tore it to bits and ate it up, Lilly-Anne may just be his pudding." The child laughed and the sound of little feet racing towards the enclosure drifted away. She smiled to herself; it was like the days of the gladiator where the public bayed for blood. *Let's hope that I disappoint them this time,* she muttered to herself as she headed back out towards the tiger enclosure.

Dressed in her safari clothing she skipped onto the stage as Pat introduced her. This was food and drink to her, she was a natural performer as her white smile melted the hearts of the crowd. It was pure theatre as Pat painted the picture and Lilly-Anne milked the applause, she was just so much better than Brandon who normally needed a big broom handle to prod him towards the cage. However, the crowd loved his cowardliness and always gave a countdown from five as Pat playfully pushed him into the enclosure.

But with Lilly-Anne it was the real deal and this time, she added a little extra showbiz by cart wheeling along the path, every successful spin leading to a massive cheer. Pat clapped along as this performance had taken his business to another level of engagement.

As the enclosure door opened he saw the other side of her, the joking now gone as she focused on the task, reading the tiger's movements and body language. She was good, soaking up every lesson that Pat had given her, knowing when to push forwards and understanding when to keep still or back away. All in all, a natural tiger person.

The tiger crouched and backed away out of sight. Turning on her microphone, she commentated to the audience about the tiger's natural behaviour as Pat watched and admired. She really had got it in abundance.

"Ladies and Gentlemen, girls and boys, Timba is now in the ambush position, waiting for us to come close, unaware that we know he is hiding. He will wait and spring out to attack us if he gets the chance." She stood tall, "But he is out of luck today." The crowd laughed as she continued. "If we stay still right here, he will lose patience, this boy always does. He just can't wait to eat a bit of Pat." On cue, Pat gave a look of horror as the crowd laughed again. Timba roared and backed out of the bush before circling back towards them.

"Now he is looking for any weakness and this is the most dangerous time for us as he is making the decision."

The tiger stopped again, never taking his eyes from Lilly-Anne. She put her hands up in the air and on command, Timba sprang forwards straight towards her, a gasp spilling out from the watching people, some children screaming before he stopped dead, one foot in front of her, and nuzzled her legs. She crouched down and grabbed him around the neck playing with his ears until he turned and strode back into the undergrowth.

"Timba has just told me that he has finished playing and if we stay any longer he will begin to get very territorial. In the words of the tiger master we have pushed our luck far enough." They backed away while a lump of meat was thrown into the enclosure from the feeding platform. The tiger pounced on the meat and devastated it in one bite with his crushing jaws.

Brandon took over the commentary as the pair of them returned to the stage.

"Ladies and Gentlemen, boys and girls, let's hear it for the incredible Pat Hunter and Lilly-Anne." Once the explosion of applause had died away, the audience filed out, still chatting about what they had seen,

"That was a superb show, Lilly-Anne," Pat showered her with praise, "and how good was Timba? He sure lived up to his part of the deal and I'm sure that he gets closer with the mock charge every time." His next words were interrupted by a smartly dressed man who walked onto the stage. Pat turned towards him with a smile.

"Hey, how can we help you? Did you enjoy the show?"

"Loved it, you have some courage Lilly-Anne," he replied, his English accent noticeable. Smiling, they all shook his hand as he introduced himself.

"My name is Father Peter Bell, I'm a part-time chaplain at a prison in Dallas where I've been speaking to Tommy Cookson."

Pat let his hand go immediately, also dropping his smile.

"I think that we need to go into my office if you want to discuss him, you realise that he killed my niece?"

"Well that's what I want to talk to you about."

Pat and the chaplain sat in the small office while Brandon and Lilly-Anne made themselves busy filming around the zoo. Father Bell relaxed back into his chair as he continued his conversation with the tiger man.

"I'm confused Pat, Tommy tried to take his life last week."

"That could have saved the tax payer some money," Pat replied, no sympathy evident as Father Bell continued in his calm manner.

"Maybe you're right, but that isn't how I look at things and in truth it never has been. Everyone deserves a chance in life. I worked with the Parachute Regiment in the UK before moving over to the USA, those boys were the toughest of the tough, most would have been sitting in a prison somewhere if they hadn't joined up. However, the country owes them a debt of gratitude, they are the same young boys who went on to join the SAS and vowed to die for their country. The point is, someone gave them a chance and they paid that trust back."

"He had a chance, he was a war hero, a Marine Sergeant. Does it come any better than that? He still managed to make a mess of his life with drink, drugs and murder."

"Drink and drugs for sure. Murder? I don't think so...."

Pat looked at him, considering what his motive was for this meeting. "You said that you are confused, Tommy's position seems clear to me."

"Perhaps, but I've seen plenty of suicides Pat. From my experience people kill themselves out of guilt or shame but by not confessing at the time by word or letter makes that act futile. They don't make peace with God or whoever they are thinking of. Tommy was just desperate with not an ounce of shame or regret. He told me that he just felt that his situation was hopeless."

Pat smiled. "Why, what do you know that a judge and jury

didn't know?"

"The truth I guess. Whatever way you look at it, the evidence wasn't examined, people wanted him to be responsible and it took just two days to find him guilty of twenty five murders. Really? What other serial killer has only had a two day trial after pleading not guilty?"

Pat opened his drawer and took out an old newspaper with Tommy's picture on the front page. He jabbed at finger at the photograph.

"Only the serial killer who killed my niece. The evidence was there, you unfortunately were not, you didn't see the families and you didn't see his guilt. The court room stank of it. He had no answers to anything and all of his witnesses lied on oath. The guy is guilty, full stop."

Peter held Pat's gaze, not ready to give up yet. "Well, it seems that you have made your mind up but could you humour me for one minute?"

Pat looked at his watch. "That's all you have I'm afraid."

"Where were you when these girls were taken? What is your alibi?" Pat's face flushed instantly with rage.

"Are you accusing me of something here because that's a dangerous thing to do...you are a priest, not a police officer."

"No of course not, I'm just asking where you were? It's a simple question."

Pat's fists clenched as he felt the frustration building, but he had to keep to his TV persona. If they had been in a bar, he would have given this guy a good beating.

"I have no idea, but what I do know is that I would have been working my butt off somewhere, not sitting on a street corner selling drugs to children or watching young girls getting murdered."

"My point is, you don't know where you were, nor did Tommy remember where he was but he doesn't have someone to look after his arrangements, and every witness he had was in the same boat. No one believed them and they were dismissed because of one lie."

Pat shook his head, the veins on his neck bulging. "Nice story Father, now if you will forgive me, I need to get on with my work," and Pat stood, signalling the conversation was over.

"I'm sorry that I've upset you but no one seems to care about him, the world has just carried on while he still pleads his innocence. I'm going to find the mystery phone and I'm going to prove Tommy is not guilty. I haven't the abilities to uncover who the real killer is, but hopefully the police will be able to put the picture together."

A sarcastic laugh filled the small room. "Ok Father, if I'm ever in trouble I know who I'm going to call. What's your plan of attack in your 'save Tommy Cookson' campaign? I'll do all I can to help and I'm sorry for seeming so aggressive, it was just a shock to hear. You know, we all thought it was over and we had the killer locked away."

"The plan contains a few thousand miles Pat, everywhere from Dallas to New York and then to Chicago for a radio interview. I have a busy two weeks ahead of me."

"Well good luck, good luck with the investigators and better luck with the radio interview. Just be careful, they are bloody sharks when they do these shows." He shook Peter's hand. "And I do wish you the best of luck, as I said before, sorry I was a little off, it's been a tough week." He had calmed down enough to appear civil again.

"I can see that Pat, and thank you for sparing me your time. Do you think that I could have a quick word with Brandon now?"

"Sure, I'll send him in, but I'm sure that he knows nothing more than he said in court."

Brandon appeared and sat down next to the chaplain who gave him a smile.

"Hi Brandon, you realise why I'm here?"

"Pat has just filled me in, how can I help?"

"Do you think Tommy is guilty?"

"Not if he really did have the phone. But I don't know and in truth I'm on the fence. Some things I heard didn't make sense and he's insistent on his innocence. When I interviewed him on the street in Chicago, before I knew anything about the case he introduced me to Melissa. Why put me in touch with her if he had anything to hide?"

"Good point."

"And why would he put himself at the scene of the crime to a journalist who he didn't know at the time? These are the things that don't add up. But then there's the necklace, how the hell do you explain that?"

"His attorney couldn't, and nor could Tommy. He didn't try to give an explanation, he just didn't know. Would you have lied if you thought that your life depended on it?"

"Damn right I would, if I thought I had a chance."

"Well he didn't, he just looked confused. As I said to Pat, I'm going to try get to the bottom of things."

"I'm sorry Peter, I have a lot of work to finish, and I've said everything that I possibly can but good luck with it." Brandon left to carry on with his work while Peter took notes of their conversation. The next conversation would be the one he dreaded the most.

Melissa was halfway through her weekly battle with the weeds, head down, kneeling on a pad and with music blaring into her headphones, when a shadow was cast over the spot which she was working on. She looked up confused as not many people had any need to come to the house.

"Hello, can I help you?" she asked the tall, slim man standing smiling at her.

"I think that I'm possibly the person who you would least like to see. My name is Father Peter Bell and I'm here asking questions about Tommy Cookson so this may be the time you kick me off your property."

"No, not at all, it depends on what information you are looking for," Melissa replied, sitting back on her heels.

"Is there any part of you that thinks Tommy might not be guilty?" She thought for a moment. "Why are you asking me that, in what context?"

"Because he tried to take his own life last week and I spent an hour and a half talking to a desperate man. I promised him that I would talk to you and look at all the evidence."

"That's very generous of you Father, do you have children?" Melissa asked as she climbed to her feet.

"No I don't. I have never married. I could never comprehend the suffering which you have faced over the past eighteen months." She let her trowel fall to the floor before responding.

"No you couldn't Peter. You said that he was desperate, how the hell do you think I have felt, or the other families who hang onto my charity for hope? And how many priests, fathers or fucking vicars have knocked on my door to see if I am ok, or spent ninety minutes sitting chatting to me? Absolutely none is the answer. So take your good intentions, Father, and stick them straight up your cassock." Putting her headphones firmly back on her head she knelt back down and weeded with extra vigour, ignoring him as he turned to leave, only looking up to check that he had driven away.

Peter sat in the departures lounge awaiting the New York flight. He had taken on some fights in his life, even picking up a weapon at one point to protect a small Forward Operating Base nestling in a mountain region on the edge of nowhere in Afghanistan, but this wall of negativity towards his questions was the toughest battle he had faced. In his mind, the worst part was over, he hadn't expected anyone to welcome him with open arms and admit that an innocent person could be on death row. But at least he had planted a small seed, something that they would think about whether they wanted to or not.

Boarding the flight, he took a plastic glass of wine from the cabin crew and dusted himself down for the next round of interviews. He had two weeks to find something useful and at least if he came home empty handed, he was going to go down fighting.

# CHAPTER TWENTY-SIX

Tommy sat handcuffed in the small, smelly cell on the van taking him to Huntsville. He tried to read a book as much as the restraints would allow while the heavy suspension banged around on poorly maintained roads. Many mixed emotions flooded his head, happy that he had been able to move away from those sadistic guards, but very confused and concerned that his next cell would be on death row. It was a step closer to his execution and felt a million miles away from an appeal and re-trial. How many people have ever been pardoned from this place? He had seen countless programmes regarding rough justice on someone, a kid who was sentenced to one year for a minor crime and ended up serving thirty plus due to other offences committed inside prison which he had little choice in. He remembered one guy on death row for a murder which his friend had committed while he sat outside in the car waiting for him to return. Very few seemed to leave custody, and fewer still had any sympathy from the public.

All his eggs sat in one tiny basket, a catholic priest on a two week vacation to find evidence. When it came to grasping at straws, he was grasping at a single strand of straw while hanging over a pit of hungry sharks smelling blood.

Pulling into an old courtyard inside the prison, he peered through the dusty van window. The place seemed bleak, like something from a period drama and at least a couple of hundred years old. The first settlers must have built it for people just like him and he wished that they hadn't bothered. His reflections were interrupted by the guard opening his cell door.

"Ok son, follow me, we're going straight through to the unit so we can deal with all that first night stuff on there. How are you feeling?" What a question, no one apart from the priest had given a shit how he was.

"I'm ok, thanks for asking. How are you sir?" The guard smiled, he liked Tommy's approach.

"Well, the unit we're heading to is where I work and I like it on there - not in a morbid way, but you guys have unique issues and I take pride in solving your problems and making the unit work the best we can. Listen, life is tough enough for you all on here so I forget the crimes, I'm not here to punish, the courts do that. I'm working on that unit to at least provide a little dignity before the sentence is carried out. I don't know if that makes any sense at all?"

Tommy nodded. "Yes, I guess so, I can't say that I'm happy to be here, but that's out of my hands at the moment."

They soon stood in the entrance to the unit, which, in contrast to the rest of the place seemed to be a newly built building. The floors were polished to a high shine and the atmosphere appeared relaxed. The guard paused before taking him through.

"Look Cookson, I'm not pretending that this is going to be easy, some of the guys know that you're on the way and they don't like the crimes that you have committed, but it's only going to be verbal. You won't come face to face with the ones who are making the most noise. We're going to have to put you on the spur with people who have similar offences, OK?"

"Are you talking about paedophiles and child killers?"

"At the moment, yes I am but you won't come into contact with them either. Just get used to the place first and we'll chat tomorrow."

As they entered the unit, a shout went up from the first cell he passed.

"Hey, come over here man, let's see how you can handle a man instead of a little girl. I will rip you to pieces you bag of shit."

The guard turned and faced the eyes glaring from behind the cell door. "Shut up Smithson, any more and I will take that TV from you." The guard was well prepared for the abuse coming but the prisoner didn't desist, another line flowing closely after the one before.

"Fucking bag of crap, what did those girls do? Fuck that man, we'll meet one day and when we do, it's on man."

Tommy ignored the name calling, he was used to the routine and he'd been told that it would happen every time he changed unit. Head down, he entered his own cell. It was bigger than any other he had occupied, and sitting on the wall was a small TV. He hadn't seen one of those for a long time.

An old white guy walked past pushing a broom, whistling tunelessly and looking every one of his seventy-two years of age. He wasn't looking at much in general as he spoke casually through the door.

"You better watch your back on here, that Smithson has been running his mouth off for a couple of days. He's saying that he's going to take you down. He probably has some kind of shank, heard him grinding something on his wall last night." The sound of the brush stroking away like a jazz drummer remained in Tommy's ears as the old guy walked away.

# CHAPTER TWENTY-SEVEN

Father Peter Bell strolled through Central Park where he had a meeting arranged over a mug of coffee and a BLT in a café. The summer sun shone onto the towering skyscrapers painting stunning distinctions between light and shade. It was his first visit to the city and the beauty of the buildings impressed him. This oasis of calm surrounded by a manmade canyon was hypnotic and he soaked in the magnificence of the setting.

A large man sitting at an outside table by a food vendor truck stood as he saw Peter approach. "That's the benefit of meeting a priest, Father Peter, you are easily recognised," he said in greeting. Peter laughed, "I do find that I have less problems getting around a strange city when I wear the collar." The man held out a hand, probably as large as Tommy's.

"I'm Alan, an old friend of Tommy's. I can't believe that the court found him guilty. We couldn't prove his innocence, but we sure as hell didn't feel that there was enough to convict him for twenty-five murders."

"That's an encouraging start Alan," Peter said as he pulled out his wallet. "Can I treat you to a coffee? I hear the bacon muffins here are not to be missed so let's order and then you can tell me what you found when you investigated."

A short while later with steaming coffees on the table in front of them, Alan pulled out a thin folder from his backpack.

"You need to realise that we have only had a few days to take a look as he was put in jail almost before we began. The first thing we looked at was the type of crime and locality; it's no secret that there was a pattern with bursts of offending and then nothing for weeks before another burst. This is repeated for an eighteen month period. Some event has started the killings and something is controlling the locations of the attacks. We have ten or eleven clusters and he returns to the same areas on roughly an eight week cycle in general. However, since Tommy was taken into custody, the attacks have stopped."

The bacon muffins arrived on the table for the men and Peter thanked the waiter before responding to the information.

"You think the two things are linked?"

"Of course, but I don't think that Tommy was the killer just looking at the evidence. A few weeks before, another guy claimed that he was framed by an unknown person. He was also a homeless drug user who travelled the country. He killed himself, do you remember?"

Peter nodded. "Yes I do, the case was reopened when another girl went missing near Dallas."

"Correct, then suddenly Tommy, just by chance another former drug user who travelled the country, is put in the frame for the killings. I don't believe in coincidence, it's another pattern of behaviour."

Peter again nodded eagerly, soaking up this fresh information before adding, "So our guy is meticulous in what he is doing?" Alan spread out a hand drawn chart and map detailing the offences.

"More than that, he is strategic. Not only does he select his victims carefully and from areas not covered by CCTV, he ensures that there is minimal chance of him being discovered. Look at the facts, all the people we identify as the victims have something in common; all are between eighteen and twenty so considered adults by the police, all are women and only one body has ever been found where we suspect his plan was interrupted by a car breakdown. He obviously has a disposal method for the bodies as not one body part has materialised, although the girl discovered in the boot had been butchered professionally. I don't want to start a panic but he may be eating the bodies, it's one avenue that we were looking at, a cannibal killer. Or more disgustingly, he is using the *'meat'* as food for others, like Sweeny Todd."

Peter put his hands to his mouth in revulsion. "Oh good God!"

Alan, seemingly not so squeamish, took a large bite of his bacon muffin before continuing. "Does that sound like Tommy? Plus, the prosecution state that some attacks happened when he came home for a week on leave. That doesn't make any sense, firstly the attacks took some planning and secondly, I was with him on at least two of these periods of leave. You want to know what we did? We went to Vegas, gambled, drank and charmed the single women. We acted as heroes and got plenty of action but we didn't kill the girls afterwards, that's for sure."

"Why didn't you tell the court that?"

"I wasn't asked to explain and the defence brushed that part under the carpet for some reason. The attorney, Mr Dobbin, seemed to think that it would put him in a more difficult position if we mentioned it."

Peter studied the maps before pushing them back to Alan. "And once he went off the rails after his discharge from the Marines, did you manage to check on his alibi in Florida?"

"What they didn't allow me to report was that I had briefly bumped into him down there where he was deeply involved in the drug scene. When I found him, he ran. He was living knee deep in shit and needles, and his friend from the next room was lying dead in a pool of his own vomit. He just couldn't face me, Peter."

"That's tragic," Peter agreed, realising just how low Tommy had fallen.

"Yep I flew down myself and spoke to a few of his old 'buddies'. They remember him staying in the area. Man, it was heart breaking to see where Tommy had ended up. They all knew him as a bit of a loner, always owing money to dealers, I even had to pay a debt for him. Trouble is that the defence attorney paid for information and told the guys what to say. The one who screwed up and lied about seeing him didn't even know Tommy, he was just trying to get a pay day. He screwed it for everyone but especially for Tommy."

"So basically a whole series of events led to his conviction," Peter summarised, "but what do you make of the necklace?"

"Peter, for me, that's obviously a set up. Apart from it being found in his room, what else do they have? Are you suggesting he only took a trophy from one person, just by chance the daughter of the woman who he'd just had dinner with? What about the other twenty-three women he's alleged to have killed, where are their trophies? Come on Peter, that is obviously a fit up and must be the police or how would they know what to look for?"

"That's what Tommy suggested to me." Peter paused before continuing. "I have an awkward question to ask you. I have no money to pay you to continue helping us but can you still help?"

"With what? We're a new business and we have no spare cash floating around. I know Tommy is like a brother, but we have bills to meet. I can't work for free - if I could I would."

Peter gave his best smile, the one that normally upped the church takings at the weekend. "I understand, but if we could find that phone, I think our guy could be cleared."

"No doubt, but does it still exist? Everything points to the main office for the newspaper throwing it away. He would have filmed what he saw without a doubt, the guy filmed everything. He was a nightmare to work with on operations." Taking a last bite from the sandwich, he pointed at Peter.

"I'll give you one week free. I'll do it myself in my own time but if I don't get anywhere in five days, it's over. Best I can do."

Peter thrust out his hand. "I'll take it. I'm flying out to Chicago tonight so here's my number. Phone me if you have anything."

The flight from New York to Chicago seemed to take no time at all with Peter deep in thought about Alan's findings. Things just didn't add up and what had begun as a hopeless mission suddenly seemed to have a renewed purpose.

Checking into a small, cheap, downtown Chicago hotel, Peter slid his case into another cramped room that smelt of cigarette smoke. He was on a tight budget and beggars couldn't be choosers. Opening the window the full six inches it would allow, he hoped that he could at least make the air breathable.

Tomorrow promised to be a good day where the interview on WBBM News Radio would give him the chance to talk about the work he conducted within prisons and the plight of Tommy Cookson. This, along with some details of his previous military life story, a subject which would make a good book if he focused himself on the discipline required to spend hours each day in front of the screen.

All it needed was for one listener to have some information about the missing phone. Who didn't like a treasure hunt? So he hoped that he might jog the newspaper into having a full on search of every nook and cranny. He wasn't a mischievous type of person but if the public knew that the evidence needed might still be sitting in a drawer, they may demand some action.

The alarm buzzed in the hotel bedroom and Peter opened his tired, red eyes. The constant roar of cars travelling through the busy intersection below his ill fitting window had ensured little sleep, and climbing under the weak, lukewarm stream of water in the shower, tested his own conviction. For a brief second he considered if this trip was a worthwhile use of his own precious time but by the time he was dry, his strength had returned. Skipping breakfast, he took the stairs down to the foyer where a lone cab sat outside, hoping to pick up a fare. He leant towards the open cab window, where a cheerful looking man in his early thirties welcomed him with a broad smile. "Hey buddy, where to?"

"Number 2, Prudential Plaza in the Chicago loop please. I don't have a clue how to get there."

"Leave it with me Father, I'll give you a good price as well. Here on business or vacation?"

"Business I'm afraid, I'm giving an interview for the radio station so make sure you listen in."

"Wouldn't miss it," the driver promised as he drew up outside one of the city's skyscrapers. "That'll be ten bucks for you. If you need a ride back call me, or the bus is a fraction of the price and stops every five minutes. I would take that route." Peter handed over fifteen dollars. "Thanks, you've been very helpful. The bus sounds fun, I'll take your advice."

The towering glass building in front of him was somewhat imposing as he looked up into the blue sky, almost going dizzy before looking back down towards the entrance. Pushing the glass doors open, Peter found himself in a massive foyer with signs for different businesses posted over a large wall behind the reception desk. Introducing himself to the man behind the desk, he barely had time to take a seat before a young woman came down and found him. She filled him in on what to expect as she led him up in the lift.

"I'm not sure how much you've been told about today but normally we give a sixty second slot which is repeated on a pod cast. How much time will you need?"

"I've flown in all the way from Dallas so it would be kind if you could offer me three minutes. I have a good story to tell." She checked the schedule. "I can rearrange two phone-in callers so I can manage a three minute window but that's all so talk fast if you have a lot of news."

The interview passed in a blur and Peter was mesmerising and charmed the producers into another two minutes air time. Once they had finished and cut to the news broadcast, he found himself surrounded by studio staff, his English accent proving a winner. The producer had a proposition for him

"Father Peter, we were wondering if you could do a sixty second slot weekly, talking about a topic of the day in a pause for reflection show? We can't pay but we can certainly promote the discussion we have just had." Peter was quick to agree as he was assured this could be done remotely and would not involve him travelling to Chicago every week. If it meant further opportunity to highlight Tommy's plight, it was worth it.

The cab driver was right and hopping on the bus back into the centre was easy. He took in the sights as the bus trundled along before deciding on an architectural boat ride along the river. Fascinated by the growth and development of the city as they cruised through the manmade jungle, he was intrigued to discover the newspaper offices were just a ten minute walk from his hotel. This was pure good fortune and pondering whether to call in unexpectedly, he decided to wait a little while to see what his interview on the radio would drum up. The tour ended back in the city centre an hour later where the smell of food wafting out from the many restaurants was too much for him to manage. He looked around before seeing a number of people heading into one particular building. *'Bloody hell, the Cheesecake Factory, the beginning of the end for Tommy's story,'* he muttered to himself.

Feeling a wave of emotion as he spotted the very place where months earlier Tommy had sat begging for change, he saw his place had been taken by an immaculately dressed woman of colour. A sign sat in front of her as she smiled a dazzling white smile to all who passed her. *'My house burnt down and I have no insurance, two children to support, hungry and cold.'* Twenty feet further down the street a man played mesmerising saxophone riffs while another performed close up magic tricks to raise a few dollars. Everywhere he looked, desperation was being played out in the awkwardly avoiding gaze of the public, and right in the shadows of Trump Plaza - irony at its best.

His appetite for lunch disappeared as he dropped a few dollars into each bowl; he didn't need the succulent steak or cheesecake dessert that he had promised himself, maybe just a sandwich so others could have a little to eat also.

Moving from the bright lights of the main streets, the classier type of begging vanished and the advances were more menacing as angry shop owners chased the beggars from their premises. One skinny man with hollow features approached him as he tried to buy a burger from McDonalds. "Buy me food man, I need food, buy me food," he mumbled as he followed Peter to a small table, still harassing for money Peter no longer had.

"I'm sorry, I have no money, I have already given all I can to others in need." A volley of muttered abuse followed before the manager pushed the beggar back out onto the street.

*The world's most powerful country, can't even feed its starving citizens in the shadow of magnificent wealth,* he observed to himself as he sat munching on the burger turned to sawdust in his mouth.

Dejected and heading towards the North Avenue beach area, he pondered the sights he had seen. It had been the same in San Francisco and New Orleans, heart breaking but what could anyone do? This had been Tommy's life months ago so how the hell did anyone believe that he could even summon the energy to plot so many murders? Survival on the streets was a twenty-four hour occupation and they were all exhausted just from staying alive for another sunrise.

The wealthier side of Chicago was a nice city, the people friendly and welcoming as he sat drinking a cold coke in the afternoon sun, watching the jet skis and paddleboards cutting their way around each other on the lake, before he finished his drink and took a stroll back through Oak Street Beach and towards his hotel. The temperature dipped as the sunset indicated that his time outside was nearly over but what he hadn't noticed was the company who had followed him throughout the day, picking up his trail on the downtown bus and watching every step he trod, never taking their eyes from the target. The young guy holding a skateboard dialled the number on his phone.

"Ok, I've followed this dude around the city but he hasn't given me one opportunity today. I'm now outside his hotel, what do you want me to do?" The voice at the other end was explicit in its instruction.

"For the money I'm paying you, I expect you to do exactly as I say. Stay outside and watch. When it's dark he will leave and head off into a vulnerable part of town. This will be your chance. Remember, take as many people with you to finish the job. As you have seen, he's not an old man. Text me when the job is done and lose the phone. I do not want a trace coming back to me."

# CHAPTER TWENTY-EIGHT

Peter dozed off reading a book, the warmth from the room just enough to make his eyes close. It was the only way to forget the hunger he was feeling. God's work was fulfilling, however the steak would have been a good option. The ringing and vibrating of his phone woke him up, and finding the room in darkness he fumbled for the light. It was nearly ten thirty and to his surprise he'd a three hour nap. A man's soft voice spoke to him.

"Hello, is that Father Peter?"

"Yes it is, how can I help you?"

"The radio station has just given me your details. I work as night security at the newspaper office and I think that I've just found your missing phone. It isn't working and is in a bad condition but it was in our office for some bizarre reason. You can come and pick it up, I have a break at eleven thirty so I'll meet you at the back fire escape door. It's painted red and is the only one there…it just means we don't have to get special permission to unlock the main reception door."

"That's great news, what's your name?" Peter asked, now wide awake.

"Davey, I'm a good catholic boy and wanted to help you. See you in an hour."

"See you there, do I knock?"

"No, just wait for me, I will be around."

In a frenzy of anticipation he got up, showered and dressed. He knew it was only a brief walk to the building, so making a coffee, he hummed soft hymns to himself. What a brilliant idea the radio interview had been, Tommy could be a free man in no time so let's see who doubted him then.

With the temperature plunging further, he pulled on his North Face fleece and headed off. The first few minutes were under street lighting but these tailed off and he began to walk in darkness as he approached an industrial area. Feeling uncomfortable he checked his phone app for directions and saw he had just five minutes before he was there. A noise in front of him made him look up and he saw three young men blocking his path. He turned to cross the road but two more stood waiting so doubling back on himself he found that route also covered by another three. Realising he was ambushed, he spoke to the group,

"Look lads, I have no money or cards on me, all I have is my phone so if you want it take it. I will not put up a fight."

"Why do we want your phone Father Peter Bell? We have got exactly what we need right here." As the realisation kicked in that he'd been set up, he held his hands up.

"Oh I get it, someone is paying you. I expected this. You're the guy with the board who's been following me all day; did you think I hadn't seen you?"

"Check out the brains on this guy," the man laughed to his accomplices.

While they wasted time with the small talk, Peter assessed his options. He had been ambushed before in a war zone and escaped so assessing his chances of success in this instance, he made a split second risk assessment. Drop the leader straight away and break through the front or take on the two guys to his side with maximum aggression? Fuck it, the big mouth had to go.

Estimating that he had three paces until he would break this bastard's nose, he put his arms behind his head and pretended to kneel in submission.

"I'm guessing that someone important wants me injured?"

"No, not injured, they want you dead," the man informed him as he produced an evil looking blade.

Half squatting, he drove forwards catching the man off guard. He stumbled backwards flailing the knife and Peter dropped him with a well aimed punch and head butt while his other gang members flapped around not knowing what to do. A sting across his hand exploded with a flow of blood and he was free, sprinting away into the night before finding his way back into a populated area. The gash looked nasty as he wound his handkerchief around it just as a passing police patrol car caught his waves of attention and stopped.

"What can we do for you Father?" an officer asked as he wound down his window. Holding his hand out in front of them, Peter fell to his knees in a blinding, twisting spell of dizziness.

Waking in the back of an ambulance Peter reflected on the attack. These guys were amateurs but had admitted that they had been paid to carry out the attack.

"I need to speak to someone, can I do it before we get to the hospital?" He asked the attending paramedic.

"Sure, but be quick." He pushed redial for Davey only to receive the unobtainable number tone. The entire series of events was a well orchestrated trap, but they had failed. He lay back, shattered from the stress.

"No good Father? Are they not picking up?" the paramedic asked as he checked Peter's blood pressure.

"No, I guess there wasn't anyone who wanted to speak to me anyway."

The phone vibrated in the man's pocket, telling him a text had arrived.

*He is wounded but escaped, what do you want us to do?* He thumbed a quick reply.

*You screwed up, he should be dead. Throw my phone away and once that's done I will pay you for your work.*

The leader turned to the rest of the gang, "Two thousand easy bucks," he told them as he threw the phone deep into the muddy waters of the river. "Everyone gets a cut when we are paid."

Far away, grinding his own phone into small pieces with the heel of his boot, the man snarled to himself, *"They will get nothing, amateurs."*

# CHAPTER TWENTY-NINE

Melissa sat in her kitchen, the freshly made cup of coffee steaming invitingly in  front of her on the table while she caught up on the local news on her laptop. Her doorbell rang and when she went to see who it was, Peter Bell stood there smiling in greeting at her.

"I thought that I'd told you to go away, I don't want to see you around here again. Leave or I phone the police," she told him, starting to close the door on him.

"Hear me out, just for one second," he replied, putting his arm out to stop her closing the door. "If you still think that I'm wrong, I will leave and never return. You have my promise."

"You'd better come in then," she said begrudgingly, holding the door open. What have you done to your hand, have you had an accident?" she asked him as she showed him into the kitchen.

"This is what I want to discuss. I was in Chicago talking on the radio about Tommy and that same evening I received a call from the newspaper office. A man called Davey spoke to me and said that he had found the phone and arranged for me to go and pick it up. On the way there I was attacked by eight young men, they knew my name and told me that they were going to kill me. One of them had followed me all day; I had spotted him but just thought he wanted my empty wallet. By the grace of God I escaped. Why were they waiting for me Melissa?" She shrugged her shoulders.

"Have you noticed what happens to people when they get too close to the truth? Your house burning down, people set up and thrown in prison, one young guy killing himself in a police cell. Do you really believe that these acts aren't linked?" Melissa stared at him in puzzlement.

"Are you sure that you heard what you say you heard in

Chicago? You must have been scared."

"Bloody right I was scared, but I still put one of them on the seat of his pants and ran like the wind. I know what I heard, they tried to trap me with the phone that's linked directly to the case. Why else try to murder me and why tell me that they were ordered and paid to do it?"

Melissa sat listening, a light bulb suddenly turning on in her head. Was she missing something so obvious? She came to a decision and stood up.

"I think we need a drink and a chat Peter, I'll put the kettle on or do you want something stronger?"

"Is the pope…. No I won't carry on with that saying, yes please, that would be lovely. Do you have a cold beer? I think I need one." Melissa walked over to the fridge and got out two beers, handing one to Peter.

"I think that we need to get the guys down here as soon as we can. I appreciate what you're doing and I think that you are on to something. My mind has been too blinkered, just hoping that it was over. Clearly it's not.

"By the guys, I take it you are talking about Pat and Brandon? They were not too thrilled to talk with me in the first place so I hope that you can turn them around?"

"Leave that to me, with what you are saying it's as clear as day. Someone is conspiring to put us on the wrong track. My money would be on one of Eric Bent's staff, they've hated me since day one when they had crimes that they refused to even investigate. It's making more sense by the day.

# CHAPTER THIRTY

Tommy sat in his cell. He hadn't had the chance to get out for fresh air for two days and the feelings on the unit were building against him. Sure it was depressing but who were they to judge him? They had all killed and he was probably the only innocent man in there. The shadow of an officer flicked past the bars of his cell.

"Excuse me guard," he called and a young woman came to his door. He hadn't seen her around so guessed that she was standing in for staff shortages.

"Can I use the library? I need to change a couple of books."

"Sure," she unlocked the door. "I'm new on this unit and don't know the regime but I noticed that the library door is open at the moment and luckily the librarian is in there. If you're quick you'll be able to change them."

Putting the books in a cloth bag, he rushed down the small corridor to the library and entered, finding three other prisoners selecting books. The man waiting to swap his at the counter was Smithson and Tommy recognised his voice as he barked at a man standing by the door.

"Kick that mother fucking door shut, we have a prize."

Trying to burst back through the door towards safety, Tommy was forced back by an unexpected punch to the nose. He held up a hand towards his nose to check for bleeding but it came away clear. This man might have muscles but he hit like a child. Smithson strolled towards him, a smirk on his face.

"Look what we have here, Cookson. I told you that we would meet up. I don't know how it happened but let's not miss an opportunity."He turned to the librarian, an old man who used to work on the unit as an officer some years before.

"You get to leave sir. We have no beef with you." The door was opened just enough to squeeze him through before three book shelves were pushed in front of it to make a barricade.

"You on the other hand are in for a long night," Smithson informed Tommy, and ripping the cables from the backs of the computers Smithson tied him to a chair in the centre of the room. Tommy remained compliant, assessing the situation. It looked like it could be three against one and he would have no chance. Smithson continued his rant. "In a moment, hell will break out in the corridor. If they try and come in, I will kill you, if they don't I will torture you and then kill you." Tommy had heard it all before and he laughed as he spoke.

"So, I don't get it Smithson...."

"What don't you get child killer?"

"First of all, the only people I have killed in my life are a whole bunch of Taliban who were breaking their balls to kill Americans, and a truck driver who tried to bust my cheeks. I keep trying to tell people, I never hurt any one of those girls."

Smithson raged, spit flying onto Tommy's face. "Bullshit, you're just trying to save your neck."

The other two prisoners watched on and Tommy could tell from their body language that they would rather be anywhere else in the world. Someone shouted through the door from the outside, "Smithson, let those people out of the room. Let's deal with the problem here and now."

The other prisoner by the door, an older black guy added his voice.

"Come on Smithson, I don't need this shit. I'm happy on here, I have a great job and an appeal coming up next year which I don't want to jeopardise."

The voice outside retorted, "It seems that you're the only guy who wants to be in there Smithson, so let's get this done."

By now Smithson was standing over Tommy. He was quickly losing control and knew it while the other two men stood as close to the door as possible, staying in clear sight of the CCTV camera. The one who had hit Tommy on the nose hissed, "Give it up Smithson, you've made your point. This guy is no threat to you." He snarled back. "You gutless pieces of shit, you wanted in on this last night and now you're ducking out."

Tommy spoke calmly. "Smithson, I have a solution. From day one you wanted me so let's do this one on one. If you win you kill me, if I win we all walk out of here. Me and you Smithson, let's see what sort of man you really are. Now is your chance."

The other two listened before the black guy joined in. "You have been shooting your mouth off for days man, this guy has said nothing back so take him up on it. I think that you're just fucking chicken, a warrior behind your door. Seen your type for the last sixteen years."

Smithson picked up a book and threw it at the two men. "Shut the fuck up."

"Come on Smithson, untie me, I want to show you what a marine sergeant is going to do to your little steroid packed body," Tommy taunted him.

From behind his cell door, Tommy had painted a picture of a larger man but Smithson stood at no taller than five ten, and although he had good definition, Tommy knew he could break that body down in seconds.

The prisoners at the door were now in discussions with the guards outside and Tommy listened while still watching Smithson's body language. He had seen these signals a dozen or more times with other Marines. The bully was suddenly lacking any confidence and every line on his face sent out the same message. He knew he couldn't deal with Tommy.

Smithson slobbered as his frustration exploded. He screamed at the other two prisoners and punched the wall.

"Pull the goddamn shelves away from the door, I don't need this bullshit."

He capitulated in a total loss of face by opening the door and walking back to his cell surrounded by five guards. One of the other prisoners untied Tommy, talking to him as he did so.

"Well, that sure put that bastard back in his box. I don't think that you did those things you're charged with did you Cookson? I think that you're a good man."

"Thanks, sorry I don't know your name, but no, I didn't do any of those crimes. Why would you think that I'm innocent anyway?"

"I know because my sister listened to a radio show in Chicago where they had nearly five minutes about your case and in a phone poll after the show nearly ninety percent of callers demanded a retrial. Some catholic priest guy was calling the evidence bullshit. He convinced my sister, and she's never wrong."

Tommy sat in astonishment; Peter was out there fighting his case, just like he'd promised. "Do you think that this problem with Smithson is over?" He looked into the eyes of the black guy as he asked the question.

"Looking at that mother fucker's face when his courage poured down his pant leg, I don't think that you'll have any more problems from him. Let's get you out of that paedophile spur and in with the real men. And my name's Jimmy, my boy here is called Curtis and we're the longest serving in this place. I guess we will see you in a few minutes." He stopped as the door opened again to another five staff standing there in riot clothing. Jimmy patted one on the shoulder.

"No need for all that stuff now Mr Clemson, Tommy here has got it all sorted. He didn't do shit and me and Curtis saw everything. I think that Mr Cookson needs to come over to our side." The officer stared at Tommy for a moment before moving aside allowing him out through the library door.

"Cookson, get back to your cell and pack up your stuff, we have a spare cell next to these two clowns, five minutes."

Tommy took a large plastic bag of possessions with him for the fifty metre walk. The last time he had walked past these cells the abuse had been horrible, this time only friendship sprang forwards as word had spread. As he passed Smithson's cell he saw that the door was open and empty of possessions. Jimmy called out through the bars of his own cell.

"That's what a fool gets if you act like a jackass on this unit, no one liked that idiot anyway, too much to say and it was all hot air. Welcome to the bright side Mr Cookson, it's going to be nice to get to know you a little better."

# CHAPTER THIRTY-ONE

Melissa prepared the table while she waited for her guests to arrive, her normal excitement for meeting up with Pat and Brandon slightly tarnished by the worry that they wouldn't believe Peter and what he had discovered but she trusted that he could explain himself to them as he had to her.

A car driving up to the house caught Melissa's attention, and seeing it was Pat and Brandon a few minutes early, gave her a chance to smooth things over before Peter arrived.

"Hey Melissa," Pat greeted her with a hug and a peck on the cheek. They went through into the kitchen where Melissa got some beers out of the fridge. Pat opened one and took a long drink. "The food smells divine, we're starving. Brandon is a hard task master out there, setting up shoots at all times day and night. When this year is done I'm sleeping for a week."

"How is it with Jenny, have you patched things up with her?" Melissa asked, knowing Pat and his wife had been going through a rocky patch.

"No, that's over, she filed for divorce last month, but that's ok, it wasn't working out and we both knew it and now have an opportunity to get on with life. How are you doing?"

"Yes, all good. Bit confused about Tommy but we'll chat about that when Peter gets here."

Brandon appeared in the kitchen holding a bag. "I wondered if I could stay over tonight please? I wanted to catch up with Jazz when we end our meeting tonight."

"Sure," Melissa agreed, "you certainly don't miss a chance young man, I take it that Lilly-Anne and you are no longer an item?"

"Just very good friends, she has her stuff to focus on and Pat and I have a book to work on. All very busy and we don't want to complicate things."

Lights moved across the room from the window as another car pulled up outside the house. Pat looked up and spotted who the driver was. "Here comes the exorcist."

"You promised to play nice," she laughed.

"The guy didn't hear me, of course I'll play nice, he's trying to help our friend get out of jail. What's not to like about him?"

She opened the door, "Welcome back Peter, and you have brought gifts!" He handed her a large bunch of flowers and a bottle of chilled, white Bordeaux wine.

"You English guys know how to make an arrival, all I got from these two were a peck on the cheek and a request for a room," Melissa laughed as she took the gifts and showed him through to the kitchen. Pat stood and shook his hand.

"Hey Peter, sorry we didn't get off on a good footing last week, let's start afresh." He noticed the bandage covering Peter's other hand. "Ouch, that left hand looks sore..."

"Just a bit, but it's healing. A fresh start sounds great to me, I have a bit to talk about with you all."

Brandon patted him on the back, "Great to see you again. My mum heard you on the radio, she told me that you had the longest interview she has ever heard on that station, they loved you."

"Hope so, just a quick question Brandon before we settle down to eat, is there a security guy called Davey who works at your building as night security in Chicago?"

"There are a team of four people who work shifts and I know them all. Three guys, Lloyd, William and Craig and an older lady who has been there for over twenty years called River. Her parents named her after her mum fell into the river and was saved two days before the birth, kind of cool name though. But no Davey at all. Sorry, why do you ask?"

"I'll explain after we eat. I'm so hungry, I haven't stopped working for nearly ten days, I'll need a holiday after this holiday." Melissa overheard his last comment as she placed the bottle of wine on the table.

"Well it's lucky that everything is ready then. You guys take a seat and pour yourselves a drink and I'll serve up."

A large leg of lamb was ceremoniously placed on a metal carving tray on the table while bowls of crispy roast potatoes and a whole selection of vegetables invited them all to tuck in.

"Pat, can you carve the meat, you are the resident expert, and Peter do you want to say a few words?"

"If you would like that, I can give a very quick blessing, it would be an honour," Peter replied.

Two hours of cooking and preparation were finished within twenty minutes, all of them chatting and laughing while secretly undoing their belts.

"Well Peter," Pat started the business side of things, "what have you discovered?"

"Ok, let me just get my notes out, I don't want to miss anything as even small details are vital. Stop me and ask questions at any time." He didn't hold back any details and discussed the difficulties with the initial chats he'd had with all three of them. They all laughed when he revealed what Melissa had told him to do with his cassock.

"But that was all to be expected," he explained, "it was the most difficult emotional part of the trip, but unfortunately not the biggest physical challenge."

The rest of the story flooded out and he hardly needed to look at the detailed notes as times and events were embedded in his brain.

"And then this brings me around to Davey," he finally said. The events in Chicago left the three of them horrified with the premeditated violence against the chaplain but this wasn't what he wanted them to focus on as he went on to explain.

"You see, events like that don't get planned in one day, whoever arranged for the phone call, apparently from your building Brandon, and the gang who thankfully were not very good at contract killings, obviously knew my movements and had some contacts in the city. I only told a small number of people."

"And who were they? This is good information," Pat said with an intense look on his face. "If we crack this we will solve this once and for all."

"Well the people I told were few, but if they have loose lips it could be many. So, here goes...everyone in this room knew my plan, however I trust each and every one of you. The warden in charge of my prison knew but she gave me her blessing so it's not her. I do work for the local communities on my day off so I had to tell Eric Bent that I wouldn't be able to work with the troubled kids last week but I also trust him.

"We don't so he's high on the list, or at least one of his men is," Melissa scowled. "That fits in with my best guess." Pat and Brandon both nodded as Peter continued with his list.

"Ok, so I'll put a question mark by that name. The next people who knew were obviously the radio station, they knew my entire itinerary for the trip, but it wasn't them, they were just making sure I turned up.

Then we come to the two biggest players in the game in my opinion, Tommy and the investigation company who are obviously not your initial thoughts Melissa. Bearing in mind I need to suspend my judgement as to Tommy's guilt, he knew every detail of my trip, including looking for the phone. He had links to the city's low life shall we put it, and somewhere along the line he has used up the money given to him from the Marines so perhaps he had paid people off. That's something like $12000 so a lot of money. If he's trying to put up a good alibi why not sacrifice me to do it? If I die in the process, it looks as though someone else is taking the blame for the killings so there is some sense in that, on top of the fact that he recommended a Marine buddy to investigate the crime. His friend told me that they were close, spent all the leave periods together in Vegas getting drunk and chasing women, something difficult to prove otherwise after all this time. And that leads to the New York team, they have no money to carry on the investigation and stone walled me until I mentioned the phone again, then they wanted my plans for the next two days and agreed to help for nothing. A great gesture, but not if they wanted to help Tommy and have me killed by a local gang while they sat in New York thereby giving everyone an alibi."

He looked up at three nodding people, "So there we have it, either in my view there is a police conspiracy to withhold and bury evidence to avoid them taking the rap, or worst still one of them is involved directly, or, Tommy and his friend from New York are up to their necks in this stuff. Until the attack I firmly believed in another parties' involvement, but just now, as we discuss it, I have a niggle of doubt in my mind."

"And what do you plan to tell Tommy on Monday morning?" Melissa asked.

"Only the facts, not my suspicions. I need to think about everything for a few days, and while my hand still throbs from a knife wound, it will be difficult to see past Tommy. In truth I'm still undecided, but more importantly, what do you three think?" A silence followed before Peter spoke again, "Ok let's make this easier, there are no right or wrong answers so let's go in turn. Melissa first."

Melissa sat back in her chair and puffed her cheeks out before letting out a sigh.

"Oh my God, this thing twists and turns like a tornado. A week ago I thought Tommy was guilty, then yesterday after we chatted I thought he was innocent, now I'm fifty-fifty between him and Eric Bent's men. I need to process it. But as for Tommy's money, that isn't an issue, he's paying rent on his apartment so it doesn't mean he has hired a hit man."

Pat spoke next. "It's a solid theory about Tommy and an accomplice as someone from New York could easily be involved. There have been a number of girls taken from that area, we know that's true, also the investigation firm would need to travel the country to do follow up work. That fits in with what you have stated Peter and if we look at the facts, that connection fits perfectly. But what do we do about it now? If we report it to Bent, and he turns out to be the man responsible, we blow any chance for Tommy. Hells bells, I'm like you Melissa, I just need to think on it. In my opinion, it's down to two groups, Tommy, or the police, and I pray to God it's not the police."

"I agree with Pat." Brandon suddenly seemed above his eighteen years. "Let's just process what we've heard and let me speak to the editor of my paper and find out if we can dig out any more information on who attacked you. Maybe the police up in Chicago can investigate, find out who the gang were, that shouldn't be too hard if one of them followed you around the city for an afternoon. If they pick that guy up they could question him about who arranged the attack and where the money was paid from. It would have been some form of electronic transfer as a guy isn't going to appear with a suitcase of cash after the attack. I think that this could be our second biggest clue after the phone evidence."

Pat spoke again. "That's brilliant Brandon, that's why I work with people like you. Do that, and let's get those clues onto the board. I truly think that this is coming to an end, I can smell it. Whoever is responsible is becoming desperate, bringing in too many people and taking too many chances. For the first time he is leaving us a trail of bread crumbs towards where and who he is."

Brandon nodded in agreement. "Ok Pat, I'll get on it in the morning. Is there anything else for now, otherwise I'm going to meet Jazz from work."

"Go get her, tiger," Melissa gave him a smile, "and take the spare key with you, I'm bushed so I might turn in early."

Peter stood and began to clear the table. "Me too guys, let me help with the washing up and I will need to get going. I've had a busy few days and my hand is not feeling great."

"No Peter, Pat and I will clean up here, you go on. Phone me next week when you have spoken to Tommy and we have processed all the things you have uncovered."

Waving at Peter's car as he drove away from the house, Pat sat on the door step; it was a warm night and the sun was just setting as Melissa came and sat next to him. "What do you really think Melissa? He has laid a bomb in our path. Every time we think that we have closure someone else opens another door."

"I just don't get it, I understand how desperate Tommy must be, but it took such a lot of coordination to plan that attack and we know that Tommy can't communicate with the outside world. How did he manage to do that?"

"He smuggled out a letter to you so he's found a way once before."

"That's true as well," Melissa agreed with a sigh of despair. Pat stood and swayed slightly.

"I've had a few glasses of wine too many Melissa, any chance of me having the other spare bed? I'll make it up."

"Sure, I had two beds ready anyway, figuring that this would happen. So sorry about Jenny." Pat sat back down, sensing Melissa still wanted to talk.

"Honestly, it's no bother, I hear that she's already moved on. One of my old friends has taken her out to dinner a few times, I live in a small town and people tell me things. I've given her the house and a promise of monthly payments for Danny so we should have a clean break." Melissa raised her eyebrows.

"That was speedy work on her part, how about you? Are you moving on?" The wine was going to her head, giving her the courage to delve a bit more into whether he was ready to look at another relationship.

"No, not yet. We have just been flat out at work so haven't had a moment to think about it. I do feel ready, just guess the time needs to be right."

She leant forwards and kissed him lightly on the lips. "And when will that be Pat?" Pat looked at her for a second. "Is that the wine or you talking?"

"It's definitely me, you're a wonderful man and when Tommy came onto me, all I could think about was you. I just wanted you to come and tell me that everything was going to be ok." He moved forwards and kissed her, rubbing the back of her neck as they melted into each other.

"Melissa, if this is all a bit fast I can back off, if not then I'm committed."

"Patrick Hunter, stop talking and just go for it."

He lifted her easily in his enormous arms and carried her upstairs into her bedroom, the door clicking shut behind them as he lowered her onto the fresh sheets. Slowly undressing her as she lay on top of her bed, she kissed him passionately before he pulled gently away. "Melissa, I need to tell you this now, we are not making love this evening, I will stay here and hold you all night, but I want to know that this is the right time for you." She sighed, knowing that he was right and this could only complicate what they were trying to achieve.

"Such a gentleman, I'm sorry that I've put you in a predicament, it just felt so natural," she explained feeling a little drunker by the second. Pat pulled his shirt back on.

"There's nothing that I would have enjoyed more, I just get the feeling that you may thank me in the morning," he said, pulling the sheets over her as she closed her eyes. almost immediately falling asleep. Pat silently left the room and climbed into his own bed, wondering what could have been.

Waking the next morning, the smell of bacon and eggs filled Pat's nose. He dressed and heading downstairs, knocked on Brandon's door. Receiving no reply, he opened it and finding the bed had not been slept in, he continued on his way, following the tantalizing smells to the kitchen.

"Morning Melissa, how's the head?"

"Don't Pat," Melissa groaned, "thank you for understanding last night, you are a true friend."

"Don't think I wasn't tempted but let's take things slowly. If you still think the same way later on, I will be very, very happy."

She just looked at him and smiled, a smile that filled a page.

"And I just noticed that Brandon didn't make his way back home last night, perhaps Jazz was a little drunk as well?" Pat added. Melissa nodded, "I did have a look in too, somehow I don't think that Brandon could show the same restraint that you did...."

# CHAPTER THIRTY-TWO

The man lay on his hotel bed, another trip away, another period of boredom and frustration. The urges were building as he hadn't tasted blood for so long and it felt forever, but these urges were different, worrying, even for a serial killer. He had never killed through the evil intent of just ending a life for nothing, there had always been a point to the slaughter, an end game of sorts. But this new feeling was one of pure unadulterated violence, tearing flesh and sinew for the act of pleasure. It was controlling him rather than him turning it on and off when he needed to. He looked at himself in the mirror. *"Who are you?"*

And he still had some unfinished business down in Texas; the bitch had been lucky last time when she was just one minute away from meeting her destiny, if it hadn't been for the kids who had shown up at the last minute. However, it had been her lucky day and events had now taken a twist with the Catholic bastard turning up out of the blue, asking all kinds of questions on one of his favourite radio shows. That had shocked him, just when he felt that Tommy Cookson was going to rot on death row until he finally met his end, this man shows up and threatens to spoil the party.

And then to top it all, the stupid kids who promised that they could deal with everything and then blew it, couldn't even take care of business, and now they had become a link between the murders and him. The only person on earth who could point the finger towards him was a nineteen year old skateboarding punk with a drug habit and bad teeth.

He showered and dressed before heading towards the Magnificent Mile and Oak Street beach. The food tasted great while looking over the lake as life passed in front of him.

Children played and others soaked up the summer sun, unknowing of the danger he presented. And suddenly, there they were, just as the last time he saw them, walking past the locals and tourists, looking for a quick buck, the nineteen year old spotting targets and lifting wallets from amongst people's clothing as they swam in the cool waters.

He knew where they would be heading, he had followed them last time. He had followed several times in fact until he understood their routines better than they did, knew the burger bar they would head to in half an hour, how they would split up half the money they stole and spend the rest on drugs. The man even knew where the dealer worked from, when he would appear and where his girls worked from to give him a little more cash. He knew everything, it was his business to know.

Waiting in the darkness of the hallway in a filthy Washington Park apartment, one of the seedier parts of Chicago, he finally heard the sound he had waited for, the wheels of a skateboard heading for the door of this slum the boy shared with his mum. Stepping out, he stood in front of the boy as he opened the door, seeing the kid brace himself as he recognised him.

"Hey, what the hell are you doing in my place? Who let you in man? I know you, you're the guy who still owes me two thousand bucks," he snarled, pulling out a blade. "Are you here to pay me?"

"Sure, I have it here." He held up a plastic bag.

"Good move man, price has doubled though for not paying when you should have."

"Ok, no issues, let's go somewhere more private where we can discuss business."

The top floor apartment in the scruffy tower block was one of the most depressing places the man had visited, the problem for the boy being that his mysterious guest had already been babysitting in there for an hour before his return.

"Hey Mum, just stopping for a few minutes, do you want me to bring food back later, around eleven?" the boy called out as he and his guest entered the apartment. There was no answer as the man pushed the front door closed behind them.

"Mum, where are you? Listen to me you silly bitch, hope you're not on that pipe again." The TV was playing loudly but she wasn't answering. "Mum?" he pushed the lounge door open, where inside there was only a small stolen TV and a ragged sofa. His mum sat tied to a plastic kitchen chair facing him, she was gagged but both of her eyes were hanging out, blood flowing over her dirty t-shirt. She was whimpering in pain.

"What the fuck?" He ran towards her before turning with the knife. "You fucking bastard, she had nothing to do with this." Lunging forwards, he missed the man with a wild slash of the blade as a hammer came crashing down onto his head.

"I'm sorry Junior, business is business. You fucked up and became a liability."

His unconscious body was now tied to a second chair as the laughing man flicked cold water onto his face. "Come on, wake up son." The boy opened his eyes and tried to focus on the face in front of him.

"Now you are back with me, let me show you how to kill someone. Obviously you failed me in this one simple action, *regard!*" He took the boy's knife and sliced it through his mother's throat, the blood splattering forwards and spraying over the wall and door. "Simple as that. And how about you, what do you want me to do with you?" The boy tried to answer but the gag bit in, preventing any intelligible sound. "I'll tell you what I'll do." the man continued, loading up a syringe with a vial of a chemical from his pocket.

"This little injection is an acid so let me tell you what will happen. I will slide this into your arm and within a minute, all of your organs will burn away inside your body. You will vomit, want to scream and then die." The boy's eyes bulged with fear as the man pulled his sleeve up and pushed the needle into a vein.

"Enjoy the ride skater boy," he muttered, standing at the door and watching blood stream from the boy's eyes.

Going into the bedroom he ransacked it before taking a few hundred dollars from the drawer. Wandering around the rooms he tried to avoid touching the soiled surfaces littered with drug equipment. In the woman's bedroom, a single mattress sat in the middle of the floor with a duvet half covering it. Condoms were discarded on the threadbare carpet while a photograph of happier times  lay on a small table, a picture of a mum and dad with a small child. *What went wrong junior?* he asked the silent apartment.

Checking himself in the woman's cheap, cracked bedroom mirror, he looked for signs of blood before walking back out into the darkness.

# CHAPTER THIRTY-THREE

Peter sat opposite Eric Bent in the police building, an uncomfortable atmosphere surrounding them.

"Sorry that I had to miss the youth meeting in town," Peter apologised. "I just needed to get out and try to put this thing to bed but everyday a new question seems to arise. I need answers, not more questions." Bent stared at him across his desk.

"I'm not sure what you're trying to achieve here Father, Cookson is behind bars so surely the case is over?"

"As I said, nothing is really making any sense. The evidence against him was unsafe, the trial was a joke and it feels as though the real killer is one step ahead of everyone all the time." The captain sat back in his chair, shaking his head in resignation that this case was still cursing him.

"If what you say is true, what are you suggesting? That he knows what we are doing?"

"He almost certainly knows what we are doing Eric, but he can't have known what your department was doing, because from my view it wasn't very much."

"What did you expect me to do? This was a national issue and I had the FBI working twenty four hours a day. The killer was a ghost Peter, this was a missing person report when it sat with me and I couldn't see how it would develop." Eric's voice raised an octave through his own frustration.

"Something doesn't seem right Eric, I'm not pointing any fingers, it's just that I have spoken to a friend of mine who works within the FBI building and they told me that they had no resources assigned to this case. Everyone's too busy chasing terror links." Eric looked at him with a resigned look in his eyes.

"I only know what I'm told Peter, what can I say in answer to your unasked question, other than no one in this building was, or is, leaking any information to a serial killer."

Peter held his gaze for a few moments before speaking. "I hope not Eric, we've always had a good working relationship and I trust you. You're a good family man."

Bent seemed to come to a decision within himself as he leant forward to confide in the priest. "Peter, I need to get something off my chest, it's been eating away at me for weeks."

"Sure," Peter answered, having sensed that this moment was coming.

"The FBI have messed up the whole investigation, I reported this stuff months ago and I was told to keep silent. Now they are trying to cover their own arse and if it ever comes out that they have allowed this monster to go unchallenged we are all finished. It could well be that Cookson has taken the rap as a cover up for total incompetence."

"They are threatening you Eric?"

"Yep, me and my family. If I talk, they say that I will go to prison as being part of the cover-up."

"That makes sense why you seem so defensive, it also crosses you guys from my list of people leaking information. But not necessarily your bosses."

"There's going to be a shit storm at some point Peter, I just hope with a little insurance policy I took earlier that I can keep out of it as much as I can."

Peter placed his hand on the back of Eric's trembling hand. "I have a plan Eric, you may not like it now, but it could save you and your men later down the track."

Tommy sat waiting in the interview room; Father Peter was running late and he was becoming impatient with waiting to hear what he had discovered. He finally arrived with a young guard, putting his bag on the table while he composed himself. He could see Tommy was eager for some news.

"Sorry Tommy, I had some business with Brandon that needed to be squared away before I could come in, please forgive me."

"No drama, I've felt a little left out in the cold for the past two weeks though. Lucky for me one of the guys in here got news of the radio interview, sounds like it went well?"

"I'd better start at the beginning and work my way through. Not everything is good, in fact we are uncovering more puzzles than we solve as we progress."

"So you didn't get the phone?" Tommy's face sank.

"I got stabbed looking for it, but I will come back to that."

Tommy sank back into his seat, Peter monitoring every expression. "How the hell? This is just getting way too deep. Who is pulling these strings? How did anyone know about the phone?"

Shrugging his shoulders Peter replied. "I guess I told too many people and it was broadcast across Chicago. Maybe a two bit hoodlum thought that he would roll me over for a few bucks."

"And just happened to know who you were and where you were? Yeah, right!"

Tommy's scepticism spurred Peter into coming out with his suspicions.

"Ok then, here we go. Someone, somewhere is leaking out information to put us off the trail and it can only be one of a few people. Melissa and her team, which is doubtful given that they have had people killed by this guy. The police, who I have just spoken to this morning and I still have doubts about the FBI side of things, or you and your New York friend. It can't be anyone else."

Tommy looked back, mouth open in amazement. "Why would I tell you everything I know, watch you go to investigate then have you killed to stop you? Are you fucking dumb? I'll tell you what, forget it. If you don't trust me Father Bell we are done here." Pushing back the chair he called for the guard, before snarling, "Or Father Bell it could be that you're being taken in by someone else, I'm already dead in case you forgot. Thanks for the help but no thanks."

The door opened and Tommy was taken back to his cell leaving Peter to sit and consider his next options, whatever they might be.

Walking back through the main prison gate and into the parking lot, he allowed himself to stop for a second to let the sun shine onto his face. "These guys will never know the joy of that feeling again," he muttered to no one in particular until a young correctional officer overheard his comment. Coming up and standing by his side, she said, "Everyone inside the prison had a choice, they don't have to be there, the majority just spun the coin and lost. But they still have a life and those people sitting on death row which you suck up to have all ensured that normal, decent, hard working families will have to spend the rest of their days in darkness." Putting her hand on his shoulder she continued.

"And that includes your own little project, Tommy Cookson. He's a killer Father, he just kept getting away with it until he slipped up and now he's crying for forgiveness. I have watched how he operates in that place, manipulating staff and prisoners, getting what he wants and I wouldn't trust him one God damn inch."

"What do you mean?" he asked but the words were lost as she disappeared back through the sliding gate.

# CHAPTER THIRTY-FOUR

Melissa sat in her office considering the things Peter Bell had mentioned over the past few days. Too many things were falling apart under examination for her liking, the entire case against Tommy was sounding as fragile as a dry leaf and there were just too many loose ends. The lack of DNA on the necklace was a distinct issue...if he were a trophy hunter where were his finger prints? The necklace had been wiped clean by someone and why hadn't anyone questioned why his fingerprints would have been absent? The police officer on the night said that it looked as though he had been keeping it as a trophy, but not touching it. That made no sense at all.

And then there were the mysteries surrounding the allegations of finding stool pigeons for the crimes, and the attack on Father Bell. She had listened to him the second time, his testament was overwhelming until his return from Chicago when everything changed again. All his two weeks of amateur sleuthing had led to was more confusion and paranoia. Everyone who seemed to be close to uncovering something was hunted down and either killed, hurt or thrown in jail. The man who was waiting for execution was the only eye witness to anything and he was locked away with no contact to the outside world apparently.

And talking of Tommy, even when confronted with all the evidence against him in the courtroom, he still maintained his innocence and still tried to contact her through the letter and the priest. Why would he do that if he knew that he was guilty? He wasn't that type of man. How, when he had nowhere in the world to call his own, did he manage to keep a necklace that was worth three hundred bucks? He had nowhere to go and nowhere to live. This final thought suddenly stopped her in her tracks. If he was in possession of the necklace then he must have had it when he was first arrested for the truck murder.

She phoned Eric Bent and as soon as he picked up the phone, she wasted no time in launching straight in to her questioning.

"Eric, I know that this sounds crazy but when Tommy Cookson was taken into custody for the first murder, you know, the truck guy, did the police take a note of his possessions?" The captain needed no announcement of who was calling, recognising her voice immediately and knowing this nightmare was just not going to go away.

"Hello Melissa! Yep, they would have listed everything. It'll be on the system here along with his description and personal details. Why do you need that Melissa? You realise that this is very off the record?"

"Yeah, Eric, I get that but humour me please, tell me what he had on him." She heard a key board being tapped, as though with one finger before Bent's voice came on the line again.

"He had the dead guy's wallet containing nine hundred and thirty dollars, a heap of bank cards and phone numbers. He had....let me see now...he had an Adidas black backpack containing a can of Bud, a green towel, and a puma sports top, a t-shirt that was so dirty it had to be thrown away and forty five cents in loose change in a pocket of the bag. Nothing else Melissa."

"And he took them with him when he was released?"

"Nope, everything was destroyed and the cash confiscated. He left straight from the court and didn't want any of that crap. Can't blame him, a military guy saw him and I believe gave him a few thousand dollars he was owed. That's all I know."

"Then where did the necklace appear from? If he left with nothing and had no address, where did Mia's chain appear from? It had no DNA on it so he can't have hidden it in his butt and it would have shown up on the scanner. It was worth three hundred bucks Eric, if he had given it to someone to look after, they would have sold it for a bag of dope the minute he went into jail. Why didn't anyone consider that piece of evidence Eric?

How can the mighty FBI not see that this is a vital clue? It feels as if they weren't even looking."

"That's a good point Melissa, when you put it like that, it does sound strange. What do you want me to do, apart from contact the FBI again?"

"Tell them if you think it's now worth it and that's if anyone is listening, but apart from that I think that we need to keep some of these thoughts to ourselves. We both know that we have a problem with keeping things secret at the moment."

Ending the call and looking back up at the map she had on her new office wall, something just didn't sit straight with her. The answer was there, as if Mia were shouting it out, but she couldn't see it. In frustration she threw her pen onto the table top. "Talk to me, talk to me," she implored, looking at a smiling photograph of Mia on her desk. The answer kept coming to the front of her brain before sliding away again like the tide, pulling the thoughts with it. Her phone rang dragging her away from the concentration haze she had fallen into.

"Hi, Melissa speaking, how can I help you?"

"Hey Melissa, it's Christine from the main office at the Chicago Press here, we are trying to contact Brandon but he's not picking up. He left your number as a contact so I wondered if you had any ideas where he might be?"

"I haven't seen him for a couple of weeks, they all flew out to India to film some tigers in the wild. He should be home again next week sometime but those boys tell me nothing."

"Oh right, that makes sense, he won't have phone reception out there in the middle of the jungle. When he gets back can you pass a message on to him? We have found the damn phone he's been looking for. I've put it in the post addressed to him at Dallas Zoo as that's where we send all of his post at the moment."

Melissa jumped to her feet. "What? You have found the phone?"

"Sure, we had enough people looking although I'm not sure why anyone would be interested in a broken old phone. One of the students working here during the Christmas break contacted us, she found it in her bag. She thought that she was in trouble and dropped it off with me yesterday morning. It has no battery life and no power lead, I tried to turn it on but it's dead."

"When did you post it?"

"Twenty minutes ago, I did it myself it as seems that everyone needs it. Should be there for when he gets back."

Hands shaking, Melissa poured herself a drink while checking Brandon's schedule. He landed at Atlanta at ten o'clock on Friday morning, another four days away. "Jesus, the answer to all of this would be sitting in an envelope on his desk. What if someone got to it first as seemed to have happened all the way through the investigation?" And with this thought in mind she picked up the phone and dialled the zoo.

"Hey, I've just posted a parcel to Brandon Jones, he's working with Pat Hunter and I want to make sure he receives it." The woman on the other end of the line gave a chuckle.

"I know him, who doesn't at the moment? We have a few things coming in for him and Lilly-Anne in the way of fan mail and the pile is getting bigger everyday."

"This one is a small parcel coming from Chicago and it's a really important delivery. Can you put it to one side and give it to Brandon yourself when he comes back? I'll tell him to come to see you. Who shall I tell him has it?"

"He calls me Mum," she laughed again. "Tell him Mum is looking after it for him."

"That's a relief, it's gone missing before so please take care of it."

"Will do, and have a great day," the woman replied with a final chuckle.

Melissa wished everything was so funny in her life and a good day was the last thing she was thinking about when a man was sitting in prison where his insistence that this phone was going to clear his name was about to be tested. He didn't and couldn't know that it had been found yet but if this video showed what he claimed then he would be a free man within the next few weeks. The monster who had really taken the girls would be exposed;

someone somewhere would be having his last few days at work, maybe his last delivery or business meeting. Kissing his wife goodbye for the final time before her life would be thrown into meltdown. Did she know what he was doing? Was she complicit in all of the crimes? Maybe the fucking bitch watched Mia take her last breath in the back of that van.

Crunching up her fists, she took some deep breaths and tried to relax. *"Focus on what you know,"* she told herself, *"don't get ahead of yourself, the phone might give us nothing."*

# CHAPTER THIRTY-FIVE

Pat sat in the Indian humidity on his hard hotel chair tapping away on his laptop. He needed to finish the financial report for the charity before the next week started and as always, was under pressure to get the figures to balance before an audit could find otherwise. They always seemed to dig that little bit deeper than was needed.

A knock on the door took him away from the screen as he opened the door as far as the chain would allow. Lilly-Anne stood a few feet away in the corridor, a bead of sweat trickling down from her neck and disappearing into her cleavage.

"Hi Pat, you phoned and asked me to come see you?" She seemed a little puzzled. Pat took the chain from the door, inviting her in. This was the first time that she'd been invited into Tiger HQ as she and Brandon called it.

"Yes, I'm just finishing up the accounts for the quarter and then I have a night time trip planned for the tigers this evening. I wondered if you would be interested in coming?" She jumped at the chance. "Cool, shall I go and fetch Brandon?" she asked as a tinge of excitement flowed through her body.

"No, not tonight. We need to have a tight team and I need someone who isn't scared by the big cats. He can stay here this evening so keep it our secret trip." She smiled, "Ok, but he's kind of going to be pissed off if he finds out."

"Well I don't plan on telling him Lilly-Anne, do you?" he asked, looking directly at her. She shook her head, keeping eye contact with Pat. "Let me go and put my boots on, I'll see you back here in five."

She raced downstairs, heart thumping with the excitement of watching tigers at night time, and a little extra thrill of being the one selected to join Pat.

Closing her door, she turned and saw Pat waiting at the end of the corridor. He waved for her to join him, his muscular frame looking impressive in his tight fitting shirt.

"How far are we going Pat? This sounds so cool," she chatted as they headed out of the hotel. He laughed at her enthusiasm. "It's only a twenty minute drive and I've borrowed a Land Rover from the tiger team. We're going to find a watering hole and sit and film for a while. If nothing is happening we'll get out and have a walk around. Stick with me though as there are two dominant tigers who hunt this area and you know the dangers. There's an old hide on the other side of the pond so we'll shack in there for a couple of hours and see what's about.

The lights of the city melted away and soon the scrub and tree lines appeared, littered by a small number of shacks for local workers which sat in the darkness, small beams of light emerging from the wooden slats which made up the walls.

Gazing around her, Lilly-Anne commented. "It's amazing Pat, these people live shoulder to shoulder with these animals and are in constant danger."

Pat's eyes stayed on the dusty road ahead as he answered. "It's not only the tigers that can kill them, these guys out here are more at risk from snake bites. They work in the rice fields bare footed, often in the darkness as they fix broken water pipes. They step on a snake and it's all over. There are a quarter of a million bites every year in this country alone." He pulled onto a dirt track leading through some dense woodland, his speed slowing right down to walking pace as he talked.

"Okay, we're in the home of the tiger right now and they will already know that we're here." Pulling over he killed the lights as they sat quietly.

"So what's the plan?" she asked, her eyes scanning around in the darkness.

"We sit here for a few minutes, get the feel of the place and get our night vision. Then we use these if we hear anything." He took out two sets of night vision goggles.

"When we hear the alarm calls from the birds around the water hole, we'll watch it from there. The hole is at two o'clock to where we're sitting, maybe thirty metres away."

They sat in silence for another ten minutes before Pat opened the door.

"Come on, let's get to the hide. We'll have a better chance to see them from there." Reaching onto the back seat he took a hunting rifle, and seeing the alarm on her face, reassured her. "Only a last resort Lilly-Anne." She nodded, a knot coming into her throat. The tigers could be sitting just feet away, ready to strike, just like in the talks she gave to the public about ambush behaviour. Just this time she wasn't in an enclosure in daylight with a tiger who was used to human interaction.

As they climbed out of the Land Rover, Pat tapped her on the shoulder, a crescent moon giving just enough light to see him two feet away.

"Let's go Lilly Anne and stay close behind me. We have around two hundred metres to cover," he whispered. An alarm call from an observant bird sprang out as they circled the large pond, swarms of insects flying in to bite any unprotected white flesh. Pat turned and put his mouth close to her ear. "Keep your eyes open, I can smell that a tiger has recently travelled around here." Her heart thumped as she peered into the darkness, almost jumping out of her skin as the same bird cried out another alarm a hundred metres behind them. Pat turned again.

"One of them is following us so we need to get into the hut asap." He upped the pace for the next twenty seconds until a black shape loomed into view. Pat took a key from his pocket and quickly opened the door. Both of them bundled inside as he closed it and locked it from the inside. He silently laughed before whispering. "That was close, one of the tigers was on our scent. If we're quick, we might see her outside as she checks us out."

Two stools sat in front of a small hatch, and taking a seat each, they silently waited until the gentle crack of a twig alerted them. A huge tiger padded past, sniffing in the night air, stopping briefly to look at the hatch. His size was so much bigger than anything Lilly-Anne had seen before, his body so muscular and athletic the power evident in the ripple of his muscles.

"Now do you see why I love these animals so much?" Pat whispered, "they are the apex predator out here and we are nothing, he could take us both out in seconds." He handed her the goggles and they continued to watch the cat patrol around the pond, stopping to take a long drink before moving on.

She sighed, "He's beautiful Pat, wild tigers even move differently to those we have in the zoos."

Pat put his hand on her shoulder as he whispered into her ear. "He has moved to the back of the hut. Without you realising it, he's set his ambush. If we set foot out of here now, he'll take one of us down."

He placed his hand onto her other shoulder, turning her towards him, his breath tickling her exposed neck as he kissed her gently. She responded, the thrill of the danger just feet away through the thin walls of the hut making her hungry for this moment. He slid his hands under her flimsy top and undid her bra, her exposed nipples aching for his attention. She stood and slid her hand inside his shorts, stroking his penis before kneeling and taking it slowly in her mouth as he smiled.

"You're a dark horse Lilly-Anne," he groaned before lifting her onto the wooden desk and pulling her shorts away from her well toned legs. "If only Brandon knew what I was doing to his girl."

She laughed, "Pat, I'm sure that you are going to do it a lot harder and longer than Brandon could ever hope for and anyway, I'm not his girl."

He knelt between her legs, letting his tongue play a sensitive pattern and she gave a groan as she lay back and enjoyed his undivided attention.

The sun crept over the tree tops as they woke from a makeshift bed on the floor and Pat smiled at her radiant face before kissing her again.

"Brandon will never know Lilly-Anne, this was a one off, okay?" She laughed, "If you say so, I'm a big girl and I can cope with one offs and as I told you last night, it's got nothing to do with Brandon.

# CHAPTER THIRTY-SIX

Tommy sat in his cell on Death Row where the atmosphere was far more relaxed than on the other units, but he was still hated by one of the other prisoners. Ironic that a multiple killer of men and women would judge Tommy because he had reached a higher number. Curtis called it professional jealousy but Tommy thought the scoring system was sick.

"You have a visit Tommy, a young guard opened his door. It's your legal team here to see you. Do you want to see them?" Tommy looked up in surprise.

"Sure, why not. To be honest I didn't even know I still had a legal team."

Shuffling the fifty metres to the interview room, Tommy considered what the visit might be about, perhaps something had come up, or who knows, maybe even Peter Bell had got his act in order and discovered something concrete at last."

Escorted into the room he stopped still in his tracks. "Melissa, what are you doing here?"

"I've come with an attorney and I've paid for her myself so don't worry." She introduced the sharply dressed woman. "This is Susan Follan and we need to talk to you about something important."

Tommy took a seat, his feet and ankle chains jangling. "OK, although I'm confused as to why you are here. I thought you'd made your opinion known to Father Bell, that none of you believes a word I say."

"Yep, and then someone tried to kill him, or was that a coincidence Tommy, along with my house burning down, or even the young guy killing himself in a police cell? I don't believe in coincidence, and I know that you didn't have Mia's necklace. It was impossible, we just didn't consider the common sense reasons why you couldn't have had it on the evening you were arrested." Tommy looked at her in disbelief as she blurted everything out

"You seem to have come to this Damascus decision so suddenly. How the fuck can you be so sure I didn't have the jewellery?"

"Because there was no way it could have been in your possession, the police would have found it weeks earlier when you were first arrested for killing the trucker, we just didn't think outside the box." Tommy looked around the box he was already locked in and considered the irony of that statement.

"I did try to explain that to my old attorney, I just couldn't get anyone to listen, including you Melissa."

She put her hands up in apology. "But that's not all Tommy, we have found the phone."

Slumping forwards he muttered, "I don't believe it, how did you find it? Everyone has tried and failed and I had totally given up on it."

She tried to smile but it came out as a frown.

"It just turned up Tommy, I haven't had the chance to look at it, but this is the important part…" His new attorney who hadn't said a word until now cut in.

"What are we going to see Tommy? Tell me exactly. There is absolutely no point in not telling us the truth as we will all see it for ourselves in a few days."

Tommy closed his eyes and concentrated. "From my memory you will see a big guy talking to Mia by the van, he then hits her with something and holds her up as she falls before he puts her in the back of a white van using one arm. He was strong and he hits his head on the top of the door frame so I knew he was a tall guy when I saw it. I just don't know how clear the film is as I was out of it." He opened his eyes and Susan continued, looking at him intently.

"Do you realise what this means for you if we find it's as you have described?"

"Why don't you tell me, I have had it with false dawns,"

Tommy replied with a shrug. She brought out some new appeal papers from her bag.

"You will get a fresh trial due to the new evidence and they will find you not guilty. We can prove that the chain wasn't in your apartment and we can prove that you didn't take Mia. It's not going to happen overnight, but it will come good. We just felt we owed you an explanation in the meantime."

He started to laugh. "It will come good? What good can come from what has happened to me? I will be forever looked at as a killer, regardless of what happens, everyone pointing a filthy finger at the drug addicted bum who watched a girl die. There's no silver lining to this cloud. I was hung up to dry while you people waited for me to be executed. Admit it, you hated me."

"Yes, but not now," Melissa said sadly.

"Even though I did nothing to help Mia, do you think that I can live with that? I would rather die in here."

Melissa had a sob in her voice when she replied. "I don't think that Tommy, you weren't to blame. People walked right past her and did nothing. And you didn't know that he was killing her, they could have just been father and daughter having an argument. You are not to blame for her death Tommy."

He placed his handcuffed hands onto the desk top. "But they weren't just father and daughter so I'll have to go to my grave with that one."

Susan took his hand gently and Tommy flinched, unused to the contact. "We can go through that once we beat the charge. It's a natural feeling just as the guys that you saved in the war blame themselves for surviving. Believe me, we don't blame you, and in time you will realise that. Now back to the here and now. Do not discuss this with anyone until we see the phone evidence, agreed?"

Tommy remained still, staring at the two of them over the table, the smell of expensive perfume assaulting his senses, but awaking the human inside him.

"Melissa, I don't know what to say; you of all people should have been the one to wish me dead but you believed in me. Of course I agree, please, let's just get this done. I just need to get out of this mad house."

# CHAPTER THIRTY-SEVEN

Pat moved through the brush with ease, speaking quietly to his handheld camera, his leather hat regularly disappearing from view much to the armed guide's annoyance as he spotted a cobra or another creature slithering under the vegetation. Lilly-Anne and Brandon finally caught up with him as he stopped just short of a large watering hole, the water looking deep and muddy as the numerous surrounding animal tracks showed its importance in the eco structure of this region.

"Look at the massive prints, this one's a really big boy, and look how the trees have been clawed. This cat must be more than ten feet high when he stretches up." He pointed the camera upwards showing the viewer the torn bark. "Whatever tiger has been here," he stopped and prodded a lump of tiger droppings, "he was here recently as the dung is still nice and warm," he told them, this time pointing the camera at the pile. "Whatever pussycat has been here is bigger than anything we have in any zoo or park, a true king of this area. I guarantee that he is the apex predator, the alpha male of this area and if we're lucky we might hear a couple of girlfriends calling out for him."

Continuing to walk forwards, camera in front of his face, the guide shouted a warning. "Pat take care, we don't know where he is but he is close, the birds are indicating that he is here." As if to emphasis his point, an Indian peafowl sent out a shrill cry, reminding Lilly-Anne of their nocturnal visit three nights before. Pat scanned the area, looking for any trace of movement or a silent shadow watching from a hidden ambush point.

"Ok, let's get the memory card from the fixed camera and see what we've got."

Brandon followed him, filming Pat's commentary as they moved carefully forward for the upcoming video he was putting together, when a burst of colour came flying out of the brush. It was the blur of a furious tiger springing at the guide who raised the rifle firing a shot into the air wildly as the enormous animal knocked him off balance and the gun bounced harmlessly down the slope before sliding into the murky water.

"Get back to the van," Pat shouted as the tiger panicked and crouched down, assessing the threat presented by the people and steadying itself ready to launch a fresh attack.

Lilly-Anne pulled the dazed guard to his feet and walked calmly backwards, the tiger not giving them a second glance. Pat stood and placed himself in the path between Brandon who had fallen to the ground in panic and the tiger as it growled, exposing the massive teeth which could carve through them both in seconds.

"Stand up Brandon and make yourself as big as you can," Pat ordered.

Struck by fear, he managed to get to his knees but his legs wouldn't allow him to stand.

"Stand up! If you don't I will kill you myself so do it quick."

He stood, making sure that he was still behind Pat. "Come to my side, we need to be as large as possible." Pat spoke without taking his eyes from the crouching beast in front of them. "Listen to me, you need to have faith in what I'm saying."

Brandon moved from the safety of Pat's massive build and stood facing the snarling animal.

"Fucking man up Brandon or we aren't getting out of here in one piece."

The tiger sprang forwards and Brandon dropped to his knees, covering his eyes, waiting for the inevitable. Pat stood firm, shouting with his arms in the air as the tiger stopped in its tracks and backed away, returning to the cover of the undergrowth.

"Get up, the tiger hasn't gone away, it's still watching us," he said as bending over, he flung Brandon effortlessly onto his shoulder.

"Let's get home, I'm not ready to die out here."

Marching forwards almost godlike, he threw Brandon onto the back seat of the jeep. "Don't worry, the same thing happened to me when I was out here with Dad. Next time you will stay calmer."

Brandon babbled, unable to control his emotions. "There won't be a next time. You saved my life out there Pat. Oh my God, you are one awesome man." Climbing into the driver's seat, Pat turned to the guide.

"Did you land in the tiger crap when you fell over or is that smell coming from Brandon?" They all laughed, mainly out of relief that they'd all survived the ambush. He glanced around the vehicle before speaking sharply to the guide.

"Where's the rifle? You had it when we left."

"That son of a bitch tiger knocked it out of my hands and it went into the water."

"Where?" The guide pointed to a spot.

"For God's sake, I am not losing a gun," Pat moaned as he climbed back out of the cab and jogged to the water's edge, plunging in an enormous arm and fishing around like a bear looking for honey in a tree. Another rumbling bellow came from out of the scrub.

"Shut the hell up, you had the chance to eat me and you messed it up," he yelled, his large hand coming out of the water with a dripping rifle. Smiling, he jogged back to the jeep and put it into gear. "What are we eating tonight Brandon? I think it's your turn to cook…how about chicken?"

Smacking the back of Pat's leather hat Brandon laughed somewhat hysterically. "Raw meat for you caveman. On a more positive note, I have the whole thing on film although I might have to edit out my crying with fear. I was such a pussy!"

Lilly-Anne put an arm around Brandon, talking like a concerned mum would do to a child. "I was worried about you, when Pat was carrying you out of there on his shoulder I thought that the tiger might bite your ass."

Pat glanced around at Brandon. "Don't beat yourself up, you didn't run, you stayed with me. When it happened to me for the first time, all I could think of was running away and hiding."

"Well that makes me feel a lot better Pat, thanks for sharing that."

"That's fine Brandon, I remember it well, it was my seventh birthday."

Brandon laughed again. "I thought that we were going to have to run for the shelter of that old shed over there," he said, pointing to the wooden hide.

"I wouldn't go near that place Brandon, people have been eaten in there," Pat told him.

# CHAPTER THIRTY-EIGHT

Melissa sat in her lounge, it was Friday lunchtime and the gang were due back in the country. Her hands shook as she phoned the Zoo. "Hi, it's Melissa Jagger, I called last week about a parcel arriving for Brandon Jones."

"Hi Melissa, yes it was me who you spoke to. I have it here, it's safe in my drawer and if Brandon gets here before three o'clock he can have it, anytime after it will have to be Monday."

"Ok thank you. It'll probably be Monday then, I think he's still on a plane."

She phoned Brandon, hoping to catch him between flights but his phone was switched off. *Damn, he must be on the connecting flight already,* she thought as she checked the flight schedules and saw that the connecting flight wasn't due to land until six that evening. Her phone rang and Brandon's name flashed up on the screen.

"Melissa, I'm just waiting to board the flight and I've just seen a couple of missed calls from you. Is everything ok?"

"All good here but I was hoping that you might be landing early, I had a quick job for you."

"Can it wait? We're all exhausted but I'll be around on Monday afternoon if that's ok? Pat's booked us into a hotel in Dallas so we have a few days to recover from the trip and I have an article I need to write for the paper about the tigers out in India. Is it ok if I come over around five?"

"Sure, ask Pat if he wants to come, I need to talk to him too."

A muffled conversation in the background was broken by Brandon speaking again. "He said he needs to fly up to New York tomorrow but he'll drop by during the week if that's ok."

"Sure, no problem. Anyway, the lady in the main office at the zoo, I think you call her Mum?" Brandon laughed. "Yes she treats me like her little boy so I told her she's just like my mum!"

"Well she has a parcel for you, so can you pick it up and bring it here before you open it?"

"A surprise! I love gifts. What is it?"

"Can anyone else hear me?"

"No, of course not."

"Brandon, do not tell anyone at all what I am about to say. Do you swear?"

"Yes, of course, you're worrying me now."

"It's the phone, the one Tommy posted to you. People have died for that damn thing and I don't want you to be the next victim."

"Hold on while I take a little walk away from the others." She waited a few seconds, hearing more muffled conversation in the background before Brandon came back on the line. "Melissa, I can't believe that they've found it, but have you thought about what you might see on the phone?"

"Yes, of course I have, it's been the only thing on my mind since I was told it had been found. I want you to bring the phone to my house, I want to see that man's face."

"There is no way on earth that I am going to sit with you and watch Mia being murdered. Have you thought about it for even one second? This guy is going to be killing Mia in front of your eyes. I am not allowing you to see that. I am taking it directly to Eric Bent. I'll pick you up and take you with me, but no way am I allowing you to see something that will haunt us both forever."

Sitting silently for a few seconds, she then spoke. "You're right, I never fully considered that I would see her last breath, I was just focused on seeing the bastard who did it. Thank you sweetheart, you take it to the police station and I'll meet you there and remember, not one word to anyone."

Monday seemed to take forever to arrive, the garden and driveway weeded into oblivion by a frantic Melissa as she tried to make the hours disappear until she could see the phone. Her stomach was tied up in tight knots and everything she tried to do to calm herself down failed to deal with the inner anxiety.

For the twentieth time she checked the clock before getting in the car and taking the short drive to the police building, her heart thumping and a feeling of nausea sweeping through her stomach. Sitting watching people coming and going, all the time wondering what the next hour would bring, she waited for Brandon to arrive.

Brandon drove over, hardly able to control his own feelings as he anticipated the difficult conversation they were going to have and pulling up outside the police station, he saw her sitting alone in her car. He knew what was coming, Melissa's wild eyes staring out at him told him all that he needed to know. She climbed out and met him before he even had time to get out of his own car.

"Brandon, I haven't slept all night. I can't do this in front of those people, I need to see it in private. Let's go home and watch it, I'm all prepared but I just need to cry and scream in the privacy of my own home." Breathless through anxiety she looked at him pleadingly.

"That was not the deal Melissa, you promised me we would go into the station and give it to Mr Bent."

Tears rolled from her sore eyes. "Please Brandon, give me a little space to grieve again?"

He capitulated, her grief cutting through his common sense approach. "Ok, but once we see it, we come straight back. Agreed?" She nodded, eyes already filling with tears again. He opened his car door and waved her in before making the short drive in silence. Melissa's hands trembled as she fumbled for her house keys before they stood in the silent lounge, the atmosphere thick with dread and anticipation at what was about to be revealed.

He opened the envelope and took out the filthy phone, its screen cracked and the case broken.

"Do you have a charger cable? We need to charge this thing up," he asked as he pressed the on/off button getting no response from the black screen.

Rummaging through the office she came out with one and

plugging it in, the phone stayed dark until it eventually sprang into life with a green light. *Charging 0%.*

"This is going to take a few minutes Melissa," Brandon told her as she paced the lounge area crying.

"I'm so sorry Brandon," she sobbed, "I just never saw it coming to this. Mia was always supposed to walk through the front door apologising for something, not end up clubbed to death in a shitty parking lot."The phone's home page opened up, it wasn't coded and a few text alerts pinged up as Brandon skipped through them. "All from drug dealers threatening to kill him, nothing else for us," he said as he checked the camera and saw the video they needed was saved, dated Feb 9th 2019. He read out the date.

"That's when she was taken, that's the video. What can you see?" Melissa demanded. Turning the screen towards her and pushing play, he held his breath. A large man in a black jacket, jeans and wool hat was holding a girl by the arm. He towered over her as two people walked past, almost brushing Mia's arm but didn't turn around and didn't acknowledge her in any way.

"That's Mia, I can tell by her clothing," Melissa almost whispered. "Shit, its grainy. Can you see the guy's face?"

Brandon nodded. "It looks like Tommy but I can't be sure."

The man then pulled her towards the van and hit her on the forehead with a hammer. Her knees buckled and she half fell before he scooped her up in his right hand and threw her into the back of the van. He followed her in and pulled the door shut. The video then stopped abruptly.

"Pretty much as Tommy described, only thing is, that could have been him," Brandon observed.

"Why would he give us the phone if it was him, and who the fuck would be filming it? That bastard is not Tommy," Melissa insisted. Brandon pressed the play button again.

"We don't know that, maybe he didn't want us to get the phone so let's not make any conclusions yet." She was now crying uncontrollably so he put the phone down on the table and pulled her into a big hug. They stood there together for a while until he felt her sobs come to a hiccupping end. "We need to take this to the police; they have the ability to clean it up and identify the killer," he told her gently. She wiped her eyes and blew her nose on a tissue.

"Let's go, we have to get Tommy out of prison and put this man in there instead," she said, grabbing her house keys and heading for the door.

"Melissa, calm down, we don't know that it isn't Tommy for definite so one step at a time."

They climbed back in the car, a feeling of deflation enveloping them both. They'd had so much anticipation about the content of the video, but still had no clarity.

Rushing into Eric's office, they broke up a meeting he was having with a number of officers. He looked up and sensing their urgency he dismissed everyone in the room. He waited for the last person to leave the office before speaking.

"By the looks on your faces you have the phone?"

"We do, but we need your help," Brandon told him. They played the video to him five times without talking until they were interrupted by a knock on his office door. Peter Bell entered and went straight to Melissa. Giving her a hug, he explained, "Brandon called me, he thought I should be here. I hope you don't mind." He watched the film intently before blurting out a comment.

"Holy God, why didn't anyone come forward? Those two mother fuckers were so close they literally brushed past them." He was unaware of the surprise to his unfatherly cussing the others showed as he continued to watch the video before Eric Bent spoke calmly.

"I don't think that Tommy is involved Melissa, he was wearing rags when he tried to see me and this man is well dressed. I need to get it sent away for cleaning up. The guys in the FBI will get that done in a day. You ok with that?"

Melissa nodded. "I've waited this long Eric, another day isn't going to break me any more than I feel at the moment."

"I'll have it sent by our secure postage service straight away and they will have it today. I'll phone you when we know anything. It may be that those guys go out and arrest this guy straight away, we just need to wait."

"Ok Eric, in the meantime, Brandon can you stay with me until we hear?" She looked over at Brandon to get his assent. Looking taken aback by the invitation Brandon weakly nodded.

"I can come back with you, no problem, I was supposed to meet up with Pat back at the hotel tomorrow but I'll phone him when he gets back from New York."

"Thanks, you know, however bad and painful that was for me, it gives me a little closure. Now I know for sure that she is gone, I guess it was important to see for myself." She took a deep breath. "That hammer to the head would have killed her outright, no doubt about that. At least that bastard couldn't make her suffer anymore. She put up a real fight but he was just so fucking big and powerful."

Peter gave her hand a squeeze. "You go back home Melissa, Brandon and I need to stay here with Mr Bent for a few minutes as we have some separate business to resolve."

Nodding, she left the office before turning back. "I'll wait outside, I would rather you drive me Brandon, I can't stop shaking."

Eric stood and hugged her, "I'm so sorry, go through to our rest area where the guys will make you a coffee. We won't be long."

Waiting for her to leave Peter spoke first.

"The cat's out of the bag Eric. Now the phone is here, the rest of your bullshit excuses for not investigating more will crash down around your head."

"I know," Bent admitted, "I just need to work out where I stand."

"To be honest, with the evidence we've gained through the investigation team from New York and from the recording of the conversation you had with the FBI, I think that you're covered. The others can answer for themselves tomorrow."

"Never trust those bastards Peter, that's what I was always taught. Keep all your evidence close to hand. Thank the Lord I hit the play button on the recorder when I did."

Brandon smiled. "And the piece written for the paper is ready, Father Peter is the most cunning fox I've ever met. Saved your ass, Captain Bent."

"Let's hope so," Bent said with a tired smile. "You guys better get going, Melissa needs all the help and support she can get."

Climbing into the car, Melissa looked drained as she spoke to Brandon. "This has been the most traumatic day of my life, I'm shattered. Sorry to drop this all on you."

Brandon just nodded. "Not exactly as I planned for my return but only too glad to be here for you."

They settled down back at the house, watching second rate TV without it sinking in as, finally, Melissa began to regain her composure. "Thanks for staying over Brandon, please tell me all about India. It looked like a great opportunity for you all."

"It was an unbelievable trip Melissa, an experience of a lifetime. I have something for you once you feel ready."

"What have you got me? Trust you to always think of others, you're so kind."

He smiled weakly, still not knowing if the time was right. "It just seems a bit inappropriate to give you it at the moment. It's our travels with Pat over this year, we have covered every corner of the country, and India was just the most amazing trip. Lilly-Anne and I made a video for you, but only when you're ready. It covers everything. I know my timing is terrible but we wanted you to have it."

She leaned over and gave him a hug. "That's so sweet of you, maybe when this calms down a bit, it will be lovely to watch."

"Apart from me nearly getting eaten…."

She laughed. "Again? How many times is that going to happen? Anyway, you are due to be going back to the newspaper soon, it must have been so much easier working there and a lot less dangerous."

"Two weeks time but I'm coming back down to write the book with Pat afterwards, mostly on weekends. We took so many pictures and have a hundred cool stories. People are going to love it."

"Where is Lilly-Anne?" Melissa sat up suddenly. "I forgot all about her with all the upset over the phone video, I thought that she was coming with you?"

"Yep, she was, however Fox News got in touch with us in India as they wanted to have a chat with her this week. It seems that she has made a big splash with the people who watched the game show and of course our videos. She's headed off to New York with Pat for an interview as they want to meet him as well for some upcoming reports. She's thrilled although it means a move to New York for her."

"And how are you with that?" Melissa asked him, knowing he and Lilly-Anne had had a thing going.

"We had a great time, but it was never going to be forever and we've kind of ended things as good friends. I just hope it works out for her, she deserves it."

Melissa nodded. "When this is over Brandon, please keep in touch, I don't want you just slipping away."

"No way, you're my third mum!"

"Second mum! I knew you before the woman in the zoo." They both giggled and Brandon was pleased Melissa was looking more herself again. She got up, still smiling.

"I'm going to have a long hot bath, can you go to the shop and buy some things for dinner tonight? I was going to do it yesterday but, you know, things are hectic still."

"Sure, I need to pop in and see Jazz anyway," he said, standing up and pulling his jacket on as Melissa went upstairs. She shouted down again, the sound of running water making it difficult to make herself heard.

"She's proud of you, couldn't stop talking about you while you were away. She has no idea about Lilly-Anne though, I don't know how she didn't realise."

"I was expecting her to mention it last time I was here but it never came up," Brandon shouted back up before leaving the house.

His phone rang as soon as he was in the car, Pat's name on the screen.

"Hey Pat, how have the interviews gone? Do you both have new jobs?"

"Lilly-Anne crushed them, they have given her a five year contract working with the news team. That girl has certainly got it."

"Wow, that's brilliant," Brandon exclaimed. "How about you?"

"Yeah, I have certainly got it too, I've been offered a five series deal working around the world in between focusing on our project here."

"That's so cool, hope the bottom line is good for you?"

"The bottom line is good for both of us Brandon. They want you too, along with another five books after this one. What do you say?"

Brandon could hear the smile in Pat's voice and didn't need to think about his response.

"I say yes, it's a no brainer. I'll need to speak to the paper first so until then it's going to have to be kept quiet."

"Sure. How's Melissa? I haven't heard from her for a while."

"Not bad considering."

"Considering what?"

"Considering that she's just watched the video of her daughter being murdered in the car park. It was fucking brutal Pat."

"They found the phone? Really? How the hell did that come to light? I honestly thought that it was gone forever….Tommy is in big trouble now, that's any appeal he hoped for gone out the window."

Brandon was silent for a few seconds before answering. "It wasn't Tommy, it was someone else. Melissa is putting everything together while the FBI are enhancing the quality of the recording. Eric Bent thinks that they will have the guy by tomorrow."

The worry in Pat's voice grew in intensity as he answered "Jesus! Ok, are you with her now?"

"No, I'm just heading to the store for food but I'll be back in an hour. Do you have a message or will you phone her?"

"No, just tell her to stay strong. I'll fly into Dallas tonight and will try to get down to see you both."

"Tonight?"

"If I can, I do have a little business to deal with so may need your help for an hour. Will Melissa be ok with that?"

"Sure, she's got over the initial shock of what she saw and has calmed down a bit now. We're eating early so what do you want me to do?"

"I told the head of the TV station that we'll be in town tonight so he wants to meet us both at ten this evening. Can you make it back for then?"

"Shit that's quick, but sure, I'll eat and leave. Where do I meet up with you?"

"Your room is still here at the hotel, wait there and I'll come and get you. He has a conference office booked for us. Nothing to worry about but he wants to pitch an idea to us. How about that Brandon? They are pitching to us!" A laugh sounded in Pat's voice at last, his friendly tone calming Brandon's tension.

"Oh my God, this is all down to you my friend, I'll see you tonight."

Driving back from the store, dreaming of stardom, Brandon cursed himself for absently forgetting what had happened earlier that day as his own needs surged to the front of his mind. The least he could do was look after Melissa while he was still staying there.

The smell of cooking woke Melissa up, she had fallen asleep on her bed after the bath and had lost all sense of time.

"Hey chef, what's cooking?" she said sauntering down the staircase in casual clothes.

"Scallops and bacon with a creamy pasta. How does that sound?"

"It sounds and smells fantastic," Melissa answered, finding that she was now ravenously hungry. I was dreaming about Mia earlier. She looked happy and she told me that we have come good for her." She stroked his hair, as he stirred the pot. "Thank you for staying, it means a lot." Brandon felt at home with her and smiled.

"No problems with that." Lifting the lid from a bubbling pot Melissa looked a little puzzled.

"We're eating very early, what's up?"

Brandon couldn't hold on to his excitement any longer. "I have so much to tell you, firstly Lilly-Anne has landed a job with Fox news."

"Wow, that's terrific, what else is going on? I can tell there's more by the look on your face."

"Pat and I have landed a massive job with a TV production company, five years of work and five books. It will be the making of me," he explained, looking at her and hoping that she would understand his excitement at this time. He need not have worried as she grabbed him in a big hug her joy at his news evident.

"Oh my gosh, I knew the public loved you all, but such a big offer....that's amazing!"

"The pay is crazy, ten times what I earn now for doing something I love, plus I get to keep the newspaper job. I can do both easy."

A slight look of worry crept into her expression. "That's fantastic, but where are you going tonight?"

"The production boss wants to pitch his ideas to me and Pat tonight in Dallas. I need to be up there before the ten o'clock meeting."

"That's late, why didn't he wait until the morning?"

"Guess that's just how it works. I need to eat and dash but I'll be back in the morning, I promise."

She nodded, after working for a large sports agency she had heard similar stories a dozen times. "No rush Brandon, but just remember, I've worked for companies who try and sign young popular stars so don't sign anything until an attorney checks it over."

"Sure, I'll bring any contract back here in the morning for you to see."

She nodded her agreement. "Ok, I'm not an attorney but I can check it over in the first instance. Let's eat and you can get going, I'll tidy up here."

# CHAPTER THIRTY-NINE

The man sat on his hotel bed, knowing he had one more job to do before calling it a day....to kill that fucking bitch, Melissa Jagger. Tonight he would take her alive and give her such a terrible death that the whole state of Texas would talk about it for years.

Laying out his tools, he carefully prepared for the evening ahead. This was the second time he had visited the house to take care of her loose tongue and he was pretty sure there was no one around to save her this time."

He looked in the mirror and ran a basin of warm water before shaving, various thoughts running through his mind. *I want to look good for this show, I want her to see that a real gentleman took little Mia and sliced her to ribbons.*

Looking around the spacious room, he checked the drawers once more for anything he had missed the first time before pulling the card from the reader. The lights dimmed as he went out into the corridor, the door closing silently behind him. He had been away for a little longer this time and pulled a large case effortlessly behind him. Pushing the elevator button for reception he cut an imposing figure as he admired himself in the mirror, checking his teeth for any hidden strands of lettuce from the fresh Caesar salad he'd devoured a short time earlier.

The young woman behind the reception desk stood smiling as she asked the usual check out questions. He passed over his credit card and settled the bill, passing her his usual $100 tip.

"We'll miss seeing you around here and hopefully see you again soon," she told him with a final smile.

Melissa sat in her office, sipping on a glass of cold white wine she had been given as a Christmas present from her old boss. Plugging in the memory stick Brandon had left her, she watched the thirty minute film featuring mainly Brandon and Lilly-Anne. They were such a good pair of presenters, it was clear why companies had clambered for their signatures, they were easy to listen to and watch and certainly smooth on the eye.

She laughed at the ridiculous competitions they set up for followers, and the effortless way Lilly-Anne mixed with both tiger cubs and fully grown adult animals, as though she had been born to do it. Brandon on the other hand always looked in a state of near panic each time he set foot in the enclosure, something not lost on the crew or the adoring public. They always begged for him to be sent back in to do any of the jobs Pat demanded.

His own unique popularity even reached a point where a special twenty second slot was added onto each show, a close up of his features while working face to face with the animals. They called it *Brave Brandon's best bits*....never anything brave, just the normal sweating and hiding behind Pat.

She jumped out of her seat when the clip from India came on, the bravery of Pat in facing down the tiger, and the image of Brandon slung over his shoulder like a child was comedy gold, but showed the dangers of the work and the professionalism and bravery of Pat Hunter. Just seeing him on film made her yearn to hold him close again.

What a beautiful gift she thought as the credits rolled at the end. And there it was, the thing that had been stuck in the front of her mind for so long as the places visited during the tour rolled across the screen. *Cincinnati, Memphis, New York, Utah, San Diego, Omaha, Philadelphia, Rio Grande, Oklahoma, Denver and Dallas.* All the main zoos in the country with tigers, all within one hour of the killings. It had been sitting right in front of her for so long, all on the map, pointing her in the right direction.

And the house burning down, the innocent people framed to try and get her and the police away from the scent and the necklace appearing at Tommy's house straight after having a meal with her and Pat. It was all becoming horrifically clear.

A noise upstairs made her jump and she walked to the door to the lounge.

"Hello, who's there?" she called as she grabbed a pool cue that was resting against the office wall.

"Come down here right now or I will shoot," she threatened, trying to hide the tremor in her voice.

"You aren't shooting anyone today," Pat Hunter said as he appeared majestically on the landing and began walking down the stairs.

"Put the stick down, you might hurt someone."

"How did you get in here? The place is locked up," Melissa said in horror, still clutching the cue.

"It's my place Melissa, I have a key." He spun it in his hand to prove the point as hate filled her face.

"I've worked it out you bastard, it was you all along."

"Well, I'm here because I knew that you had worked it out, or should I say were about to work it out, and your little buddy Brandon is half way to Dallas at the moment so he won't be helping you."

Anger filled her senses, momentarily taking away any fear she might have of him.

"Why did you do it, why kill my girl?"

"Why kill anything? It's just become part of me, and it's a part of the life cycle. It's a necessity, apex predators hunt to survive. The tigers taught me the finesse of the hunt and the kill, I just followed their lessons."

"Where is she? Before you kill me, please tell me where you dumped her body."

"I only left one body, I didn't set out to kill anyone in anger. The framing of Tommy, that was epic Melissa, but definitely not my best moment, that is still to come I think. But the girl in the boot was a disappointment, she left too many clues. All that work and I had to leave her because of a car breakdown."

"So where are they?" Melissa demanded again, "Tell me."

"I'm going to do better than that, I'm going to show you exactly what happened to Mia and every other girl I took, a number of different locations which you have just worked out, but the same basic ending."

She rushed forwards swinging the cue and striking him on the shoulder. It smashed in two pieces and fell hopelessly onto the floor. "Bad move," he told her as he grabbed her arm and punched her hard in the face as she struggled.

"My oh my, you have some fight in you," he panted as reaching into his belt, he brought out a hammer and slammed it into her head. She buckled, knocking a chair over as she fell to the floor unmoving.

"I thought that you might like to see my signature move with the hammer," he told her unconscious body, "let's go, we have a date to keep."

His phone rang as he was tightening the plastic ties around her wrists and ankles. He stopped and answered it.

"Hey Brandon, what's up buddy?"

"I'm stuck in traffic and I'm still more than an hour away if it ever clears. I'm going to miss the meeting. Sorry." Pat smiled as he looked down on Melissa's limp body.

"No problems, some things have come up for me and I'm out of town at the moment. Carry on to the hotel and I'll get the guy to come over at nine in the morning. We will have some breakfast and chat tactics, how does that sound?"

"Perfect Pat, you sure are a great boss to work for. See you tomorrow."

"Sure thing buddy, stay safe and I'll see you later." He put the phone back in his pocket before continuing.

"Now where was I, ah, the gag. This bitch never stops talking so better make it super tight." Her head flopped onto its left hand side as he spoke, still deeply unconscious. He pulled her up onto his shoulder, still talking to her inert body.

"When that phone video comes back all crystal clear with me smiling at the lens, I guess that I'm going to be in hot water. The problem is Melissa, I don't think that you're going to be around to see it."

The suspension of the white van creaked as he threw her body into the back like a bag of trash for the dump, and locked the door. She wasn't going anywhere just yet.

The traffic on the freeway had eased as he pushed on towards Dallas; the zoo gates officially closed at six, however this evening there was a special night time show for the families of veterans who did not make it back from the different conflicts and war zones. It happened every year and the local celebrities came out in force. He reached the gate with a few minutes to spare and greeted the zoo night watchman who was just starting his rounds.

"Hey Arthur, we just got back in from India and I have some cool things for the kids. I'm going to park up and leave the van tonight and I'll unload it in the morning. I probably won't see you on the way out, but look after my babies tonight."

"Just like every God damn night Mr Hunter, you take care now and I'll see you in the morning."

His personal office complex was next to the main enclosure. During the peak seasons he often left his office and walked across a small walkway twenty feet above the main feeding area smiling and waving to the crowd. From there he thrilled the customers and video followers by hanging meat ten feet from the ground while the tigers leapt up and grabbed it.

He also had the advantage of a parking space for the van, right up close to the tigers but just out of the eye of the public which was perfect for what he had in mind.

A group of excited kids had gathered watching the tigers prowl the enclosure boundaries hoping for a late night meal while the guide for the evening kept a keen eye on the time.

"Ok folks, we need to get back to the cafeteria in the parking lot as the animals need some peace and solitude after such a busy day. And we have a lot of free burgers, hot dogs and milkshakes, with so many e-numbers you won't sleep for a week." The kids cheered and the mums thanked him as they headed off towards the exit.

Waiting another few minutes in the dark, Pat opened the van doors where Melissa was still unconscious, lying on her front breathing shallowly, blood oozing from her head wound and down the gully at the side before heading towards the door.

Dragging her out by her feet, he threw her back up onto his shoulder and carried her upstairs. He needed her alive as she had to see what was happening. It was pointless if she didn't understand what his mission entailed. She needed to see, understand and be terrified. She had pushed so hard to find the killer but now the killer had found her.

The hum of the large padlocked fridge was the only sound in the building as he carried Melissa down into the food preparation area. She finally awoke with a jolt and tried to buck her body out of his grip, a futile gesture of defiance as her brain registered the ordeal she faced. Pat looked down at her face as he saw her movements and realised she was conscious again.

"Glad that you're back with me, I didn't want you to miss out, given all the trouble that you have gone to in your hunt for the truth."

He lowered her none too gently onto a swivel chair before taking the padlock key out of his pocket and opening the deep fridge. "Ok, commentary time. This is where we keep meat or dead animals from the zoo, it's the biggest fridge I have ever seen Melissa so just watch and learn what we keep in here."

Pulling out a huge metal drawer he hoisted a large black body bag out almost effortlessly and slapped it down onto the stainless steel cutting board.

"Let me introduce you to my latest Dallas attraction," he said, unzipping the bag and pulling it clear from the body.

"She was a nice girl, tried to sell me a factory unit a while back, you might remember her name, Sophie I think." Melissa sat watching in horror, her eyes bulging.

"I needed to do some cutting before I could get her into the car, a bit of an error stealing one that was too small for the job." Arranging her arms and legs beside the torso, he continued to talk.

"You see, it's very important for me to get the cuts of meat right," he continued as he took out a bone saw and began sawing.

"I like that familiar sound of the blade cutting through flesh and bone, you know I nearly became a butcher when I was younger…." Melissa vomited, coughing loudly as it trickled back into her mouth from the tight gag. He stopped and helped her clean up, undoing the gag for a second. Jerking her head away from him she screamed.

"You are a fucking monster!" Her head felt as though it were splitting in two as she bellowed. Stars flashed before her eyes and just for a second she thought that she was going to pass out. Pat scolded her like a child.

"Shush, you'll get Arthur wondering what all the noise is about," he said, replacing the gag. He continued his gruesome commentary along with the cutting. "If you get this bit wrong Melissa, the whole joint suffers. Who knew an ass could cause so many problems? Thank God for the pulley system in the factory….I hope you noticed how neatly the legs have been detached?" He held up the dissected rectum to show her, as if in a show and tell session at primary school. She couldn't look anymore, the pain she felt across her body and emotions were crushing her. Mia would have lain on the same table, with the very same saw dismembering her. Meanwhile Pat continued, immune to her distress.

"I'm sorry that I don't have a happy ending for you, I know what you were hoping for, your daughter to walk back into your family home one day. But she is long gone. Mia was in here for a day, but she was dead, in fact she died in the van. Don't worry she isn't here anymore Mellissa. Jesus, even my own niece went the same way but as I said to you earlier, it's just part of the circle of life. Hopefully you understand that now. My tigers need to eat, I did it all for them."

A crushing pain came over her entire body in a surge again, and fighting the darkness she tried to stay awake, until she couldn't fight it anymore and drifted away onto oblivion. Almost on cue, as the last cuts were made, another deep bellow of a hungry tiger came from the enclosure, "Nearly there, another two minutes," Pat called to his beloved tigers.

Placing the human flesh into a large plastic bin next to the table, he moved over to the chair and untied Melissa before lifting her unconscious body effortlessly and strapping her onto the metal surface. "You're next, just this time I think that I will cut you up alive so you can appreciate my skills. That will be a first for me."

Outside, the tigers who fully understood the routine were anticipating the meal. They knew that whenever the van came at night time they ate fresh meat and pacing up and down, their roar became louder. He turned and shouted out to the enclosure again.

"Yes girls, just be patient."

Arthur wasn't so patient and stomping up to the enclosure, he cursed that they were still all out. The tigers kept the whole zoo awake at night with their constant roaring when they were left out all night, not to mention the people in the houses which bordered the zoo grounds. He phoned Pat's number.

"You better answer Mr Hunter, those damn tigers better not keep me awake again," he muttered as he waited for the call to be picked up. It went straight to answer phone.

"God damn it, the one night I need him, he turns the phone off. I only saw him an hour ago," he cussed as he then tried Brandon and got through straight away.

"Brandon, I need someone to come and put the tigers away, they are creating havoc with the other animals. They sound like they do at feeding time, but there's no one there."

"Phone Pat, Arthur, it's his thing," Brandon told him, having just gone to bed in his hotel room.

"He ain't answering, and if someone doesn't get down here soon I'm reporting you for tiger neglect, they shouldn't be out all night."

"OK, I'm on my way. Give me ten minutes, I'm at the hotel."

Arthur was waiting for him as he pulled up in the car, he had worked at the zoo as night security for nearly forty years and needed to be listened to when he had a complaint.

"I haven't heard anything like it, either you shut them up or

I'm getting the gun out the safe. I can then shut the mother fuckers up real quick." Brandon knew Arthur would never harm any of the animals and that his bark was worse than his bite....unlike the tigers he was going to have to deal with alone.

"Leave the gun where it is Arthur, I'll deal with it, just give me five minutes. If I'm not back, come looking for me, the tigers will possibly be tearing me to bits. You know how nervous I get and they never do anything I tell them. Those animals only ever listen to Pat and Lilly-Anne."

"That's because they smell your fear Brandon, the whole country sees it three times a week, it's hilarious."

Brandon laughed. "Like I said, five minutes Arthur, and if they get me, tell my mum I died a hero."

Brandon walked through the zoo, he loved the place in the dark, but even he was surprised that the tigers were out prowling and so restless. He looked into their enclosure spotting the problem immediately.

*'Damn, the sleeping enclosure doors are shut, they can't get inside.'* He needed the key from the office safe and he thought for a moment, trying to remember the combination. He checked his saved phone numbers under tiger, *54262 gotcha!*

Opening the door, he sensed immediately that something seemed wrong. The entrance leading downstairs to the meat preparation room was open, the cellar light on. "Hello, anyone down here?" he called from the top of the stairs.

"Hey Brandon, it's Pat, come on down. I have a problem."

"Why didn't you let Arthur know you were here? He's going crazy and I could have stayed in bed," he complained as he stomped down the stairs. He stopped as he entered the room. Melissa was lying face down and naked, her blood oozing onto the floor, while nylon straps tied her down. He froze momentarily, trying to process the scene.

"What the hell is going on Pat? What have you done to her?" he gasped as horror filled his face. Pat carried on tidying up around him as he spoke, as if nothing was wrong, before looking up.

"Well, I guess this is one of those moments Brandon where

you are either with me or against me, your move."

"Fucking against, every day of the week! Untie her, what has she done? Oh wait, Jesus Christ it's you! It was you all along."

Pat stood with his arms out stretched as if welcoming Brandon to be part of the scene. "Yes, it was and still is but our partnership doesn't need to end now. She's the last one, no more. She just stopped all of our plans, our dreams. Help me and it will never happen again, I promise you." He looked hopefully at Brandon.

"You sick bastard Pat, I believed in you, I worshiped the bloody ground you walked on. And all this time, it was you who killed the girls, you in the video. You were the last person on the planet I would accuse. You are one of life's good guys so why?"

"Well Brandon, this feels like a real James Bond moment when the bad guy explains the plan," he managed a weak smile. "I saw my dad do it the first time when Mum cheated on him. I was around fourteen and he killed her stone dead with a hammer, and took me with him when he fed her to our tigers. It was amazing, they finished everything in one night, and he was happy. And because he was happy, I was happy. It turns out she had cheated on him throughout the marriage, from when she was eighteen, one man after another so he eventually had enough and killed her. Everyone thought that she had run away with a lover, my little sister was taken into the care of a relation as Dad didn't want her around, she was too much like her mum. That's how it started, and after that we killed another person, a complete stranger and then after that, three more, until dad died of cancer. You see, he just didn't teach me about tigers, he showed me the joy of killing like a tiger and keeping our cats well fed. I tried to hold it back but it was too strong, it was in my blood. You are like my son Brandon and we have a plan together. I saved your life more times than I can remember so you owe me that. We will both be as rich as we ever dreamed of so it's up to you which way it goes, wealthy or dead, you choose."

Brandon's face gave the answer long before the punch connected with his jaw. He crumbled onto the floor, Pat instantly trussing him up and gagging him.

"Looks like it will be one more meal after her, you spineless coward. And to think I ever thought that you would be man enough to join me. I should have left you to die in a pool of your own piss in India, you dickless bastard."

Brandon tried to climb back onto his feet but the plastic ties stopped him. A large hand shoved him back down with a heavy stamp from a boot following.

"Stay there you bastard," Pat told him as grabbing a rope, he tied him tightly to a wooden beam.

"You try to move and I will kill you where you sit."

Pat heard a noise behind him and turned just in time to see Melissa's leg twitch as she regained her senses and tried to move her head to see what the commotion was behind her.

"Oh at last," Pat smiled, "let's go. Now you can see firsthand where Mia and the other girls ended up. Carrying her out into the cooler night air, the enclosure door slid open before he closed it behind them as the second door opened and the tigers stood and watched. He dragged her in towards the pond, chasing the cats away as he did so while they roared their appreciation to him as he left her and hurried away past them.

"I was going to cut you up alive, but on second thoughts, I'm going to let my babies do it for me. Bon appetit my babies."

Hurrying back to his office and out onto the viewing platform, he looked down in amazement as the tigers nuzzled Melissa, gently pawing at her body, warm breath blowing over her face as they looked at their meal. Then they lay down, as if refusing the sacrifice. The big female stared straight into her eyes from feet away. She had a look of sadness or maybe kindness but whatever it was Melissa was still alive. Pat shouted an instruction down at them.

"Eat her, you thankless bastards, eat!"

As he spoke, a spotlight shone up at his face from the path below taking Pat by surprise. He looked down expecting to see Arthur.

"Dallas Police, stay where you are, hands in the air," he was ordered. He took a step forward and the officer repeated the order.

"Sir, do not move."

He inched forwards again and vaulted the railings, falling twenty feet into the enclosure, his ankles splintering with a sickening crack as he hit the hard floor, rolling in agony before looking over at Melissa. He smiled through the pain as he tried to kneel, a large blade glinting in his hand.

"If they won't do it, I will," he snarled through his pain. He crawled towards her, pointing the knife towards her throat and then, almost in reaching distance he stopped.

"All you had to do was accept that Tommy was guilty, that's all Melissa and we could have had a life together," he screamed at her, spittle flying from his mouth, some hitting her on the face as he raised the knife and lunged forwards.

The horror in her eyes told him one split second before the powerful jaws crushed around his head, and the second tiger joined in the frenzy as they tore flesh and bones apart. They fought for the chance to feed first, snarling and striking out at each other with razor sharp claws.

Melissa tried to shrink into the ground, making herself as small as she could in the hope that Pat was the bigger deal but the female tiger sprang back during the melee knocking Melissa aside before she crouched down while the male ate first. Her tail swished in impatience and smacked into Melissa's head as she lay motionless and for this one second Melissa was forgotten about. The tigress slowly edged forward and was allowed to feast on the exposed stomach contents and she ate, oblivious to anything else around her.

The familiar grind as the enclosure door slowly opened alerted Melissa to help arriving, but both tigers ignored it, the blood lust taking over every sense as they continued to rip Pat to pieces. Brandon ran in, crouching low as if to make himself a small target, realising that he had just this one opportunity. Once they had finished with the kill, Melissa would be next as every instinct in the animals would make them kill her.

Arthur stood guard with his weapon swaying uncertainly from left to right as hurriedly Brandon took a knife and cut through Melissa's restraints as the tigers finally noticed his presence, "Run!" he shouted, dragging her to her feet and pushing her towards the small exit. "Arthur, start shutting the door," he yelled as they dived through and a paw smashed into Brandon's calf. He felt himself being dragged back inside the enclosure before Arthur joined in on the tug of war as a shower of blood sprayed the wall and the blast from the rifle made the tigers scatter. The door closed and Brandon and Melissa lay panting on the straw.

"Arthur, that was a long five minutes," Brandon managed a weak smile at his saviour.

"Hush your mouth Brandon, you're a lucky son of a bitch I bothered at all. I figured that with all that noise you deserved to be eaten, but I wanted to check anyway, and I sure as hell wasn't coming without my friends."

# CHAPTER FORTY

The morning light coming through the hospital window brought Melissa to her senses, her head still thumping. It had been two weeks since the attack and she'd had two operations on her brain to deal with the wanton violence inflicted by her daughter's killer. A maze of wires and tubes disappeared into every space on her body, one tube in particular hurting her throat and making her gag as she tried to breath.

A figure sitting in the far corner of her room caught her eye, a big, hulking sleeping man, dressed in an old tracksuit. Drink cans and wrappers lay under his chair and her eyes widened as he stirred and stood before opening the door and waving a nurse into the room. Before she knew it a team of doctors had gathered around her and when she looked again he was gone.

"Don't try to talk Melissa, just relax. We've been breathing for you for a little while and now we just need to take some of the tubes away," she was told as they removed the tube from her throat making her gag and cough. One of the nurses saw her looking over at the chair.

"That man who was sitting there, he hasn't left your side for ten days and nights, not for one second apart from a five minute shower every other day. We insisted on that after the first few days and if we hadn't brought him food and drink I think that he would have starved to death. He said that he was your brother, we couldn't be sure but he was very loving towards you. He spent hours reading books to you and stroking your hair. We all fell a bit in love with him to be honest."

A tear fell from her eye and drifted down her crumpled cheek as she lay motionless while the medical team worked around her. Thoughts drifted through her confused mind as she tried to remember what had happened and how she had ended up almost dead, just like her beautiful daughter but all she could recall was darkness.

"Ok, Melissa, we just need you to stay nice and calm, everything is ok and you can just breath normally now. We'll be back in a minute," the nurse smiled at her, squeezing her hand. She lay still, listening to the nurses speaking to each other in the corridor outside the door. She strained to catch a word of what they were saying as she drifted off again into a light sleep.

"Melissa!" The voice was almost a whisper. "Melissa, are you awake?" It was Brandon's gentle voice creeping from the chair previously occupied by the man.

"Brandon, what the hell are you doing here?" She was shocked that he had managed to get into the room without her noticing.

"I had to have a couple of operations on my leg, that tiger made a big impression on my calf."

Lifting her sore neck an inch off the bed, she looked down and noticed the heavy surgical bandages around his leg.

"How the hell has a tiger attacked you, what did you do this time?"

"It's a long story and maybe it's best forgotten. We both had a close call so let's leave it at that for now."

"I don't remember anything after seeing Pat in my house which was a shock. Why was he there, is he here?" Her confusion was starting to grow again.

"No, he is not here, I'll explain when you're ready but your doctor has told me that you need to rest. I have to go back to my room soon too."

"And Tommy, I thought I saw him in my room when I woke up but why is he out of prison?"

"It's a long story too but you were right about Tommy, he was a good guy. The police found out who the real killer was, and he won't be bothering us anymore. They searched his private locker and he had another twenty seven pieces of jewellery hidden, One for each missing girl."

"Who was it, was it Pat?" she slurred. He looked over, about to give her the answer but she had fallen asleep.

# CHAPTER FORTY-ONE

Tommy arrived back in court with his attorney, Ms Follan. Father Bell was sitting at the rear of the room reading but he put down the book and nodded as he saw them arrive. Susan Follan turned to her client.

"Now listen Tommy, you know what's going to happen and that it's just a process that we need to go through. The judge will find no evidence against you and dismiss the case. If he thought otherwise you wouldn't be out of prison on bail would you? And you certainly would not have been allowed to sit by Melissa's hospital bed for the past two weeks."

Tommy nodded before asking, "Is it the same judge who put me onto death row without listening to the evidence?"

"No, he's no longer allowed to hear the case, in fact he's not allowed to preside over any cases anymore. We call it being disbarred in our circle. He can't practice law anywhere within the country, but hear me out, I have someone who we need to meet after the case."

"Sure," Tommy agreed as the judge came in and the case began.

The courtroom was a world apart from the one Tommy had sat in a few months before. Gone were the packed jury and media attention as he sat with just his attorney with him, looking at the new judge and Peter watching from the public benches. The proceedings took less than five minutes before the case was dismissed but the judge did not however leave her seat. She addressed Tommy directly.

"Mr Cookson, while you have obviously had the most traumatic time imaginable at the hands of our legal system, I would like to offer an explanation as to what I intend to do." She looked at him apologetically.

"As we speak, the police have arrested four people in

connection to your period of imprisonment. Three of these people are correctional officers from the Dallas prison which you were assigned to. They are to be held in custody pending a trial in which you will be asked to give evidence. "Is that clear?" Tommy smiled hearing the news.

"Yes judge."

"The fourth person arrested at his home this morning is the original trial judge and again you will be asked to present your evidence although that will be just a formality. His actions are, after all, recorded on camera and written record. You were not given a fair hearing and it is the opinion of the investigation team who collected all the facts, that if the evidence against you were explored as it should have been under US law, you would have been found Not Guilty.

You will of course be eligible for a substantial settlement for harm caused to you and your reputation. Mr Cookson, regardless of what the trial Judge Martin Searle said to you. You are a war hero and God bless you sir." She stood and left the court room.

Susan Follan shook Tommy's hand as another smartly dressed man joined them.

"Mr Cookson, my name is Mark Jenson from the legal firm Jenson, Jack and Jacobs from New York. We would like to represent you in claiming damages against the US Government for the traumas caused to you both physically and mentally. I have only one question for you based on the work that I have already completed."

Tommy shrugged his huge shoulders, not knowing what to expect this time. "And what question is that?"

"What are you going to do with the thirty million they have already agreed to settle?" Tommy took a deep breath and slumped into his seat. He thought that he might cry but this quickly drifted into a laugh.

"Where do I sign?"

# CHAPTER FORTY-TWO

Melissa and Tommy sat watching TV in her newly built home, it had been a long time coming but the sense of joy she felt moving back in was overwhelming.

"It should be on next," she said in a hushed tone as they watched the news report.

"Today in New York City police arrested a prominent judge from his home as he slept. After a month long investigation by the FBI it is thought that serious breaches of law were exposed spanning two decades. A government spokesperson confirmed that Judge Martin Searle was arrested at 06.30 this morning and is assisting the police with all investigations. This coincides with the release from Death row of Mr Tommy Cookson from Dallas, a decorated war hero found guilty of crimes he did not commit."

The camera cut to a group of veterans waving flags in the road outside the court.

"Local groups of military veterans celebrated the victory outside the courtroom and praised the actions of Melissa Jagger and her charity for uncovering the true story and setting an innocent man free.

The allegations of an abuse of power from such a prominent judge have led to some unrest within the city of New York where Judge Searle once sentenced a young black man to life on the evidence of a corrupt police sergeant." A film clip of an angry mob smashing Macy's window and stealing clothes was shown before returning to the young reporter.

"A police crackdown and possible curfew have been suggested by the mayor's office and a full investigation into the conditions faced by prisoners in Texas and New York prisons has begun. This is Lilly-Anne reporting for Fox news, Times Square."

They looked at each other with pride bursting from their

bodies.

"Looks like one of our babies is doing alright for herself Tommy." He nodded energetically.

"She is doing well Melissa, and Brandon sure as shit is doing well too, Mr *'best selling'* author. He better remember us when the film company comes calling."

Melissa waved her hands at him. "Think I'll give that story a miss Tommy," she said before adding, "I think that Jazz has fallen on her feet with that young man, especially now her dad, Captain Bent was given such a good early retirement package. Not sure what he did to deserve that but still, maybe he did things that I didn't see."

"The Lord and Peter Bell move in mysterious ways Melissa, I think there are a lot of things we didn't see." He sat forward on the sofa and turned to face her.

"I have a proposition for you, see how you like this. What if I said that we can move the charity operations up a notch or two?"

"How do you mean?"

"I mean our own office in town, with a couple of staff to help us."

It was Melissa's turn to sit up as the importance of what he was saying hit her.

"You used the plural twice in one sentence there Tommy, what do you mean us?"

"Well, I have some money to invest and I have my eye on buying the building overlooking the police headquarters, right in the police station's line of sight. We could maybe call it 'The Mia Foundation' and help families all over the country. It would be our place, but somewhere people would know they could come to for help."

"And where do you fit in, apart from deep pockets and a huge heart?"

"I want to do it with you Melissa, we could make a big difference. Our story has run for a long time but some families are just setting off on their journey. With your experience and my backing we can set a new standard for caring for the forgotten victims and their families."

She thought for a second before holding out a hand. "Seems fitting and feels the right thing to do. I think that we have a deal, partner."

"Hell yeah, let's do it for Mia."

# ACKNOWLEDGEMENT

Thank you for reading my latest book...if you enjoyed it, please take the time to leave me a review on Amazon as for us indie authors this is very important for getting our books noticed. If you didn't enjoy it then maybe try one of the other five I have published to date....they are all different!

 A big thank you must also go to Chris Rodgers, who on hearing the title and topic of my book offered one of his beautiful tiger photos for use on the cover. My research on the behaviour of tigers certainly gave me an increased sense of awe and appreciation of these magnificent beasts.

Finally, a big thank you again to Adrian Whiting for his invaluable advice on all things concerning police procedure.

If you would like more information on my novels, or to read excerpts from each of them, please visit my website www.adrianodonnell.com

# BOOKS BY THIS AUTHOR

## High Risk

The Byfield Trilogy, Book One

## Resolution

The Byfield Trilogy, Book Two

## Between The Shadows

The Byfield Trilogy, Book Three

## Vengeance Is Calling

An Ernie Stocken adventure

## Thicker Than Water

An exciting novel of brotherly love and ultimate deception

Printed in Great Britain
by Amazon

32059270R00169